EVERY
LAST
ONE

BOOKS BY CAROLYN ARNOLD

Sandra Vos series

Save Her Life

Detective Amanda Steele series

The Little Grave

Stolen Daughters

The Silent Witness

Black Orchid Girls

Her Frozen Cry

Last Seen Alive

Her Final Breath

Taken Girls

Her Last Words

Missing Before Daylight

The Wildfire Girl

Her Deadly Rose

Hidden Angels

Three Girls Gone

Brandon Fisher FBI series

Eleven

Silent Graves

The Defenseless

Blue Baby

The Secret of the Lost Pharaoh

The Legend of Gasparilla and His Treasure

Standalone

Assassination of a Dignitary

Pearls of Deception

Midlife Psychic

CAROLYN ARNOLD

EVERY LAST ONE

bookouture

Published by Bookouture in 2025

An imprint of Storyfire Ltd.
Carmelite House
50 Victoria Embankment
London EC4Y 0DZ

www.bookouture.com

The authorised representative in the EEA is Hachette Ireland
8 Castlecourt Centre
Dublin 15 D15 XTP3
Ireland
(email: info@hbgi.ie)

ISBN: 978-1-83618-060-9
eBook ISBN: 978-1-83618-059-3

*To William (Bill) Arnold
for sharing your ingenious inventions and sense of humor with
the world.
You also had a way of seeing people for who they were deep
inside.
You will be forever remembered.*

ONE

9:50 AM

Founders Hospital
Washington, DC

Gail squeezed her daughter's hand tightly while looking at her. The girl's eyes were shut, and wires and tubes overwhelmed her small, fragile body. Sensors on her chest fed to a monitor and captured her heart rate. Gail watched her daughter's life force as the line dipped up and down in a somewhat erratic pattern. If she stared at it too long, her own heart would tick up speed and her mind spin with thoughts. All of them were propelled from a place of fear and uncertainty. But she couldn't afford to give in to them. The heart transplant had to work. It just had to. Without the operation, she would die. Two extreme swings of the cosmic pendulum.

Though as much as Gail tried to keep positive, it didn't stop the doubts of the unknown from slinking in. Her daughter's fate was in the hands of the surgeon, and Gail had to accept that fact or go mad. It wasn't like she had the skill to carry off the operation herself.

Gail pinched her eyes shut, and images of her daughter's

smile flooded her vision. The sound of her laughter filled her ears. All of it snatches from brief pockets of time. Memories. But there would be more like them. There just had to be.

But where was Dr. Cowan? They were just over thirteen hours out from surgery, and she said she'd drop by that morning to check on Phoebe.

Gail glanced at her daughter, hesitant to leave. *Afraid* to leave her in such a fragile state. But she had to find out what was going on.

"Mommy will be right back." She kissed her daughter's forehead and left the room.

There was a lot of traffic in the hallway. The soles of running shoes from rushing nurses and doctors squeaked on the linoleum as they moved past. Phoebe's room wasn't far from the nurses' station, but this level of chaos was unusual.

Gail spotted Nurse Torres talking to a colleague. Torres had been by their side in the past few weeks since Phoebe was admitted, awaiting her donor.

"Are you for real right now?" Nurse Torres asked.

"I'm being serious. There's a situation." The other nurse looked at Gail over Torres's shoulder.

"Excuse me, Nurse Torres," Gail said.

The nurse turned to her with a face stricken with fear. "Ms. Chapman, you need to return to your daughter's room, lower the blinds, and lock the door."

"I was just looking for Dr. Cowan. She said she'd come by to see Phoebe."

Nurse Torres laid a hand on her forearm, looked her squarely in the eye when she spoke. "Please, for your safety, and that of your daughter, do as I say."

Her words sent shivers down her spine, chilling her right through. "What's going on?"

"There's no time to explain. Please. Go." Nurse Torres took her upper arm and guided her back to the room.

"I don't understand. What's—"

Two nurses scurried past, talking to each other, not mindful of their volume. "I heard there are gunmen in the hospital."

"Complete lockdown," the other said.

Next thing, a coded announcement came over the speakers. Then the main lights went dark, and emergency lights came on.

A surge of panic rolled up Gail's chest into her throat. "Phoebe." She jogged toward the room, and the nurse kept pace next to her.

Nurse Torres shut the door and locked it behind them.

"Mommy?"

Phoebe's tiny voice had Gail running to her daughter's side. "It's okay, baby. It's going to be okay." This couldn't be happening. Everything had to turn out all right. Phoebe was getting her new heart today, and the surgery was going to go smoothly. There had to be some mistake.

But the nurse was hustling, grabbing at the strings for the window blinds. Each set clattered down as she made her way along the wall and to the door. She completely blocked out the view to the corridor, and with only the dim emergency lighting, the room was dusky like twilight. It felt suffocating, and Gail went to open the vertical blinds on the outside window.

"No." Nurse Torres thrust out a hand to accompany her directive. "It will lighten up the room and draw attention to us. Emergency protocol states locked doors, lights off, and we're to stay quiet and out of sight."

Emergency ricocheted in Gail's head. Panic swelled her throat. This couldn't be happening. Not when Phoebe was so close to being saved.

TWO

9:50 AM

Jordon Maddox woke up that morning with plans of making things right. His focus would be off until he did. As it was, his girlfriend's announcement from last night continually played in his mind, like a haunting refrain. "I know we didn't plan this, but I'm pregnant."

The last part of that statement packed the punch. Just two little words that would forever change his life.

His first reaction was utter fear. There was no doubt his girlfriend would make a wonderful mother. She was loving and caring, the qualities that made her a terrific nurse practitioner. But he wasn't too sure about himself as a father.

Am I even ready for this? Are we?

He had his next five years mapped out. It was an approach to life he'd started in high school. It saw him through college, earning his MD, becoming an intern and attaining a residency. He'd decided on a specialty and had his sights on heading up the neurology department by the time he was thirty-five. That was only two years out.

It would take all his focus, ambition, and drive to pull it off. If he succeeded, he'd be one of the youngest department heads to ever work at Founders Hospital. He'd put in the hours, and his mentors believed in him, praising him as one of the best attending doctors they'd ever seen. He was so very close to realizing that goal. But a baby... There was no way he could turn his back on Maria or their child.

That's why he showed up at the nurses' desk on the fourth floor that morning.

No roses in hand, though he'd thought about doing that. But she told him last night that she didn't want to tell anyone else until after the first trimester. He came to deliver her favorite cupcake, red velvet, and a decaf coffee from her favorite shop. When he was brave enough, he had something else for her in his pocket.

Maria lit up when she saw him and kissed him on the cheek. They tucked into the nurse break room for a few moments. Two nurses were in there who Jordon knew, but they stuck to themselves. Leah Winters was making herself a coffee, and Colby Mahoney was on the couch reading a printed newspaper like a man in his sixties when he couldn't be older than Jordon. They passed him a look for being there, as if he should know nurses sought refuge from doctors within these four walls. But he was tolerated because of Maria.

"This is for you." He handed his offering over to her, and she took it with a grin.

"Georgetown Cupcake? I'd say someone is trying to make up for last night."

"Is it working? I was a complete and utter... well, I should have responded better than I did." He'd gone quiet in the immediate aftermath. *I'm pregnant.* Truth be told, he'd hoped he could sink into the couch and disappear.

"You were in shock." She kept her voice low.

"To say the least. But I'm hoping we can talk more tonight after work?"

"Yes, of course. But speaking of work, I need to get back to it. I'm sure you have patients who would love to see you."

"Don't tell me that a little girl has stolen your heart," he told her.

"You know Phoebe has, but there's still room for you." She tapped a quick kiss on his cheek and was off, her fingers filtering through his. "As for this treat"—she held up the cupcake box—"I'll eat it later." She put it into the fridge before leaving the room.

He stood there, watching her leave and feeling like a coward. Pushing his hands into his pants pockets, his left one wrapped around a small box. His great-great-grandmother's diamond ring, a family heirloom.

Marriage might not have been in his five-year plan, but it was in the next segment. He loved her without a doubt. She was his future, the mother of his children. Did it really matter if the timing was moved up? Not that he had any plans to propose here. He'd already imagined the perfect setup. A baseball game at Nationals Park with them being invited to the pitching mound by her favorite Washington Nationals player. They'd go down there, and he'd propose to her right there in front of the world. She'd love that more than any other grand romantic gesture.

His phone rang, breaking his thoughts. He should get moving on his rounds anyhow, but he answered after seeing the name on Caller ID. It was best to take her calls, or she wouldn't leave him alone. "Hello, Mother," he said. "I'm kind of busy if you can keep it short...?" He left the break room and stood outside in the hall.

There seemed to be far more people roaming about than normal. Nurses, patients, and visitors were cluttering the hall-ways. All of them were hustling too. *What the...*

"Make time for me," his mother commanded. "I just wanted to make sure that you're set to come here this Saturday. It's your father's birthday dinner. A lot of important people will be here."

Of which he had no doubt. He could protest that it was five days away, but his mother wasn't wired like most people. She was a perfectionist and everything she had her hands in was planned to exhaustion. "You know I'm coming."

"What's going on there? It sounds busy."

"It is." He was having a hard time making sense of the foot traffic.

"He's got a gun," a man said to him quickly while he kept walking.

"Did that man just say…?" his mother asked.

His heart jackhammered as he stepped out farther and looked down the corridor. There was no sign of Maria. Maybe she'd gone to check on her youngest patient. Wherever she was, she needed to be safe. *Please be locked inside a room, out of sight…*

"Jordon?" His mother raised her voice. "Talk to me."

"I don't—" Then he caught sight of a man waving a gun around in the air. He only stopped walking when a voice came over a walkie-talkie that he carried.

"Secured," it said.

The man pulled a device out of the backpack.

Jordon tucked against the wall and slid along it, hoping to find the door for the break room.

"There's a gunman on the fourth floor," he whispered to his mother. But she was gone. The call was dropped. He couldn't be sure how much she heard.

The lockdown code was announced over the speakers, and the emergency lights came on.

Shit, shit, shit!

"Get in here!" Mahoney said, urging him into the break room.

But Jordon was frozen, locked in eye contact with the gunman.

Time stood still. A part of him refused to back down, but he didn't want to die. And if this man found out who he was, he could be in serious trouble.

He spun, storming back into the break room and turning around to throw the lock. But he was too late.

The door thrust inward, knocking him to the ground. He scrambled to get to his feet, but the gun was leveled at his face.

"Get up nice and slow, or I will put a bullet in your head."

THREE

9:50 AM

Sometimes a person does things in life they never thought themselves capable of before. Scaling a mountain, swimming with sharks, jumping out of an airplane, or closing a big business deal. Most people will never kill but that's what I'm prepared to do. I have nothing to lose, and I'm about to find out just how far I'm willing to go, but it's certainly far too late to turn around. Things have been put into motion, and it's not just me caught up in this.

I approach a woman in her mid-thirties, a pleasant smile on her face. I mimic the expression, even letting it touch my eyes. A nameplate on her desk identifies her as Pamela.

"Hello, can I help you?" Pamela asks with a tone balancing kindness and authority. She's the gatekeeper. Behind her is the office of the most powerful woman in the building. Megan Beal, the chief executive officer of Founders Hospital.

"Yes, I'm here to speak with Ms. Beal." I offer a smile, this one more tentative.

"I'm sorry, but she's currently unavailable. I can schedule an appointment for you at a future time. I'd just need your name and what you wish to discuss."

A cold sweat washes over me, and my stomach churns. I wrap my fingers around the handle of the gun in my pocket. Coming here, I knew that would be her answer, even why Beal is *unavailable*, but Pamela is my ticket inside. "I need to speak with her. It's urgent."

A smile again. This one, patronizing. "As I said, she's not available."

Voices have me turning to look over my shoulder. Two doctors are walking down the hall, their stethoscopes dangling around their necks, the instruments swaying with their gait. They round the corner out of sight. I didn't want it to come to this but am prepared to do what I must.

My heart pounds as I pull my weapon, just enough to direct her gaze there. "I'm not asking."

Pamela's face goes white while her mouth gapes open and shut, open and shut, open and shut. It's like she's locked in fear and shock. I can't take the risk she'll do something stupid.

"Don't even think about screaming," I say clearly, slowly, and at a low volume. "Now, I'm only going to ask nicely one more time. I need to speak with Ms. Beal. Is she in this hospital?"

Pamela is nonresponsive. Her facial expression, her body language. I'm not even sure if she's still breathing. It might be a few seconds, but the passage of time stretches out painfully so.

"Pamela," I prompt using her name, hoping that will jolt her out of her daze.

Pamela nods.

"Take me to her." I don't need to make a display of the gun again. Pamela's gaze is fixed on the pocket where I had lifted it from a moment ago. "Come on, no need for you to get hurt."

Pamela stumbles to her feet, her long legs unsteady like a newborn foal.

"Just act normal. We'll walk side by side." I force a smile again. My heart is beating so fast, I hear it behind my ears.

She walks to my right where I have the gun in my pocket. We pass some doctors and medical technicians, all in their distinguishable uniforms. One woman smiles brightly at Pamela and glances at me, cocking her eyebrow. I turn to Pamela, hoping my movement is discreet enough, but I need to censor her response. I don't like what I see. It's a flicker, a transference between the two. I tighten my grip on the gun, about to pull it out, but the other woman keeps walking. I don't dare to look back to see if she's been alerted. If she has, all of this could fall apart before it begins.

Pamela continues to take me down the hallway, leading me to the large boardroom. She puts her face in the door's window, and CEO Megan Beal dismisses her with a wave.

"Open the door," I seethe while I nudge the gun into Pamela's side. "Get us inside, or they'll be mopping you off the floor."

Pamela is trembling as she reaches for the handle and cracks the door.

Beal shoots her a glare and tosses a hand of surrender in the air, motioning for a board member to keep us out. But I push Pamela into the room and roll in quickly behind her, leaving my back to the door and blocking the exit.

"What is the meaning of—" Beal's mouth snaps shut as her gaze goes to the gun in my hand.

Same too for the rest of the eyes in the room.

Twelve faces, mostly strangers, though I wager every one of them is powerful and corrupt. Except one. A red-cheeked twentysomething seated next to Beal at the head of the table. Her fingers are suspended over the keyboard of a laptop. No doubt the minute-taker for this meeting, a boring and thankless job I've done before.

Beal goes for the phone on the table in front of her.

"Go ahead. It won't do you any good, because in five minutes or less, this entire hospital will be locked down. And soon the phones won't work either. Same for your cell phones. Put them on the table. *Now*."

The suits scramble to pull them from their pockets and concede to my direction. It makes me feel powerful, but I let that emotion roll over me. I don't want to lose focus.

I take slow, cautious yet confident strides toward Beal, but talk to the room. "If one person goes for the door or leaves, I will shoot everyone who is left. Got it?"

Mumbles of acknowledgment echo around the room. All but one person is ready to do as I say. Beal is looking at me like she pities me, and anger heats my chest. I shake her. "You understand?"

Her pretty face contorts into an ugly mask. "What do you want?" Asked with an impatient tone, like I'm a bug she can easily swat away. It's like the gun in her face doesn't even exist.

I press the muzzle against her forehead. Yet, still, her expression barely falters. An arrogant show of strength, no doubt. "It's up to you. You have the power to decide how this is going to go, but I will be heard."

My voice is overridden by one coming over the speakers, and suddenly the lights shut off and emergency lights rise in their place. The sunlight coming through the window takes on more power, but I need to close the blinds.

I head over to the window and slide them shut and turn around to face everyone. A smile touches my lips when I go to speak. "You all might as well get comfortable. You're going to listen to me and listen good, or people will die." I take out my walkie-talkie to update the rest of my team.

FOUR

10:20 AM

FBI Washington Field Office

That morning's run along the Potomac River through Georgetown Waterfront Park felt like it belonged to yesterday at the pace time was going. It was a quiet Monday, but Sandra was under no illusion that set the tone for the rest of the week. With her job, things could go from a crawl to lightspeed in the blink of an eye. There still wasn't anything else she'd have chosen for a career. Working at the FBI's Washington Field Office was where she'd been for the last fifteen years, and fourteen of those as part of the Crisis Negotiation Unit. When her skills as a negotiator weren't called upon, she played a role in taking violent criminals off the world stage.

A major drug kingpin was taking up her time these days. He was in the wind and had left hundreds of bodies in his wake, not just from his product but a shootout between his gang and a rival one. The guy was good at being invisible, she could give him that, but eventually he'd resurface, and she'd be there ready to draw a target on his head. But until that happened, she was at her desk proactively trying to narrow down where he might be hiding out.

The office space comprised of several desks, with no partition in sight. Some days she would kill for a cubicle, but privacy wasn't a thing in a business where everyone had information at their fingertips. Her fellow agents near her were on their phones or tapping on their keyboards, including the colleague she was closest to, Brice Sutton. He was one of the latter, fingers flying, though she could swear he backspaced more than he made forward progress. Only a few here were also part of the CNU, and Brice was one of them like her.

"You've got to move. Right now. Both of you." Elwood Rowe, the assistant director of the FBI's Critical Incident Response Group, also their boss, came storming up between her and Brice. As if *both of you* wasn't specific enough, he was pointing at them as he'd said it.

She straightened, and so did Brice. "What is it?" she asked.

"Founders Hospital is on lockdown. At least one gunman on scene. The Metropolitan Police Department has responded, but we've been called in to assist with the negotiations."

"The MPD's Emergency Response Team has their own negotiators," Brice said.

"Thank you, Agent Sutton, for that wealth of information. I had no idea." Sarcasm dripped from Elwood's words. "But since you called me out, there is more to this. The director received a call requesting that we put our people in there. MPD will supply the command vehicle and officers to round out the team, but Vos, you'll take lead. Sutton, you're second and support."

His directive left her with more questions. For one, it would take some special pull to get the CNU called in for a fresh crisis incident where local law enforcement should be able to handle it. "A call from whom?" She was certain there was more than was being said, and to be a successful negotiator she needed to be armed with as much intel as possible.

Elwood took a deep, staggering breath. "I should have known you'd ask. Ilene Maddox."

"As in Maddox Industries, one of the largest pharmaceutical companies in the United States?" Brice cut in.

"The very same."

"And how does she know the director exactly?" Sandra asked.

"Her husband and the director are golfing buddies and belong to some fancy dinner club. They also donate tens of thousands to the FBI. Does it matter? Go." Elwood thrust a pointed finger toward the exit.

Brice took a few steps, but Sandra stayed put. "And how did she come to know about the situation?"

"What is this? A hundred questions?"

"The more I'm armed with going in, the better." There was a pull to get to the scene, but she needed to balance this with her hunger for answers.

"She was on the phone with her son, who is an attending doctor. Name's Jordon Maddox. They were mid-conversation when their call was cut off. Just before the line went dead, she heard someone say, 'he's got a gun.'"

"And what floor does he work on?" she asked.

"He's assigned to the fourth. That doesn't mean that's where he was when the hospital went into lockdown," Elwood said, impatience coating his tone. "But it's likely."

"All right. Let's get going." She turned to Brice. "I'll drive."

"Why wouldn't you?" he said.

"You can if it means so much to you."

"Just get your asses there," Elwood barked, shaking his head.

It was impossible to park close to the hospital, but it was standard to shut down the surrounding vicinity in a case like this. Word was out judging by the crowds gathered behind a cordon line and the MPD officers battling to keep people back.

Sandra approached one officer facing off with a woman in her mid-thirties.

"My sister's in there. You need to let me by," she told him.

"Ma'am, you're not going anywhere," the officer said.

The woman stepped forward, and he held his hands out to stop her. She tried to circumvent his efforts and wound up being grabbed by her upper arm.

"Ma'am, behind the line, or I will have no choice but to arrest you."

The woman let out a scream. "You can't just keep us here like a herd of cattle."

"Ma'am, one more outburst and I will—"

The woman turned around to face the crowd behind her. "The police are keeping us from our loved ones. We need to fight back."

At first the crowd seemed to ignore her, but then the energy shifted. What was merely curiosity-driven now crackled with the hint of revolt. The situation needed to be cooled down quickly before it escalated any further.

"FBI!" she called out, stepping to the tape and putting her back to it. Brice stood beside her. "You are all here because you're concerned about the people in Founders Hospital."

There were mumbles of agreement. Some voices of contempt.

"You want the people inside to be safe. You want to be safe. So let the police, and us"—she gestured to Brice—"do our jobs."

The confrontational woman came up to Sandra's face. "Why should we trust you?"

Sandra remained calm despite the woman being close enough she could feel her warm breath on her face. She slowly drew out her business card and held it toward the woman. "My name is Sandra Vos, an FBI negotiator, and I assure you I'm going to do all I can for a peaceful resolution here today. What's your name?"

The woman took her card, holding eye contact with Sandra until she looked down at the text. "Remy Bishop. My sister, Janie DeSilva, works in there. I was supposed to meet her for coffee, but I was running behind like I always am, and now... this." She flailed a hand toward the police officer.

The woman didn't realize how fortunate it was that she was late. "Remy, I'll do what I can, all right?"

"Just promise me if you find out that she's okay, you'll let me know. I'm going crazy out here. You have my name. You want my number?"

Agreeing was a potential minefield with so many listening in. She couldn't take everyone's information, but seeing the desperation in the woman's watery eyes tugged at Sandra's heart. "Sure."

Remy gave Sandra her number, and she keyed it into her phone in the notepad app.

"Thank you." Remy backed up.

With the situation now de-escalated, Sandra turned to the officer.

"That was pretty impressive, Agent Vos," the officer said, while lifting the barricade tape for her and Brice to slip under.

The compliment washed over her because praise didn't matter. Results did. "We all have the same basic need to feel safe. I just appealed to that."

"Whatever the case. It was impressive."

"Could you direct us to the person in charge down here?" She preferred to move forward than remain stuck in this uncomfortable exchange.

"You bet. Lieutenant Rick Kreiger." He then directed them to where the mobile command center was parked, one street up and one across.

"Thank you," she said before leaving him.

"Anytime, Vos."

As they followed the officer's directions, Sandra's mind was on the assurance she made to the people at the cordon line. She would do all she could for a peaceful resolution. That was always her goal, but seeing that swell of people made it sink in just how many lives were on the line. And how many families and friends would be affected by what transpired here today.

Brice looked over at her. "I could have gotten us here in less time."

"Small talk right now? Really?"

He shrugged. "Never hurts."

She could argue that sometimes it did. Like now when she was balancing the load of responsibility on her shoulders. But playing along may ease some pressure. "Are you saying I drive slow?"

"I didn't have to. You just did."

She shook her head and smiled at him. For years, she'd kept Brice Sutton at a distance. It wasn't even personal. She liked to keep her private life just that. But when her sixteen-year-old daughter, Olivia, was taken three months ago, her relationship with Brice took on a new dynamic. Sibling-like at best, cantankerous at worst, but he proved himself as someone she could rely on. Working with him on a crisis incident like this would be a new experience, as they'd never been paired up in that capacity before.

She pulled out her phone and texted a quick note to Olivia that she had been called to an incident. She'd be in class now, but she'd see it during break period. After hitting send and watching it go through, she muted her phone and put it in her pocket.

As she and Brice approached the street in front of the hospital, the incident took on more structure. Everyone in sight was with the MPD. She wondered if her boyfriend, Eric Birch, was here somewhere. He was a detective for the Criminal Investigation Division, but in cases like this all available manpower was called in to assist.

There were a few ERT BearCats around and officers in tactical gear loaded for war with their thick bulletproof vests and combat boots. Such a contrast to her and Brice. They wore vests too, but their primary weapons were their minds and the laptop in Brice's messenger bag.

She spotted the mobile command vehicle just as two officers stepped in front of her and Brice. They both eyed the FBI logo embroidered on their vests.

"We're looking for Lieutenant Kreiger," she told them.

"You found him." One of the officers pointed ahead of them at a man with a silver mustache standing next to the vehicle.

"Thanks." She walked past them and right up to the lieutenant. One of his hands was on a hip, while the other had a death grip on a to-go cup. "Lieutenant Kreiger?"

"That's me." His posture tensed, becoming defensive like a caged lion bracing to attack. "And I take it you're our FBI negotiators?"

"What gave it away?" Brice teased while pointing at his vest, but the lieutenant didn't look amused.

He took a slow draw from his coffee cup.

She hadn't expected the red carpet to be rolled out, but some professional courtesy would have been appreciated. "Special Agent Sandra Vos," she said, extending her hand, to offset the lieutenant's lack of a cordial greeting.

He left her hand hanging there. "And you?" Kreiger swiveled his head toward Brice.

"Special Agent Brice Sutton."

"Well, welcome to the circle of hell. The hospital is in complete lockdown. No way in, no way out. I've had officers block off a three-block radius, and we estimate approximately eleven hundred people inside between patients, staff, and visitors."

The life of every last one rests on my shoulders... "That's a lot of people."

"It's a big hospital. Eight floors."

"Does the hospital have an emergency protocol in place with the MPD?" Sandra asked, knowing that many large facilities set this up to prepare for worst-case scenarios.

"It was in progress but not yet finalized."

"I assume the hospital has security, though..." Sandra was curious how things had escalated to complete lockdown.

"Standard hospital security has one guy posted at every door and one guy watching camera feeds all day. We haven't heard from any of them."

"They must not have looked suspicious until it was too late." That was all Sandra could think of to explain the silence.

Kreiger continued as if she hadn't spoken. "A woman called nine-one-one from inside and reported a woman with a gun. She got as far as that before she was cut off. We have no idea what floor she was calling from."

"There's at least two, then," Sandra said. "We were told there was a man with a gun on the fourth." She based that on Elwood's summary of Maddox's call with his mother.

Kreiger gave her a tight smile. "Then you know about Jordon Maddox, not that I'm surprised. It is why you're here."

Sandra wasn't walking into the trap.

"Hmph. Well..." Kreiger narrowed his eyes, drank the rest of his coffee, and tossed the cup on the ground.

Did he just... Olivia would have had a conniption fit if she were here. If he didn't pick up his trash when they left the area, Sandra would. "I assume that the nine-one-one operator tracked the call. Do we have a name? We could find out the floor that way."

"No dice. Been down that road. The woman works for the Snack Co. and would have been filling the vending machines inside. There's no way to know which floor she was on when she made the call."

The dead ends keep coming... "What caused the dropped calls? Do we know?"

"Oh, yeah, we know. A scanner detected a Wi-Fi jammer which is affecting cell phones inside the hospital. Thankfully, it has a relatively limited range. It only reaches out about fifty feet around the structure. As you probably know, there's no way of knocking out a jammer remotely. Hands must be put on the device. It either needs to be destroyed or turned off. But that's not all. The hospital's phone and internet system has been knocked out too. I don't know all the technical ins and outs on that. Just that neither would be affected by this jammer apparently. All of it is hard-wired, from what I understand. Hopefully we can get more information once the hospital's emergency director arrives."

"Well, often large institutions use a VoIP, or Voice over Internet Protocol, which routes and carries calls over the internet," Sandra said. "Usually when one goes down, they both do. Whether the plug was pulled or a virus was uploaded, both would require the person to have access to the hospital's mainframe."

"Then we could be looking at an inside job. Well, this Luis Rigby should be here soon. That's the emergency director," Kreiger added when she must have looked confused. "Thankfully, he was off today. From what I understand he's going to see if the service provider for the phone system can reactivate it remotely."

In the meantime, no means of communication presented a challenge. How to talk down the situation without a means of doing so? But she'd been in this position before and got creative. "With at least two armed persons inside, it's likely they are communicating somehow. Possibly using walkie-talkies."

"Uh-huh, and Gibson, that's our intelligence officer, has a

scanner running for radio frequencies. It's programmed to over-look activity on police radios, but if any others activate, he auto-matically gets ears on the conversation. From there, he'll use a triangulation scanner to pinpoint the source of commu-nication."

As for the scanner Gibson was using, she was familiar with the technology. It wasn't without an Achilles' heel, though. Radio frequencies needed to be in use to detect them. That meant they were dependent on when the perps inside wanted to chat with each other. But the first time they did, they'd have a way in.

"And what about the security video?" If they could get their hands on that, they might be able to identify their gunmen.

"Separate system, and the footage is sent directly to an offsite surveillance company that stores the video. Getting our hands on it is a priority too, and Monica's on that. So far, she's been bashing her head trying to get anywhere with them."

So much for getting a look inside and having the chance of running facial recognition. It was hard to know if they were looking at professionals here, but it had the markings of a planned and coordinated attack.

"And who is Monica?" Brice asked.

"Harding. She'll be acting as scribe today."

The scribe made typed records of all conversations between negotiator and subject.

"Well, let's get a move on. I'll introduce you to the team." Kreiger nudged his head toward the command vehicle and started walking toward it.

Sandra went to pick up his tossed coffee cup at the same time Brice did. She gestured for him to go ahead. If the brief interaction with Kreiger was any indication, he was a big personality she'd have to navigate. But he was the least of her concerns.

FIVE

10:41 AM

Most mobile command vehicles were the same. This vehicle had a round meeting table with a half-moon bench, and four workstations with computers and other electronic gadgetry. Whiteboards were secured to the wall, while an alcove was stocked with essentials to fuel long negotiations. There was a coffeemaker and a kettle for tea, cups, coffee condiments, and a small fridge.

Sandra looked at the markerboard, and the information was sparse and reminiscent of what she and Brice had already been told.

Two armed assailants—one man, one woman

Man believed to be positioned on the fourth floor

Lines of communication down—jammer and hospital lines

That last barrier was a huge problem and one that needed to be overcome as soon as possible.

"Neal?" Kreiger said, causing a man with red hair to turn

around. He was standing at one of the workstations, watching over the shoulder of a man wearing headphones. The scanner was on his work surface next to a laptop. The seated man must be Gibson, the intelligence officer. Kreiger went on. "I trust you can handle the intros, et cetera. These are the FBI negotiators. I'm going to follow up on those blueprints." Kreiger left the vehicle.

So much for him introducing us... That was the first she'd heard about blueprints, but getting them was a standard request during a crisis incident.

Neal came over to them and eyeballed the coffee cup in Brice's hand.

Brice raised the cup. "I assume you have somewhere this can go."

Neal took it from Brice, shaking it to make sure it was empty before tossing it into the recycling bin in the alcove. "Let me guess? Rick's?"

"It was," Brice said.

"The logo gave it away. His favorite coffee shop. I shouldn't say this, considering I don't know either of you from Adam, but the guy's a freaking litterbug. It irritates the livin' hell out of me."

Sandra smiled. "Special Agent Sandra Vos."

"Lieutenant Coleman. Feel free to use my first name and call me Neal like everyone else. And you?"

"Special Agent Brice Sutton."

Neal nodded. "Well, this is the dream team you'll be working with."

There were two other people in the vehicle.

Neal gestured toward the man. "That's Gibson Farmer, our intelligence officer."

The man turned around, offered a token wave, and smiled. He appeared to be in his late forties, like Sandra. She was forty-seven, but she liked to think the wrinkles around her eyes weren't as defined as his. That might have been denial blended with wishful thinking. She was aware of the grays that kept creeping up in her blond hair.

"I can help you out, Gibson," Brice said. "Whatever you might need. Pulling backgrounds, phone calls... As support for Special Agent Vos, part of the job is providing psychological profiles. Obviously, identities and backgrounds aid with that."

"Offer accepted," Gibson said. "Right now, I'm monitoring the scanner for radio transmissions to see if we can latch on to our perps."

"You can help me with backgrounds," the woman said, holding out her hand to Brice, then Sandra. "Monica Harding, scribe, though I'm stepping up to fill multiple roles right now."

Her smile created fine lines around her mouth. Otherwise, no gray hairs or wrinkles in sight. She had brown hair and a smooth complexion. It was refreshing to be working with another woman, as it wasn't that common in this field. "Nice to meet you," Sandra told her.

"Likewise."

"So who are the backgrounds on?" Brice asked, pulling his laptop from his bag and claiming the workstation next to Monica.

"Officers are gathering plate numbers from the parking garages and vehicles parked on the surrounding streets. They're forwarding these along, and we're pulling backgrounds on the registrations to see if anything flags."

Sandra admired the proactive approach. "Good idea. Especially with the street parking. It could be more appealing to our perps, offering greater ease of getting away."

"Not that anyone is getting far," Neal said.

"True enough, but that's not how the human mind is wired to think." Unlike animals, people consciously planned for the future. If the people inside had any intention of walking away from this, they would have thought this through.

Even against logic that would tell them a clean break wasn't likely.

There was a knock on the vehicle's door, and Neal walked past them to answer. Sandra looked over his shoulder and spotted a uniformed officer and a male civilian next to him.

"Luis Rigby, the hospital's director of emergency management," the man announced.

"Welcome to the party," Neal said, backing up.

Luis stepped into the vehicle. Dressed in pleated pants and a light jacket, he was anything but the picture of composure. His forehead was glistening, his hair poked out from behind his ears, and his glasses were sliding down his nose. He had a zipped leather portfolio tucked under his right arm.

"You've got a mishmash here today. The MPD and the FBI."

The man's eyes jabbed toward her and Brice. Sandra chalked it up to nervousness. Their presence often made people uncomfortable.

Neal quickly ran through the introductions. "Here, take a load off." Neal gestured to the bench seating. "Coffee or anything? Would that make you more comfortable?"

"I'm fine." Luis offered a tepid smile and pulled his portfolio from under his arm as he sat down.

"Yes, we won't bite. I promise." Neal was grinning and let the expression travel to Sandra.

"Though, this one might." She jacked a thumb toward Brice, trying to lighten the tension.

Luis looked at him, and Brice was shaking his head. "She's playing with you."

"Oh." Luis pushed his glasses up his nose.

Luis struck her as a touch socially awkward, but it was hard to know if that was the stress of the day having that effect. Most people, even those in emergency management, weren't emotionally prepared for situations like today.

"You seem a little out of sorts," Sandra said, showing empathy.

Luis met her gaze. "You could say that, but..." He took a deep breath, smiled, and sat back, shoulders square. "My job is to ensure that procedures are followed in cases where something like this happens."

"Has it ever happened before?" She had asked to show interest, already knowing the answer. Helping Luis realize his nerves were perfectly normal.

"No, and now that it has, it's nothing short of overwhelming." He pushed up his glasses that had slid down the slope of his nose again.

"Well, you're safe here, and we intend to resolve this peacefully before anyone inside is hurt." Sandra was running on the presumption no one had been injured, but her softened tone appeared to soothe the man.

"Thank you for saying that." His shoulders relaxed, and he withdrew a slim laptop from his portfolio.

Sandra didn't miss the look shared between Neal and the other MPD cops. Monica pressed her lips and nodded.

"We understand you were working with the service provider to reactivate the hospital's phone system remotely. What are they saying?" Neal asked.

"That it *should* be possible, but it all depends on how it was knocked out. The good news is they can see the network, so someone didn't just pull the plug."

"A virus then?" Sandra asked.

Luis nodded. "Most likely."

"But how would someone infect the server? Emailing a bad file or link?" Neal asked.

Luis shook his head. "This is a highly sophisticated system. It scans all incoming mail and locks out potential threats."

"Technology isn't foolproof. It could have missed one," Neal said.

"I'd say the chances of that happening and aligning for today are slim," Brice put in and added, "I think we're best to assume someone shut it down from the inside."

"Suppose you might have a point," Neal conceded.

Sandra turned to Luis. "How hard would it be to plant a virus on the mainframe to crash the system?"

"Difficult to impossible, but if this happened, it was definitely an inside job. To start, the server is locked inside a dedicated room with retina scanners on the door. Once inside, the person would need to bypass the passwords and understand code to directly upload malware. But if a virus was used, that's potentially good news for us. The service provider may be able to restore and reactivate the system. In the meantime, they are supposed to get me a link to access the last uploaded information. The system backs up automatically ten minutes to every hour."

"We need to know who last accessed that room," Sandra said. "And when."

"Five staff have that clearance. I can get you what you need once I have that link from the provider."

"What floor is the server on?" Sandra's mind shot right to the fourth floor.

"The sixth."

That could be where the gunwoman was posted, the one that prompted the woman's call to 911.

"On another topic, we've been trying to gain access to the security cameras, but Monica hasn't had any luck with the company yet," Neal said.

"I'll see if they respond faster to me."

"That would be great," Neal said. "The sooner we can get eyes inside, the better."

"Just before you get on that, Luis, could you run us through the protocols for lockdown?" Details and facts were crucial. She'd rather be overloaded with intel than on the short end.

"Sure thing. Overhead lights go off, and emergency ones come on. Exterior doors and the ones between levels lock. Personnel are trained to get all patients into their rooms. Doors are to be locked, and all the blinds closed, including ones on exterior windows. Any visitors are escorted into rooms and told to stay put. Staff are also to find a place to hole up.

"Ambulances receive a computerized message in their rigs and are rerouted to Howard University Hospital. Any surgeries underway during the time of a lockdown will continue as long as it's safe to do so. The hospital has several walkie-talkies, which doctors and nurses use to communicate transfer of patients, among other things. They are instructed to keep off the radios during a lockdown."

"I can confirm no one is saying a word," Gibson said, clearly keeping one ear on the conversation.

"And what about elevators?" Brice asked.

"They shut down, and the doors to the stairwells lock."

"What if there was a fire?" Gibson asked from his work-station.

"A fire wouldn't prompt a lockdown."

"But a fire could be started after the place was locked down. Hey, I'm just saying." Gibson shrugged.

"I have the ability to unlock doors and resume the elevator remotely," Luis said, not indicating that Gibson had rattled him. "There is always one person off shift that does. The trick is the system needs to be up and running."

"Does anyone inside have a keycard that overrides all the locks?" Neal asked. "Or does the system need to be responsive for that too?"

"It sure does, but in answer to your other question, no. Otherwise, that could make them a target. If they were taken out, their card stolen, criminals would gain access to the entire hospital. Only a few of us have standard keys and codes to unlock the main entrance, myself included."

"By knocking out the system, the gunmen must not be concerned with unlimited movement around the hospital. Or they didn't know about this restriction. Are these protocols public knowledge?" Sandra asked.

"They are on the hospital website along with the entire emergency response notebook. We need to think about the safety of all our patients and visitors. It's there for them to see before coming."

Sandra imagined the hospital was prepared for several contingencies, but there was no need to squander time exploring the others right now. "What's on the fourth floor?"

"The fourth houses the cardiology and neurology units."

"Critical patients," Brice said.

A knot formed in Sandra's gut, but she pushed the sickening feeling aside. The job demanded her focus, not her emotion. "Which I suspect was intentional, just like their reason for being here today. Just like their reason for shutting down communication. They want to make sure we don't interfere with their plans."

SIX

11:01 AM

There were a few misdirects with Gibson hearing radio communications, but none of them came from inside the hospital. Sandra was waiting impatiently for some beacon of hope, a way to connect to those inside. She considered asking if there was a bullhorn she could get her hands on, but there was no point. Even if it was powerful enough to reach the gunmen inside the hospital, the problem was with logistics. In this situation, it wasn't like they could drop a throw phone at the front door and have a gunman come get it. Not with all the floors locked down and with the hospital system being offline.

Uniformed officers kept Brice and Monica busy pulling information on vehicle registrations. For Sandra, every passing minute felt like twenty, and she caved and pulled out her phone to check the time. She saw she had a missed call and a voicemail from fifteen minutes ago. It was from Dana Ford, her mother's nurse. If she hadn't silenced her phone upon arrival, she would have heard the call.

Sandra's heart sped up, and she excused herself from the command vehicle. Margo Davenport and her late husband adopted her and her twin brother, Sam, when they were twelve.

She was seventy-one and battling Alzheimer's. Some days, it felt like Sandra was living suspended over a precipice prepared to lose her. Not that one was ever ready for the loss of a loved one. And she should know. She'd buried both her parents, and her precious twin brother. Sam was stolen at fourteen years old when he was shot during a hostage situation. After him, she'd lost William Davenport, their adoptive father.

Outside, she didn't bother to listen to the message because the only reason Dana would call was if something was wrong.

Listening to each ring, waiting for Dana to pick up, was painful.

"Hello? Sandra?" Dana eventually answered, saving her from the brink of voicemail.

"Tell me everything's okay." Her words rushed out.

Dana hesitated. It was slight but telling, warning Sandra that the news to come was going to be upsetting.

"Your mother fainted and—"

Sandra's world closed in around her. "Is she okay?"

"When your mother fell, she broke her wrist. It twisted when she landed."

It seemed strange that a fall was all it took for that to happen, but bones typically became more brittle with age. "When did this happen? Where is she now? I'll get there as soon as I can." Sandra was prepared to rush to her mother's side. She hadn't established contact with anyone on the inside. Brice could assume the lead, and another secondary negotiator could be brought in.

"It was just within the hour, but please, don't worry yourself too much. We're at Howard University Hospital. Guess there's a situation at Founders."

Howard was only a sixteen-minute drive away. "I'm there actually."

Dana was quiet for a few beats, then said, "Stay. There's no need for you to upset your workday. Mrs. Davenport is receiving good care. Her wrist has already been bandaged, and they've given her some medication to help with the pain. She's content enough, but she's in quite a dazed state. I'm sorry to say that it's more than likely she won't remember you right now. She keeps asking me why I'm hanging around."

Sandra detected sorrow in Dana's voice at that admission. She was technically an employee, but she lived in Davenport Manor with Margo. In such proximity, a bond had developed. The way Dana referred to Margo formally wasn't the true reflection of her fondness for the woman. And Sandra knew Margo hadn't been well lately. Sadly, refusing to acknowledge that ugly truth didn't change things. She was torn between staying and leaving. No one would judge her if she left. She pinched her St. Michael pendant, as if it could tell her the right thing to do. It was passed on from her father, a career cop, after he died in the line of duty. Then it was passed on to her twin brother. When he was murdered, Sandra took it as her own. It never left her neck. Wearing it made her feel like the two of them were always with her. And her late mother too, who overdosed after her husband's death to ease her grief.

"Ms. Vos, I sense your struggle, but she is being taken care of. There's nothing you could do for her if you were here anyhow. You can help people where you are."

It was uncanny how Dana had read Sandra's mind, but this wasn't the first time. A part of her realized Dana was being logical. Really, there wasn't anything Sandra could do for Margo. It would be about herself and appeasing her conscience. Margo was in good hands between the doctors and Dana at her side. Here at Founders, Sandra could make a difference. "What's next then? Do they know why she fainted?"

"That will be the next step. From what I understand, they'll be doing bloodwork and some other tests to see if they can determine the cause."

"They don't know?" Sandra's breaths were shallow, as if the

permission for the next inhale depended on what came out of Dana's mouth. She really had to pull on her training to remain calm when a personal crisis came up.

"No, but please don't let it stress you out too much. We should know soon and be able to address the matter. My mother always told me that worry is a waste of time. For all our greatest fears, rarely do any of them come true."

Dana was right, but Sandra was still fighting against her fear. Another loved one leaving her behind. She cleared her throat. "Did they say how many tests, or how long they would take?" Sinking into mission mode would keep her moving forward.

"No, but you must know what hospitals are like. They operate on their own schedule."

"All right. But, please, *please*, call me the minute you know anything more."

"Of course, Ms. Vos."

"Thank you."

Dana hung up, and Sandra remained standing there. She needed a few minutes to process everything before she returned inside the command vehicle. Reason argued that in Margo's muddled state, Sandra's arrival would only compound her confusion and frustration. It was hard to admit, but the most loving thing was to let the doctors do their job, while she did hers.

As she held her phone, she considered texting Olivia about her grandmother. She decided against it for now, pocketed her phone and went back inside the vehicle.

The energy was far different from when she left. Dare she say there was the hint of victory?

"Luis got the system link," Neal told her when she walked back in.

Finally some good news... But her thoughts drifted to her mother, lying in a hospital bed sixteen minutes away. On the upside, her emergency had come after the lockdown, or Margo could be inside Founders right now. This gave Sandra more empathy for those whose loved ones weren't so lucky. Like that woman at the cordon line whose sister was in danger. In large-scale incidents like this, she knew it was more conducive to focus on the few, not to be overwhelmed by the many.

"Just give me a minute, and I'll find out who last accessed the server room," Luis said as his fingers tapped on his laptop. "It shouldn't take too long." He drummed his fingers on the table. A few moments later, he was declaring success. "Ah, here we go." He leaned forward. "It was Stevie Cross."

"I've got this," Brice said, and started clicking on his laptop, likely pulling Cross's background.

Sandra didn't miss that Luis had said his name slowly, but she'd circle back to that. And if Stevie was behind the system shutdown on the sixth, was the gunwoman posted on another floor? "At what time?"

"This morning at nine thirty."

"And when do we figure the system went down?" Brice asked.

"Ten on the dot," Luis said, and shrugged when everyone looked at him. "The provider told me that."

"Okay, so Cross could be one of the gunmen inside, or he conspired with someone, let them into the room and left before the lockdown." Sandra's mind swirled with all the possibilities. Cross could have been blackmailed for his help or paid for it.

"All right," Brice began. "Stevie Cross, fifty-five, no criminal record, single, lives alone. Boring as vanilla."

Sandra winced at the judgment and looked at Luis. "When you said Cross's name a moment ago, you said it slowly. Is there something about him that concerns you?"

"It's just that…" Luis looked at her and swept his gaze over the rest of them. "Stevie isn't the most sociable of people."

"Can you elaborate on what you mean by that?" If Cross

was in on this, presumably he had some social skills because he had at least two accomplices.

"Just that. He sticks to himself."

So how does that fit with him working as part of a team? "Is there anything about him that makes you think he'd be involved in something like this?"

"I don't know how to answer that. Do we ever really know anybody? I mean, that's what they say." Luis resumed typing on his laptop, but Sandra wasn't sure what he was checking for. She trusted he'd share if or when it mattered.

After hearing Luis's assessment Sandra leaned more toward her earlier theory of potential blackmail. If so, they'd need to discover what Cross had done that someone saw fit to exploit. There was another possibility that may be easier to prove. *Follow the money* was an adage for a reason. "Brice, what is Cross's credit score?" People with money problems were typically easier to manipulate.

"I didn't check, but one second..." Brice tapped away again. "Oh, his score's in the toilet."

Sandra made eye contact with Brice. "Cross could have been paid to get someone into that server room. Was he due in to work today?" She directed the question at Luis.

The emergency director lifted his eyes from his screen to meet Sandra's. "That's what I was just checking. And, yes, Stevie was scheduled to work today, but he never clocked in."

"Yet, he accessed the server room..." Sandra was feeling more confident in her assessment by the minute.

"Remember I told you five employees have access?" Luis began. "Cross was the only one on the schedule today."

"He'd be guaranteed to have time alone, undisturbed," she said.

"It seems Mr. Vanilla wanted to add a little excitement to his life." Neal pulled his phone from his pocket. "One way to find out. I'm going to get an officer over to Cross's place ASAP."

SEVEN
11:30 AM

Metropolitan Police Department, Homicide Unit

Detective Eric Birch was sitting at his desk, trying to transcribe his scribbled notes into the system when his cell phone rang. "Birch," he answered without looking at the caller's identity.

"It's Sergeant Medina. I'm not sure why I even bother trying to take personal time," he griped as a way of greeting. "*Trying* being the operative word there."

Alex Medina was his boss and out of the city today for his grandchild's birth. His daughter was having a scheduled C-section. For him to call, this had to be something urgent. "Everything all right?"

"There's a loaded question. Keeping it to business, you've probably heard about the lockdown at Founders. There's over eleven hundred people inside."

"I have." It had dominated most of the chatter around the station for the last hour and a half.

"Listen, you know how it is in situations like this. Every available unit and officer, regardless of rank, is boots on the ground. I wouldn't pull you into this if there was an option. I know you're working the Gordon case."

Don't remind me... Thomas Gordon was pulled from the Potomac with a gunshot wound to the chest three weeks ago. No wallet or jewelry, and it presented like a fatal robbery. With little to go on, the investigation file felt bound for cold storage like Gordon's body. A break from the murder could only help perspective. "Just name what you need."

"Those on scene have a potential suspect for you to check out. It's unknown whether he's still inside the hospital or if he served as an accomplice and left before the lockdown. You have authorization to enter and search his home."

"This person's name?"

"Stevie Cross." Medina provided the man's address.

Eric wrote this down on the page in front of him. "Why is he a suspect?"

Medina brought him up to speed.

Access and a lousy credit score. Check.

Medina added, "If, by chance, you find him, treat him as hostile. We don't take chances."

"Which you don't have to tell me."

"And watch your steps, period. The FBI's been called in to help with negotiations. Guess some rich boy is inside. Something Maddox. Name ring a bell for you?"

"It does actually." Eric was certain he'd seen it in the news that morning. Some humanitarian story.

"Well, you know how the world works."

Eric could fill in the gaps. His boss got especially moody when people pulled on their privilege. Even more so when the FBI became involved. Eric wondered if Sandra was one of the FBI negotiators called to the scene. "I'll request an officer or two to accompany me."

"And hopefully you can get them. Most of MPD's resources

are out scouring the area around Founders Hospital, collecting plate numbers."

Officers, *resources*, interchangeable. "Understood. And who do I call with my findings?"

"Lieutenant Coleman. He's acting as team leader today. You have his number?"

"I do." Neal Coleman was an outstanding cop, worthy of respect.

"Great. Don't call me."

Medina ended the call before Eric could even think about asking his boss to elaborate on personal matters. Hopefully all was going well with his daughter and the birth.

Eric saved what he'd been working on and backed out of the system. He wasted no time signing out a car and driving across the city to the address of Stevie Cross.

Eric knocked on Stevie Cross's door and rang the bell. No luck. And not a surprise, really, when it was highly probable that he was inside Founders Hospital.

While Eric was armed with a warrant to breach and search the home, he wanted to sweep the perimeter before heading inside. He walked along the side of the house and stopped next to a window. The curtains were pulled back, and he peered inside.

Cross was sitting in a stuffed armchair in the corner, leaning forward and gripping his head in his hands. There was a bottle of bourbon on the side table and a rocks glass with little left in it. Cross was doing some day drinking.

He must have sensed Eric's presence because he lifted his head and looked straight at him. Did a double take.

Eric tapped the glass and smiled. *Busted!*

Cross staggered to his feet. The front door was open by the time Eric got back there.

"Stevie Cross, I'm Detective Birch. We need to have a little talk."

Cross shrugged, acting nonchalant as he backed up and waved for Eric to enter.

Eric stepped just inside the door, finding the man's reaction to him unsettling. He'd rather meet with outright hostility than lukewarm hospitality. "I'm sure you know why I'm here."

Cross met his eyes. Small, little black beads sunken into a doughy face. Silence.

"Let me lay it out for you then. You turned up at Founders this morning, though not clocking in for your shift. When you were there, you accessed the hospital's server room. Tell me what you did in there."

Several seconds passed in silence. It was like the guy was stoned.

"You better get talking," Eric pushed.

"Someone stole my keycard."

"And your eyeballs?" *Does he not realize I know about the retina scanner?* Eric motioned for Cross to spin. When he didn't, Eric yanked his arm to make him turn, and then snapped on handcuffs. "You're coming with me."

"Please, don't do this. You're making a mistake. I was made to do this."

Eric spun Cross around again, continuing to hold one arm. "Creative. I've never heard that before." Given the situation, Eric wasn't in the mood to give the guy the benefit of the doubt.

"I mean it. Listen, I never meant for this to happen. The whole lockdown thing, the system crash."

"Who said anything about a system crash?"

Cross wet his lips. "I told you someone made me. I just opened the room. The guy did something with the mainframe."

"Did what, specifically?"

"I think he uploaded a virus."

"You think? You'll need to do better than that."

"Ya know, to take out the phones and internet."

"And that's all?"

Cross swallowed roughly. "It could be worse than that."

A cold sweat blanketed Eric. "How much worse?"

"It might have jeopardized medical charts and records."

People will *die...* "Tell me what he uploaded and how to override it."

"I couldn't tell you. This guy, he—"

"Give me a name," he snapped.

Cross flinched.

"I don't care if he promised to come for you and your family. I have a promise for you too. I will make sure you go to prison for a very long time, and trust me, you'll be at the bottom of the pecking order. I suggest you get talking."

"Brent Hartley."

"Just like that?" Eric remained skeptical. Cross hadn't been willing to name anyone a moment ago, but put against the wall, he served someone up.

"Yeah, it's the truth."

Usually when people made that claim, the opposite was true. Eric played along. "So this Brent Hartley uploaded the virus?"

"Ah, yeah."

"And who is Brent Hartley?"

"He used to work at Founders until they canned him a few weeks ago. Guy's not happy, I tell ya that."

Eric wasn't moved by Cross's story because that's how it sat. Like fiction. He hauled Cross out of his house, only giving him time to slip into a pair of shoes before he rattled off the Miranda Rights.

EIGHT

12:03 PM

Sandra couldn't be happier that there were two potential suspects for today's events. Now they just needed to find out more about Brent Hartley. Ideally that intel would prove useful for negotiations. Once she established a means of communication anyhow.

When Neal's phone had rung a few minutes ago, he put it on speaker for everyone to hear. At the sound of Eric's voice, her spirits lifted. She couldn't help but speak up and say she and Brice were there, but he didn't seem surprised.

At the time of his call, Eric had just brought Cross to the station for interrogation. But Cross had requested a lawyer. Eric volunteered to go to Hartley's residence to see what he could find out.

Brice stopped tapping on his laptop. "Okay, so Hartley is fifty-nine, no criminal record. Single, lives in the city." He turned the screen so everyone could see his driver's license. The man was average in every way. Brown hair, brown eyes, medium build.

"As that detective said," Luis began, "I can confirm Hartley was a hospital employee in the admin offices. He was let go three weeks ago for stealing office supplies. He lost his full pension with his termination."

"It seems a rather severe punishment for lifting some pens and paper," Brice said.

"According to his file, it wasn't just one offense. He'd been stealing over a length of time. His option was to leave quietly and take the hit on the pension, or the hospital was prepared to file a lawsuit against him. The hospital doesn't want to give the message employees can help themselves to hospital property."

"Understandable, but I can see how this guy might feel backed into a corner." Brice looked at her. "No job, no pension, no source of income, but how does that translate to him paying Cross to get into the server room? One would think he'd be strapped for cash. And does this guy even possess computer knowledge?"

"It would be foolish to assume he doesn't just because he worked as a paper pusher," she said. "Hartley could study computers in his time off. Today could be about getting his job back or his pension," she said. "Desperate people don't think rationally, as you know."

"And if Hartley is on the sixth floor, who is he working with? Just two friends or others we don't know about?"

"He could have hired help," Brice said. "There is the possibility this is simply about retaliation. He's attacking the hospital, like they essentially attacked him. Though I'm still not sure where he'd get the money to pay anyone."

"And Hartley's not all we're dealing with here," Sandra said. "Luis, were you able to confirm the patient system was unharmed?"

Luis nodded. "Yes, I just received that confirmation via email."

"One thing going right, at least," Neal said.

There was a knock on the door, and it opened immediately after. Kreiger stepped inside with an officer holding a few bags of food.

"Hope you don't mind that I sent an officer on a lunch run. Hopefully y'all love mumbo sauce."

The smell hit before Kreiger's words, and it had Sandra's stomach growling. Mumbo sauce was a Washington staple and typically accompanied comfort food such as wings or pulled-meat sandwiches. She'd run harder and farther along the Potomac tomorrow morning to make up for the indulgence.

The officer set the bags of food on the table and left with a dip of his head.

"Help yourselves." Kreiger grabbed a container and dropped onto the bench of the booth. He opened it and took out a pulled-beef sandwich. "What's the latest on this end? I haven't heard anything about communication being established yet." With that statement, he shot a look at Sandra.

"We're all still working on finding a way in," Neal said, stepping in on her behalf. He then opened the lid on another container and licked his lips.

Sandra filled him in on the leads so far.

Kreiger bobbed his head. "Some headway then. We've had some too. We got our hands on the blueprints, and ERT's studying them. If all turns to hell, we need the fastest and safest route inside."

"Which is even harder when we'd be going in blind." Including herself in the summary hurt, but it would build some camaraderie. "We don't know how many gunmen we're dealing with or where they are all positioned."

Kreiger's mouth was full, but he raised his sandwich to show his agreement.

Everyone else helped themselves to a container and started eating.

After Sandra finished, she stepped outside for some fresh air. The hope was a few minutes to herself would clear her mind. But there was no luck ditching the nagging thoughts about her mother. She took out her phone, and there was a text from Olivia.

Okay, be safe. If u r late, I'll go to Avery's.

Avery was Olivia's best friend, and the girls were practically inseparable.

Sandra stared at her daughter's name, wondering if she should mention the news about Margo. *If I were in her shoes...* This had her selecting her name and calling.

"Mom? What's up?"

"Liv, there's something I need to tell you."

"I responded to your message. Did you not see it? And if you're busy with a negotiation, why are you calling?"

Sandra's heart pinched thinking about the reason. She could come up with something to explain the call and back out of telling Olivia. But if she were in Olivia's place she'd want to know. It was a two-way street. Sandra couldn't expect her daughter to communicate openly if she didn't. "I have some sad news." She paused there. Not because she'd intended to but anxiety gripped tightly around her throat.

"Mom, you're scaring me."

"I'm sorry, sweetie. Everything should be all right, but your grandmother fainted this morning." She pushed past Olivia's gasp. "But Dana's with her, and the doctors are taking care of her."

"I don't understand. But she is okay? Right?"

Avery asked Olivia in the background, "What's going on?"

"It's Grandma."

Hearing her daughter's voice sound so fragile, stung. "She

should be fine," Sandra rushed out, trying to salve the wound. "Dana said the doctors are running tests to tell us if there are any underlying reasons that caused her to faint."

"When you know, I want to know."

"I promise."

"Grandma's gonna be all right, Mom." Now it was her daughter reassuring her.

Sandra squeezed her eyes shut. Her girl had been fortunate not to have lost someone, and Sandra didn't relish the time when that innocence would be taken. "Well, if I had any reservations, I wouldn't be at work. Let that assure you." Guilt snaked through her at the white lie. Sticking around here didn't stop bad feelings from making inroads. She was using her work to preoccupy her mind, or at least keep her worrying at bay.

"Should I go and see her?"

Sandra thought of what Dana had told her about Margo resting peacefully. Also what she'd told her earlier about her being disoriented. "It might be best if we catch up with her a bit later today or tomorrow. She needs her rest, and she's a bit confused."

"I can't believe she's going through this. Isn't the Alzheimer's enough?"

Sandra glanced heavenward. That was a question for a greater being. "Life doesn't always play out how we want. Speaking of, sweetheart, I need to get back to work."

"I love you, Mom."

"I love you too, Liv." Sandra got out her entire reply before Olivia hung up. A rarity that told Sandra that Olivia was clearly just as shaken as Sandra. But regardless of her personal turmoil, Sandra had a job to do. Lives depended on her.

Sandra tried Dana's number and listened to it ring until she landed in voicemail. She ended the call without leaving a message. There could be many reasons Dana couldn't answer. It didn't mean her mother was dying. *Nothing to worry about...*

She pushed off the command vehicle and went inside. Brice raised his left eyebrow, a creepy expression of his that he pulled out when he was shocked or curious. This time she'd side with the latter, but she wasn't getting into her personal life with him right now. "Tell me what I missed."

NINE

12:05 PM

Jordon watched the hands on the clock roll around. Though two hours in this room felt like twenty. He'd never felt so caged in all his life. His parents' wealth ensured the world was laid at his feet. A blessing and a curse because he wanted to make life on his own terms, putting in the hard work and netting his accomplishments. His father understood, but his mother not so much. Since the call with her was dropped, he imagined she'd spun out calling on everyone she knew for favors to find out what was going on with her little boy. Something he'd always be in her eyes despite the advancements he'd already made in his career.

He could hear his mother now. "Jordon, you'll always be my baby boy."

The gunman hadn't stopped pacing except for a few short breaks. His eyes were clear, his pupils not pinpricked or dilated. Jordon could rule out drug use, but the man was antsy regardless. Though taking over a hospital at gunpoint was bound to do that to anyone.

Jordon was just happy the gun was out of his face. But he didn't miss that the gunman kept it close, holding it in his hand as he moved around the room. He had taken his backpack and set it on the counter, though.

Colby Mahoney lost interest in his paper a long time ago and was sitting stiffly on the couch. Jordon knew he was married and a father of one. Leah Winters had dropped behind the couch when the gunman burst into the room but had since been directed to take a seat. She was only in her mid-twenties and a mother herself to two girls. They kept looking at Jordon as if he could rectify the situation.

But he had no plans on being the hero. He'd watched enough crime dramas to know the hero was always killed. No, he'd stay seated on this cushioned chair, still and subservient until the cops shut this down.

After all, his five-year plan certainly didn't include being shot in the hospital where he worked. And it certainly didn't include risking Maria's life or their baby's.

There was at least one other gunman who had spoken over the man's walkie-talkie. There could be more, including others on this floor.

Jordon kept returning his gaze to the gunman's backpack. He didn't seem to worry about it as much as keeping a hold on his gun. But Jordon didn't miss that periodically the man would pass a glance across the room. It was one of those times that Jordon followed his line of sight and noticed something was sticking out of the back flap on the bag. Definitely an electronic device. Probably a Wi-Fi jammer. Jordon was quite certain it was what the man had in his hands when the call with his mother was dropped. It was probably why his phone still didn't have any bars. But how could he expect to get his hands on it without getting a bullet in the back?

The gunman stopped his pacing and picked up Nurse Mahoney's newspaper from the coffee table and started flipping through the pages. Mahoney met Jordon's gaze, and he didn't care for the flicker in the nurse's eyes. He had a tendency of being impulsive in his work, sometimes rushing ahead without approval from a doctor. Jordon shook his head, hoping Mahoney would take the direction.

Instead, when the gunman turned his back, Mahoney slowly got off the couch.

Stupid man! It would only take a split second for the gunman to turn around and pull the trigger. Just a split second...

Winters quietly hissed at Mahoney and passed a panic-stricken look at Jordon.

Their efforts to caution their colleague were ignored as Mahoney hurried toward the gunman, the soles of his shoes slapping on the floor.

Jordon watched in horror as the gunman spun. The rest played out in slow motion. Almost as if time stood still.

The blast of gunfire, followed by Mahoney's screams. They came through dampened to Jordon's ears as if from a thousand miles away.

Winters jumped off the couch and hid behind it. Her hysterical cries sounded like they were coming from a great distance.

Jordon's ears were ringing but he noticed that the man was standing there looking from Mahoney to his hand, as if the gun were a foreign object and he was trying to make sense of what had happened.

If Jordon was going to do something, with the gunman in a trance, now might be the time. He hurried over to the backpack and lifted the electronic device out. It was a jammer, just as he'd thought. Now, he just needed to find the power switch and turn it off.

"I'd put that back in the bag if I were you." The man's voice rolled over Jordon's shoulders as if dry ice, sending chills through to his toes. He braced for the feeling of a bullet tearing through flesh and bone, while a projection of his future played out in front of him. Maria in a white dress smiling and saying, "I do."

"I said, put that back!" the stranger roared.

All Jordon had to do was smash the jammer to the floor, but he froze. Just because the man hadn't shot him yet, didn't mean he wouldn't. Jordon didn't want to die. He wanted the chance to prove himself as a great father. To be a great husband. He raised one hand in surrender. "I'm putting it down."

"No funny business." The man's voice trembled this time. Regret at shooting someone, or riding an adrenaline high because he had. Maybe both. But it was possible Jordon was being too generous to assign this man feelings of empathy considering what he was doing, what he had done.

Jordon put the jammer on the counter. It was out in the open, and should he get a clear opportunity to destroy the thing, he would. His fear be damned.

"Back to your chair. Now!" the gunman barked, guiding Jordon back to the chair he'd been in before with a wave of his gun.

Jordon sat down and got his first look at Mahoney. The nurse was back on the couch, a hand over his upper left arm. Blood was pouring out between his fingers. That location shouldn't have struck anything vital, but the bleeding needed to be stopped or it would be fatal. Jordon gestured toward Mahoney. "Let me help him. I'm a doctor."

The gunman narrowed his eyes and contorted his face into a sneer. "You're going to stay right where you are. I obviously can't trust you."

In a burst of rebellion, Jordon wished he had just smashed that device and really pissed the man off. But to what end? A bullet in the head? And while he might be on the losing end of a physical altercation, he had his brains. "You don't want him to die. Trust me on that. If the police find out, whatever you have planned here will be over. You'll be happy if you don't leave in a body bag." Courage rose within him as he continued to speak. His mouth was running off like he was a rebellious teenager again.

"Fine." The man nudged his gun, pointing toward Mahoney. "Help him. But don't try any funny business."

And there it was again. *Funny business...* It must be the man's adopted colloquialism. Jordon hurried across the room, taking his white coat off as he walked. He lifted Mahoney's left arm and fed the coat's sleeve around it, planning to use it as a tourniquet. Mahoney cried out as Jordon tugged on the fabric and tied it off tightly to staunch the bleeding.

Mahoney's eyes were clouded over with shock and spiked with adrenaline. For now, his body's natural defenses were shielding him from feeling all the pain, but that would only hold out for so long.

"He needs medication to help with the pain and surgery to remove the bullet," Jordon told the gunman.

The gunman shook his head. "That's not happening. You help him as best as you can. Otherwise, we're not going anywhere."

"Then he could die. Is that what you came here to do today? Kill people?" Jordon was shaking with his own dose of adrenaline, and not doing well at keeping his mouth shut. It was a weakness his mother tried to rid him of since he learned to talk.

"It's none of your business what brought me here. Get back to your chair."

Jordon left Mahoney with hesitance but tapped the man's hand before leaving his side. It was the best he could do for assurance. He'd done all he could for now.

He dropped back into his chair, feeling powerless. If only there was a way to get the man separated from his gun... But he'd witnessed how well Mahoney's efforts had gone in that regard and wasn't in a hurry to try it for himself. Not considering how close he'd already come to getting shot himself. And the gunman's aim was bound to improve.

The next few moments passed in silence. Mahoney was wincing and hissing but breathing evenly. Less blood was seeping through the fabric of Jordon's coat. The situation seemed to be stabilized. For now anyway. But would it hold out long enough for help to arrive?

It had already been two hours since the lockdown went into effect. If his mother had heard him before the call was dropped, she'd make the police turn up. But what if she hadn't? Did the cops even know the situation here if people weren't able to call out?

Jordon's eyes drifted to the jammer. Even if they were aware, without a means of communication, the cops would remain in the dark. They would stand down. In the meantime, things would play out however these people with the guns wanted. Jordon had to get to that jammer and turn it off.

The gunman had returned to the newspaper, almost as if nothing had happened. As if he hadn't shot a man. The observation was chilling.

Was Jordon brave enough to take a chance? After all, he knew well that life could change in a flash. Not just with his patients, but look at poor Mahoney on the couch. He wouldn't have expected to be shot today. Life was unpredictable. And in case he didn't survive this, he wanted Maria to know exactly what she meant to him and that he wanted his future to be with her.

Jordon discreetly slipped his cell phone from his pocket. No bars, as expected. He still brought up the text thread he had going with her, tapped out a message, and hit send. Even if she didn't get it immediately, she would eventually and then she'd know just how much he loved her. He pushed his phone back into his pocket just as the gunman looked up from the paper.

He was looking straight at Jordon, and his cold, calculating eyes lit as his lips curved into a smile. "Well, I'll be."

A sickening dread settled in Jordon's core. Call it a gut feeling, but his mother and her insatiable philanthropic causes were going to get him killed. Usually he wasn't roped into being a face among them, but last week, he was involved. His mother awarded full medical scholarships to five students who otherwise wouldn't be able to afford the schooling. The announcement garnered media attention and netted an interview at his family home. His mother touted him and his accomplishments for inspiration.

"This is you." The gunman held up the photo of Jordon smiling next to his mother. He walked over to Jordon, closing the distance between them to a few inches. The man laughed. "What do you know? My life has just changed for the better."

Jordon should have known the man would discover his identity sooner than later. But he could use this as leverage. "Let everyone else go. Hold on to me."

Nurse Winters gave Jordon a hopeful look, as if he was her savior, but she ought to hold on to her optimism. Jordon noticed the gunman's face was unchanged. There was a calm, somewhat eerie peacefulness to it. Unsettling.

"Please, let them go," he petitioned again.

The man shook his head, all the while smiling. "This is so much bigger than you and me, kid, but you are a godsend."

Jordon bristled at being referred to as a gunman's gift from God. He was just religious enough to take offense.

The man went over to his backpack and dug out a walkie-talkie. He was smiling as he spoke into it. "I just got us some more insurance."

TEN

12:15 PM

Sandra tossed the stir stick into the garbage, took her coffee to her workstation next to Brice, and sat down. Maybe if she adopted an optimistic mindset, she'd be rewarded. She certainly wasn't when she'd returned to the vehicle. No one had any updates to give her.

Kreiger had left them after eating to rejoin ERT. Brice and Monica continued pulling registrations and backgrounds on vehicles in the area. Luis's efforts with the security company hadn't paid off yet, so they were still without eyes on the situation inside.

Gibson raised his left arm in the air and snapped his fingers. Everyone looked at him. Neal came over, standing at their backs and literally breathing down Gibson's neck.

Gibson didn't say or do anything but lower his arm for the next few seconds. Sandra watched as a window flashed up on his computer screen. "Bingo. Okay, so there was just a transmission. Two parties. A man and a woman. Trajectory puts the communication inside the hospital."

A thrill ran through Sandra. "What was said?"

"It was short and sweet, but the system automatically

records activity." Gibson took his headphones off and hit a button. The recording came over the speakers in his laptop.

"*I just got some sweet insurance,*" a man said.

"*Stick to the plan,*" a woman hissed. "*And get off the radio!*"

Short and sweet was right, but it confirmed that early 911 caller's statement. "So there *is* an armed woman inside."

"But we still have no way of knowing what floor she's on," Brice said.

"I'm curious about that man's voice." Sandra looked at Luis. "Did that sound like Hartley's?"

Gibson played it again.

"Nah, I wouldn't say so. Guy sounds about the same age, though."

Sandra could hear that too. Or as she'd describe it, the voice belonged to a mature male. "So this could be the man from the fourth floor. Or someone else we don't know about yet."

"Well, if it's the guy from the fourth, we know that Jordon Maddox was on that floor," Brice said, turning toward her.

Her colleague's implication chilled her. Maddox's wealth and prestige would make him a target and provide the gunman with leverage. Or *insurance*, as he'd put it. The man would feel protected and invincible. "I need a walkie-talkie ASAP."

Gibson reached overhead to a cabinet and pulled one out. He powered it up and twisted the dial to the right frequency. "You're all set."

As she took the walkie-talkie, she was blasted into the past.

"Peanut, do you copy? Over." Sam's young voice comes across the radio with my call sign. It was Mom's nickname for me because I was smaller than Sam when I was born. When he uses it, I feel closer to her. It helps even more as I was lying awake in the dark, staring at the ceiling, feeling uncomfortable in this new place. The house, the smells, and the foster parents are strange. All these things keep me up.

"I copy. Over," I say back, wishing we shared a bedroom, but we're not allowed with me being a girl and him a boy.

"What is your situation? Over."

"I wish you were here. Over." A hot tear splashes my cheek.

"I am here. Always. Now, sail off into Dreamland, and I will meet you there. Copy? Over."

"Copy. Goodnight, Sam. Over."

"Goodnight."

The recollection replayed in less than a second, but the passing memory had left its mark. It didn't feel like she'd ever get over the loss of her brother.

"Okay, so is everyone ready?" She looked at the team.

"Born that way," Brice said. Not that his cocky response surprised her in the least.

Gibson and Neal all nodded that they were ready. Monica, the ever-diligent scribe, had her fingers over the keyboard of her laptop ready to record the conversation.

Moment of truth... Sandra was thinking this as she pushed the button on the walkie-talkie. She was *on the air.* "Hello there. Anyone on this frequency?"

The silence stretched out for a few seconds before there was a response. "Go away. This is a private channel."

She nodded at the team, and Brice nodded back. That voice was the man they'd just heard on the playback. She was on with one of the perps. "This is Sandra," she said, purposely not rushing to identify herself as FBI. "Who are you?"

"Not born yesterday."

At least he responded. "Everyone out here is worried about you in there. Is everyone all right?"

"Everyone's fine. Now get lost."

"That's great news. How many are with you on the fourth floor?" She paused, having a feeling she'd lost the guy. The urge was to rush in, but she remained silent, to give him a chance to speak. After a minute, she said, "Hello? Can you hear me?"

Nothing again for another minute.

"He's gone," Gibson said. "He either turned off his radio or switched frequencies."

"I'll let him be for a few minutes and try again." While she wanted more details on his *sweet insurance*, negotiation was a dance. Coming out with the question would have gotten the man's back up more than it already was.

"At least you made contact with one of the perps on the inside," Monica said. "And he didn't deny being on the fourth floor."

"Still, it's been a few hours and all we have is this." Gibson scribbled on the markerboard and pointed at his takeaway. *No injuries on the fourth.* He wrote that next to the addition of *perps using walkie-talkies to communicate.*

Sandra's mind stuck on *perps.* "This hostage taker isn't the shot caller."

Brice shook his head. "Not with the way that woman barked at him to stick to the plan and get off the radio."

"If that woman is the shot caller, why didn't she speak up just now with you there?" Neal asked.

Sandra could think of one explanation. "She's not ready. If you think about it, they've gone to a lot of effort to shut down lines of communication. Not just with a Wi-Fi jammer, but in also wiping out the hospital's phone system."

"They're obviously trying to accomplish something here, but they must realize they need to talk to us for that to happen," Neal said.

"Unless they don't," Sandra served back. "Whatever they are after may be inside those walls. Going dark prevents us from interfering."

"They can't expect us to stand around out here forever," Neal pushed out.

Sandra thought it best not to point out they were likely quite confident they'd be granted some time. There were a lot of lives at risk and no law enforcement agency wanted anything rivaling the Waco Siege of '93. With that incident everything was handled wrong from the start, and eighty-two people paid with their lives. "I doubt they do. My focus needs to be on how I can get the hostage takers to see that talking to us is their best course of action. I'm going to try again."

Her attempt was met with failure, and Gibson confirmed there was no radio activity whatsoever. Changing frequencies wouldn't help. With the clock steadily ticking forward, it was drilled in how the timeline was out of their hands. Many people inside were already ill, in need of medical attention or medication at regular intervals, but they wouldn't be getting the help they needed. Just like how her brother had died because he hadn't gotten treatment soon enough. But if it wasn't for those patients, all the innocent lives, she'd have a tougher challenge in holding off ERT officers from breaching.

Gail kept lifting the phone receiver, but every time she did she was met with silence. The line was dead, and her cell phone didn't have any bars. If that wasn't unsettling enough, being stuck inside this room was making her claustrophobic. The brightest thing in here was the readout on her daughter's heart machine. Otherwise, emergency backup lights spread shadows into the corners. "What is going on? Why can't we call out?"

"I don't know," Nurse Torres said, her eyes blank.

Gail couldn't just stay here while her daughter's life hung in the balance. She left Phoebe to peek through slots in the blinds out to the hallway. Maybe she could spot a reason for hope that this would be over soon.

"Please, ma'am, get away from there." Nurse Torres came up behind her and beckoned her away from the window.

"We can't just be expected to stay holed up in here. I don't see anything." A stamp of frustration, like a petulant child, but her nerves were stretched and frayed.

"It doesn't mean we're safe, Ms. Chapman. Please." The nurse came over to her, holding out her hand.

If she expected Gail to take it and step away, she had another think coming.

The heart monitor started beeping wildly. Gail turned to watch in horror as the line spiked and dipped. Phoebe was pale and sweating. "Do something," Gail begged the nurse.

Torres was already at Phoebe's side. "She's arresting, and there's only one thing that can help her."

"What?" Gail screamed out, fear gripping hold of her. She should know, having been here before, but it was like her mind had left her.

The nurse remained calm, soothing her daughter, rubbing the hair back on her forehead. "It's okay, sweetheart. Everything will be okay."

"Why aren't you doing anything?"

The machine continued to beep. The spikes had lower peaks, but the rhythm remained erratic.

"Do something!" Gail never felt more helpless in her life.

"She needs a defibrillator, and..." The nurse's eyes widened, and jabbed toward the door.

"They're out there?" Gail blanched. She never understood why one wasn't always in the room near her daughter, just in case. Probably due to budget restraints. Money determined life and death.

Torres nodded. "But we can't go out there."

"To hell with that! Tell me where, and I'll go get it."

"I can't let you do that."

Gail got in the nurse's face. "Tell me where to get one! Now!"

"They're on wheeled carts next to the nurses' station, but I told you, *we can't go out there*."

"I'm not just going to stay here and watch my daughter die."

"You go out there and run into the gunmen, you could both die."

"I don't matter. Only Phoebe!" To hell with being swallowed by hopelessness. Her baby's life was on the line. She stormed out the door, ignoring the nurse's protests at her back.

Voices came to her ears from down the hall, transmitting scared, nervous chatter. Gail looked back over her shoulder at the room, and Nurse Torres was peeking out through a crack she made in the blinds. Spotted, she let the slots fall back into place.

Gail crept down the hall toward the nurses' station, keeping a lookout for the gunmen. The voices she'd heard were coming from inside a room with a plaque on the door that read *Nurse Break Room*. It sounded like there was an altercation inside. Was a gunman in there, just mere feet away, with only a door standing between them?

Not my problem, she told herself. She just had to grab a cart with a defibrillator and get it back to her daughter. She saw them next to the desk. Her hand was on one when there was a loud bang.

She ducked to the floor behind the desk, her ears ringing and her heart thumping furiously. *Gunfire!*

It came from inside the break room. The earlier chatter and scuffle transformed into screams and crying.

Not my problem, she screamed again in her head while she stood. She planned to just grab the cart and run. But there was a charging tray with three walkie-talkies on the desk, and she snatched one. She couldn't call out on the phones, so maybe this would work.

She grabbed the closest cart and pushed it back to the room in a run. When she was within a foot of the door, Nurse Torres threw it open and swept her inside.

Eric was used to multitasking, and leaving one suspect to speak to another wasn't unheard of. Cross was waiting on his lawyer anyhow.

Brent Hartley's place was a modest row house, painted purple. The street was lined with some cherry trees, their pink petals at their peak. By next week the ground would be littered with them, and they'd be blowing everywhere.

Eric banged on Hartley's door. Stacks of boxes and totes blocked the front window. Hartley was a hoarder. Eric arrived with full clearance to enter the home, just as he had with Cross, and he was prepared to do that. He'd just have to find another way in.

Just as he went to step away in search of another entry point, the door was cracked open.

Eric froze. He hadn't expected a response. The consensus was that Hartley was holed up on the sixth floor of the hospital. Eric's hand hovered over his holster, prepared to respond with force.

A man in his late fifties tucked his head through, and it was Brent Hartley. The breathing version was a match to his license photo with some imagination. This one had greasy hair matted to his head and beady eyes. Hartley and Cross had the latter in common.

"What do you want?" Hartley asked.

Eric pulled his badge without taking his eyes off Hartley. "Detective Birch. You're Brent Hartley?" Asked purely for the record.

"Yeah."

"I need to talk to you about an incident at Founders Hospital."

"Hold up. They said if I went quietly, they wouldn't press formal charges or take me to court."

"This isn't about the office supplies. You may have heard about the lockdown at Founders Hospital." Eric decided he'd feel him out before dragging him down to the station and sticking him into an interrogation room. But he'd do it from the step. A peek over Hartley's shoulder showed a narrow path wormed to and from the door. Entering would be taking a risk to his personal safety. In more ways than one. It was hard to defend oneself within a square foot of space, and who knew what bacteria was thriving in there?

"I don't watch or listen to the news."

"You were let into the server room where you uploaded a virus to take out the hospital's system. Then you left before the place was locked down."

Hartley's face paled, and his mouth gaped open.

Eric snapped his fingers. "Hartley. You need to get talking and fast."

"I have no idea what you're talking about. I've been home. Founders fired me three weeks ago."

As a veteran detective, Eric trusted his ability to read people. There were only so many types of personalities, and during his career, it felt like he'd seen them all. Hartley looked baffled. "Are you telling me you have no ill will against your former employer? They fired you and took your pension." Eric tried to entice a reaction for a better gauge on the man.

"I hate them, but as you can see, I'm here, not there."

He made a solid point, but he could have hit and run like Cross had. Eric imagined it was possible for the virus to be time-delayed. "See, the problem comes in because your claim of innocence doesn't line up with what I've been told."

"Then you were lied to. You said a virus? I don't know jack about computers, unless working Word and Excel count. Certainly nothing like how to infect the hospital's system."

"Why would someone tell us you did this when you didn't?" Eric could think of one reason. That Cross wanted to waste Eric's time. While he was busy chasing false leads, the real culprit remained unidentified. But he had to see this through. "Come on, we're going down to the station."

"Seriously? I'm not saying a word until I get a lawyer."

"As per your right." Eric cuffed him and had him taken back to the station. He followed the police cruiser, hoping Cross's lawyer had arrived so Eric could talk to him and ideally make some progress.

It turned out Cross was ready to go, and Eric made up a coffee and headed to the observation room for a look at Cross and his attorney through the one-way mirror.

Cross paced, appearing more frayed than before. He kept running his hands down his face and raking his greasy hair with his hands, contributing to the problem.

Eric entered the room without knocking, and Cross flinched and paused mid-pace.

"If you could sit..." Eric gestured to the empty seat beside the lawyer and set the coffee there.

Cross sat down and eyed the offering with skepticism.

"Go ahead. I brought it for you." Eric turned to the lawyer. "Sorry that I didn't think to bring you one."

The lawyer smiled tightly and slid his business card across the table. Eric didn't pick it up, barely glanced at it, but caught the name. Gaylord Pearson. His parents must have hated him.

The lawyer leaned forward, but his rigid movement told Eric he was poised for a fight. "My client is ready to talk if you can guarantee his safety."

"His safety? What about the eleven hundred people inside of Founders Hospital right now?"

"My client has nothing to do with that."

Eric was the one to smile tightly this time. He could lay it all out, how they might not be in this mess if not for him, but attacking Cross would shut him up. Eric was forced to dance. "We'll disagree on that. But let's say your client has reason to be concerned with his welfare. Before I can give you any guarantee, I need to hear what he has to say." Eric leaned back in his chair, crossed his arms as if disinterested. In truth, Eric saw all this talk of fear for his life to be hyperbole. Especially if he were meant to believe Brent Hartley was violent.

Pearson gestured at Cross for him to speak.

"I was told that if I didn't cooperate, I would be hurt. I'm just as much a victim here."

Eric bristled at that claim. "How is that?"

"I was vulnerable. This person knew about my gambling debts." Cross met Eric's eyes.

"So this is about blackmail now?"

"Ah, yeah."

"And *this person* being Brent Hartley?"

Cross rubbed his chin on his shoulder and looked at the lawyer.

"Because that's what you told me. You let Brent Hartley into the server room, and he uploaded a virus. I have to say, I've talked with the guy, and he's not scary to me. Not too smart either."

Cross was refusing eye contact.

The telltale sign of an unskilled liar. "It wasn't Brent Hartley, was it?"

"No."

"Why tell me that then? To waste the taxpayers' money? Drag things out for everyone?"

"I... I don't like the guy."

Eric licked his lips and leaned forward, shook his head. "That's not why. You're lying, Mr. Cross."

"Not about how I feel about him." The second the words left Cross's lips, he snapped his mouth shut and remained still.

Eric resisted the urge to smile. Cross as good as admitted he'd lied about everything but his feelings toward Hartley. Eric turned to Pearson. "I'm not sure what your client told you, but there's no denying that Cross got into the hospital's server room. The scanner needed his eyes. The rest is up for debate."

"My client is not disputing that part, but he was there under duress."

"Honestly, I'm losing patience. Who threatened you? Made you do this?"

"I don't have a name."

"Fine. What did he look like?"

Cross turned to his lawyer.

"It's best that you tell him all you know," Pearson advised his client.

"He was in his fifties, scruffy, a white guy."

"Seems rather vague. How did he find you?"

"He, ah, just came up to me at work last week."

All the filler words Cross kept using didn't bode well for his truthfulness. "Uh-huh. Let me be honest with you. I think you're still lying to me. And Mr. Cross, there's nothing much I hate more than a liar. Either we start having honest communication or I'm out of here, and you'll be facing decades, if not life in prison." Eric paused for effect, then added, "If anyone dies today, you will go away for murder."

"What? No, that's not— I didn't do it."

"When you opened that server room, you became an accomplice to a felony. Have your lawyer explain that to you if you're confused." Eric got up and left the room. Cross might not be talking, but the search of his home might speak on his behalf. All Eric knew was Hartley had to be cut loose, and Cross warranted closer scrutiny.

It felt like everyone in the room was watching him. Jordon should be used to the spotlight being born a Maddox, a sole heir at that, but it never got any easier. He wanted to make his mark as an exceptional neurosurgeon to help people, not for fame or money. If the latter was his driver, he didn't need to get up and do anything in the morning because his trust fund was sizable enough to finance generations.

Mahoney was looking pale and clammy, and his breathing was becoming a little choppy.

"Let me look at him again, see what I can do." Jordon made the petition while not holding out much hope.

The gunman waved his weapon, directing Jordon to Mahoney on the couch. Jordon first inspected the wound and saw that the bleeding had slowed to nothing. The fabric of Jordon's coat hadn't gotten any more soaked with blood. That was a good thing. Jordon pulled his stethoscope from around his neck and listened to Mahoney's heart. The beats were even but a bit on the slow side and indicative of low blood pressure. "He needs surgery and medication, or he could die." If the gunman obliged to the latter, Jordon *might* be allowed to leave the room.

"Neither is happening."

"Do you want him to die?"

The man put the gun in Jordon's face, and he withdrew, holding up his hands in surrender.

"Hello there. Anyone on this frequency?" A woman's voice cut into the room. It was coming over the walkie-talkie. It wasn't the one who a moment ago had told the gunman to get off the radio. This one was different. Jordon felt a bud of hope in his chest.

"This is Sandra. Who are you?"

The gunman's gaze became a blank stare before he started to pace again. He put his back to them, and Jordon eyed the jammer that was still on the counter. With the man distracted, he might be able to spring to his feet and smash the thing before the gunman had a clue.

Jordon quietly made his way over there, having just enough time to retrieve the jammer and race back to Mahoney. Jordon pushed the jammer under the couch in a fluid motion as he got down on his knees.

The woman said over the walkie-talkie, "Everyone out here is worried about you in there. Is everyone all right?"

Sandra had to be a cop or negotiator. There might be hope for a rescue yet. Jordon wanted to scream that a man had been shot and needed surgery. But to what end? The gunman would need to hold the button down to open the line of communication. And then Jordon would need to feel especially lucky.

"Everyone's fine. Now get lost." The man tossed the walkie-talkie into his backpack.

Jordon went cold. He was going to notice the jammer was missing. Jordon tensed and made eye contact with Nurse Winters.

The gunman had gone still. The room was quiet except for Mahoney's panting.

Please don't notice... But Jordon knew it was too late for that wish to come true when the gunman turned around and leveled his gaze at him.

"You!" the man hissed. "Where is it?"

"Where is what?" Jordon pretended to be immersed in Mahoney's care, oblivious to whatever crisis the gunman was undergoing. But he saw the judgment in his adversary's eyes. It was a fair one, but bitter in these circumstances. He was an excellent surgeon but a terrible actor. And an even worse liar.

"Don't play dumb with me. Where did you put the jammer?" The gunman was quickly at Jordon's side. The gun was aimed at his head. "Hand it over now."

It was like the device was sending out a pulse that Jordon could feel. If he destroyed it, this nightmare could be brought to an end. Or would it make it worse? But the police needed to know what was going on in here. People needed to reach their loved ones. Just as he would give anything to speak with Maria and lay a hand over her stomach and talk to their child. He beamed them both as much love as possible, hoping they'd sense it. The man holding the gun may rob him of everything.

"I said, hand it over." The muzzle was pressed against his skull.

It was still warm from shooting Mahoney. The gunman wasn't the image of a violent character, but his actions confirmed his capability.

"I'll get it for you. I'm sorry, I shouldn't have taken it."

"Damn right you shouldn't have."

"It's just… It's under the couch. I must reach for it." Jordon dragged out the situation, moving slowly, trying to scheme some way out of this. A way to bring it all to an end. Though there was at least one other person with a gun. The woman who had yelled at the man over the walkie-talkie a moment ago. He could swear it was the same one who had said, "Secured," at the beginning of this. Well, she sounded vicious. What would keep her from storming into this room? But Jordon had the answer to his question the moment it had formed. She must not be on this floor. And with the lockdown, she wouldn't be able to come in here.

"Hurry up," the gunman urged.

Jordon never cared for being rushed. It was a pet peeve, and a possible weakness. But the gunman's prompting only made him want to rebel. He surprisingly kept a cool head until he rose to his feet, putting some space between them. The device was in his hand, and the gunman had lowered his gun, his guard down, to take it from Jordon.

"You want the jammer?" Jordon asked. "Here it is." He hurled it at the gunman's head.

Startled, the gunman ducked out of the way just before the device hit him, and the gun dropped from his hand. The jammer sailed across the room, smashed into the wall, and fell to the floor in a jumble of pieces.

"You little shit!" the gunman roared after witnessing the aftermath.

Jordon took advantage of this distraction and went for the man's gun, but he couldn't see it anywhere. *Where the...?*

Nurse Winters was in the corner of the room, her back to the wall, holding on to the weapon. Her hands were shaking, and she could barely keep her arms raised. "Leave us alone!" Her cry was ear-piercing.

The gunman smiled, a maniacal and evil grin that belonged to a villain in any movie. "Do you think I have anything to lose? Go ahead. Shoot me." The man raised his arms, and Jordon was unsettled by this dark twist.

Winters looked at Jordon, then let her gaze slip past him to the gunman. "I will. I swear."

"This doesn't need to get any worse. No one else needs to get hurt," Jordon said, not just to the gunman but to the nurse as well. He walked over to her with his hands up, cautiously taking steps forward while watching over his shoulder. "Give me the gun, Leah. It will be all right."

Tears were streaming down her cheeks. She sniffled and handed Jordon the weapon.

He could finally breathe. Not realizing how he had been taking shallow breaths. "She's right, though. You're going to leave us alone. This is over." Jordon turned as he spoke to fully face the stranger, leveling the gun on him.

The man was standing behind Mahoney, his arm around his neck. Mahoney batted at him, but his strength was clearly fading. "It's only over when I say it's over. Now hand me my gun, nice and slow, or I will strangle your friend here."

Jordon played the scenarios through in his head. He could pull the trigger, but he wasn't a skilled shot. The stranger was leaning over Mahoney, and his head was too close to the nurse's. If Jordon fired the gun, he just may end Mahoney's life as easily as take the stranger's. There was the chance he could pull it off. But was it a risk worth taking? Maybe Jordon could lure the stranger away from Mahoney to hand him the gun. Or... Instead of surrendering the weapon, he'd pull the trigger. Yes, that might work.

Jordon kept some distance from the man, and as it had worked in his thoughts, the stranger put a bit more space between himself and Mahoney as he reached for the gun.

In his mind, Jordon pulled the trigger. The stranger went down. The nightmare was over. Or was it? There was that woman out there... And Jordon was being barraged by the Hippocratic Oath. *Do no harm.* If he shot this man, he was no better than him. Jordon didn't want murder on his conscience, justified or not. Unlike his sick patients who didn't survive surgery or treatment, this death would be deliberate. At his hands. The very hands that were skilled at saving life.

No, he couldn't do it. Jordon held out the gun, putting the handle toward the man.

"Smart guy," the stranger said as he took his weapon back.

Jordon stood there numb, silent, paralyzed by self-chastisement and second thoughts. Maybe he'd been too quick to assume he'd be haunted if he'd killed him. He was accustomed to death, having it around him. He had money for therapy. Not that it mattered. There was no going back. The moment had passed.

"I want all of you to hand over your phones. Now!"

Winters was sitting on the floor crying and shaking. Mahoney's eyes were glazing over.

Jordon took his phone out, hoping like hell the message to his girlfriend had gone through, and gave it to the man. "Do you have a phone?" Jordon asked Winters.

She pointed toward the couch, and Jordon fished in the cushions for her phone and surrendered it. When the transfer was made, Winters let out a strangled cry.

"And yours." The gunman nudged his gun toward Mahoney, and the man flinched.

"Get that away from him." Jordon rushed to his defense, and the gunman turned on him with cold eyes.

"Give me one reason I shouldn't shoot you after what you did," he barked.

Jordon raised his hands and backed up. His entire body was quaking. Not with rage, not with fear, but self-criticism. He should have shot the bastard when he had the chance.

The stranger raised the gun on Jordon. "Don't think I won't shoot you. I'm sure it will be easier the second time."

FOURTEEN

12:30 PM

Gail stood back and watched in horror as the machine attached to Phoebe's heart nearly flatlined. She opened her mouth to cry out, but all sound was smothered in her throat.

Nurse Torres powered up the defibrillator and approached Phoebe armed with the paddles. "Stay back," she told Gail just before she applied them to Phoebe's chest.

Her daughter's body flopped on the bed like a lifeless puppet. Her complexion was deathly pale, and her lips a shade of blue. "Please... please, help her."

The nurse repeated the process and powered the paddles again. The heart monitor stopped screaming, and Phoebe's heart rate picked up again. While it was a touch erratic, it had a relatively stabilized baseline.

Tears were falling down Gail's cheeks as she moved toward her daughter. Phoebe's eyelashes fluttered, and she opened her eyes. "I'm here, baby. Mommy's here." Gail swept back some of her daughter's hair from her forehead. It was wet and plastered to her flesh, but at least her color was returning.

"I can't believe that you... that you did that, went out there.

Do you realize how reckless you were in doing that? You could have killed yourself, killed the rest of us."

Gail's heart was still pounding from the experience, but she'd do it again. "We're all scared, but there was no way I was letting my baby die."

"I heard a gunshot. Where did it come from?" She was speaking stoically and staring blankly at the floor.

"Hey, are you all right?"

"Just tell me. Where was the gun fired?" Torres slowly lifted her eyes to meet Gail's.

"It was in the break room near the nurses' station."

Nurse Torres touched her neck, her fingertips toying with the collar of her uniform, and tears beaded in her eyes.

"For what it's worth, I don't know if someone was hit." Gail would keep the fact she'd heard screams to herself. That's if Torres hadn't heard them herself.

Torres nodded while chewing her bottom lip.

Gail glanced at Phoebe. Her sweet girl was now resting peacefully, her little chest going up and down while the monitor tracked her heart. Stronger, more even dips and peaks. But she knew it wouldn't stay that way. Gail took the walkie-talkie from the pocket of her sweater. "I grabbed this from the nurses' station. We can call for help now."

"No, you can't." Torres's face blanched.

"Like hell I can't, and why wouldn't I?"

"If you do, there's a good chance the gunman will hear you and come right here. You don't want him in here with Phoebe."

Gail felt a jab under her ribs. "Then what are we supposed to do? Wait and do nothing?"

"Pretty much. Yeah. Police are already out there. I peeked outside and saw them."

After she told me to stay away from the windows... "Then they must have heard the gunshot. Why aren't they coming in?"

A ding sounded from the nurse's pocket.

Gail lit up. "Was that your phone?"

"Actually... I think it was." Torres reached in and pulled the device from her pocket. "It's a text message."

"Then the phones are back up. Or at least cell phones. I can call the police and tell them someone was shot."

"You just said you didn't know if someone was hit." Torres looked up from the screen of her phone. Her expression shadowed.

"I don't, but the police will come much faster if they think someone is hurt," Gail said, rushing to backpedal.

"No, you can't lie to them." Torres's gaze fell back to her phone.

The hairs raised on Gail's arms. "Bad message?"

Torres shook her head, sniffled, and put her phone away.

Gail saw the bars on hers and called 911.

Sandra had talked over the walkie-talkie several times in the last forty minutes, trying to lure a response, but nothing worked. If they were even still listening. Thirty-five minutes had passed since Sandra got through to the man over the radio. His words "everyone is okay" continued to haunt her because she had no foundation of trust with him.

The door to the vehicle swung open and Kreiger stepped inside. "Good news, everyone. The jammer's been knocked out. Bad news. There are so many calls flooding nine-one-one, they're overloading the system. But there's one woman currently on the line about to be patched through to here. She says she's on the fourth floor, and there was a gunshot."

Where they knew one gunman was positioned. But no one had heard gunfire. The concrete and steel of the structure must have prevented the sound from reaching them out here.

The vehicle's phone rang, and Gibson answered. "Yes, I understand." Gibson spun his chair around. "I have the woman from inside, a Gail Chapman, on a shared line with the nine-one-one dispatcher. You can pick it up there." Gibson pointed at the headset dangling on a hook in Sandra's workstation.

Sandra wasted no time putting it on her head. "Gail Chapman? This is FBI Special Agent Sandra Vos. Are you somewhere safe and hidden?"

"Yes, in my daughter's room. But, please, do something. He has a gun." Her breaths were fast and jagged, and if Sandra didn't help calm her down, she'd go into a full-blown panic attack.

"You've got the door locked and the blinds closed?" As much as Sandra wanted details, the women's safety was the priority.

"Yes."

"And it's just you and your daughter in the room?"

"And Nurse Torres is here." Gail's inhales were hungry gasps for air. If she kept going like this, she might pass out.

"Gail, you need to do something for me. Okay?"

"Okay." Tentative.

"Just take a few deep breaths."

"I am..." She panted. "Breathing."

"Just deep, calm breaths," Sandra reiterated in her soothing late-night DJ voice.

When Gail's breathing slowed, Sandra spoke again. "There. Are you feeling better?"

"A bit, but he has a gun."

At least this time when she doled out the situation recap, she was much calmer than before. "How many men are there with guns?"

"Just the one that I know of."

"So you never saw or heard this man talking to anyone else? An accomplice?"

"He was talking to people. I think they're with the hospital, though, and he... *he...*"

"You're safe, Gail. Talk to me. He what?" Sandra remembered Kreiger said this woman heard gunfire, but she wasn't going to rush her.

"I went out there... in the hall. The sounds came from the nurse break room."

Sandra looked over at Brice, who had picked up his headset and was listening in too. "What did you hear?" she asked Gail.

"There was a bunch of talking. Men's voices, two or three. I think one was the gunman. Then there was what sounded like a scuffle, the gun went off, and there was screaming." Her breathing deepened. "I think that he... *that he* might have shot one of the men. One screamed, and that's also when I heard a woman cry."

Sandra sensed the energy shift inside the vehicle. Injuries changed things and would have ERT wanting to move in, but there was nothing standard about today's incident. "Do you know if anyone was seriously hurt?"

"A man was shot."

"There was a gunshot," another woman said in the background, presumably Nurse Torres. "That's all you know for sure."

"You weren't there," Gail said. "You didn't hear the screams or crying."

"Ms. Chapman, did you hear anything else after the gun was fired?" Sandra asked calmly, taking back the reins of the conversation.

"No, but someone could be dead."

"You sound scared, and that's understandable. But, please, focus on what you heard. Did anyone cry out that someone was killed?" Sandra slid her gaze to Kreiger, who was watching her closely with squinted eyes. The expression defined a wrinkle in his brow line.

"No."

There was some hope in that. Logic would suggest someone would have blurted this out in shock. While injuries ramped up the urgency, murder advanced things to the next level. "Please run me through when you heard the gunfire. Why were you in the hall?"

A few beats of silence, then Gail told her about her daughter arresting and how she went to get a defibrillator.

Sandra was touched by the story, but she couldn't allow herself to get weighed down from it. Her focus needed to be on resolving this incident. Even asking about the daughter's well-being would be too much. It could be assumed the child was helped, or the woman would be past soothing. "I'm so sorry that you and your daughter are going through all this. So you heard all this take place from the hall outside the nurse break room, but you didn't see the shooting happen?"

"That's right. I just heard it."

Sandra made eye contact with Kreiger again and shook her head. "Did the man see you? Know you were in the hall?"

"I don't think he even knew I was out there. And I hurried back to the room with the cart." Sniffles traveled the line.

"You're doing great, Gail."

"What are you waiting for? Get in here and put an end to this. He shot someone. I *know* that. I mean, why else fire a gun? And with doctors and nurses locked up in the rooms, he won't get the help he needs."

"I assure you, Gail, that we are doing all we can to bring this to a safe resolution for everyone."

"What does that even mean?" Gail tossed back. "If you don't do something fast, my daughter is going to die!"

Sandra may have been wrong to assume the situation with the daughter was resolved. Clearly, her daughter had a weak heart. She could arrest again. There was a clatter from the other end of the line, and Sandra thought the connection had been lost. Following more scrambling and scuffing noises, another woman's voice came over the line.

"Hello? Is this nine-one-one?" the woman asked.

"The nine-one-one call was patched through to me. I'm FBI Special Agent Sandra Vos. Who am I speaking with?"

Gail was sobbing in the background. Getting through her eyewitness account must have pushed her past her stress limit. From the sounds of it, she was already dealing with a lot before a gunman entered her life.

"Nurse Torres?" Sandra said, wagering a guess.

"This is."

"What did Gail mean when she said that her daughter is going to die?"

"Her four-year-old daughter, Phoebe Chapman, is scheduled for a heart transplant tonight at eleven PM. She's in a very critical and fragile state. Without that donor heart, she will die."

SIXTEEN

1:01 PM

The stakes just got higher. A little girl's life was teetering in the balance. She needed that heart transplant if she was going to survive. While Sandra had a point of focus with Jordon Maddox, now she had another one. An innocent child. All the time Sandra had been speaking with Gail, she imagined the daughter to be older, even an adult.

Sandra spoke with the nurse for a few more minutes and provided her with her number. If something happened, Torres was to call Sandra. That's assuming the jammer would remain offline. They didn't know if it was just switched off or destroyed.

"Luis, would you have a first name for Nurse Torres?" Brice asked the hospital's emergency director.

"One second..." He tapped away and soon after said, "Maria."

Brice brought up her background. "Twenty-nine, single, lives alone. Clean record. Here's her pic." He gestured to the screen, and looking back at them was a beautiful Latina woman.

"And here is Gail Chapman," Monica said, having brought up her background. Gail was pretty but plain, Caucasian with light-brown hair. "Gail's thirty-five, lives alone as well. She's a single mother." Monica caught Sandra's eye.

That would make losing her daughter more devastating. Sandra's bond with Olivia was strong, and she credited much of that to the two of them spending so much time together. Olivia's father was a good man, but not a good fit for Sandra in the long run. They had never gotten married, but he was a part of Olivia's life when he was in Washington. Nolan Copeland was with the FBI's Hostage Rescue Team, and his work took him for stints around the world. Sandra looked at the hospital emergency director. "Luis, there is the chance this won't be resolved in time for Phoebe Chapman's operation. If it's not, what will happen to Phoebe's donor heart?" She was nauseous even thinking about the answer to that.

Luis took a deep breath and let his gaze pass over everyone in the vehicle. "It would depend on the situation but considering that the operation is planned, it's likely that they are taking the donor off life support to harvest the organs at a pre-set time. That's usually within a couple hours of a transplant."

There might be some hope then... "So if we could get a hold of the transplant coordinator at the donor hospital, tell them what's going on here, we might be able to postpone this."

"It's possible. Though it's also possible the heart would fall to the next eligible recipient. It depends on timing, and there's the family to consider on that end."

Sandra put herself in their minds. They were preparing to say goodbye to their loved one. Prolonging that would only extend their agony. She didn't want to play God, but she would do all she could to get that heart to Phoebe as it was arranged. She suspected other organ recipients were lined up too and wouldn't be eager to postpone life-saving surgeries. "Could we call them?"

Luis nodded. "I'll see what I can do." His phone rang, and he took the call at the table.

"It's infuriating sitting out here while people are dying inside," Neal said.

"Rather a pointless comment when it's a hospital and people die here every day," Kreiger pointed out. "But this guy on the fourth discharged his weapon, and we have a witness swearing that he hit a person. That changes things."

Sandra agreed, but sure hoped he wasn't going to suggest they blow past protocol and swoop in early.

"This woman is dealing with a lot. She thinks someone was hit," Brice inserted. "She didn't see it."

"No, but she heard it. The yelling, then the crying, and the silence. You're telling me that doesn't sound like someone was seriously hurt?" Kreiger pressed his lips and popped his eyes as if that reasoning was indisputable.

Sandra straightened her posture. "We can't know the extent of this person's injuries. As Special Agent Sutton just said, this witness never saw anything. Sounds can be misinterpreted."

"Sure. Let's play. Name one hypothetical." Kreiger gestured toward her.

It took her a few seconds. "He fired the weapon, but didn't hit anyone."

"And the crying?" Kreiger volleyed back.

"A natural fear response."

"Huh."

"Do you dispute that?" Brice said, stepping in.

"We don't know. I suppose that's the bottom line. But being in the dark isn't the place I want to be. You like being a mushroom and fed shit, all the power to you." Kreiger flailed his arms, coming close to brushing the roof of the vehicle with his fingertips.

"It's frustrating not knowing everything, sure," Sandra said, feeling like she needed to de-escalate things inside the vehicle. It wouldn't be the first time.

"Everything? I'd settle for *something*." Kreiger rubbed his chin. "We don't have any eyes or ears inside and have no way of fixing that with the barricaded doors. The perps aren't talking to us through the radios, or even to each other. And now we have a four-year-old girl who will die if we fail." By the time Kreiger finished his recap, he was breathing heavily. And it was no wonder after that emotion-infused summary.

Sandra could argue that nothing had changed. Phoebe was in that condition all along. They just hadn't known. And there were likely many other similar cases inside at this moment. "We're best not to get ahead of ourselves."

"She's right, Rick," Neal said. "It's not over until it's over. We think we're going to fail, we will."

Kreiger waved a hand through the air. "New-age nonsense? From you? That surprises me."

"How do you think we reach any goal in life?" Sandra asked.

"What?" Kreiger's face bunched in confusion.

"Attaining a goal always comes from putting our minds on what we want. And that's what we're going to do today. What I do every time there's an incident like this," she said.

"Me too," Monica said, backing her up.

Soon after, Brice, Gibson, and Neal added their voices to the chorus.

"Fine. But I sure hope something changes and soon, or I might not have a choice but to suggest that ERT move in." Kreiger went to the alcove and made himself a coffee.

Luis raised a finger in the air, drawing everyone's attention. "I've got good news."

"It's about bloody time someone had some," Kreiger mumbled.

"That call I just took was from the hospital's service provider for the internet and phone system. They've been able to get the works back up and running." He pushed his glasses up his nose. "They were able to root out the virus and clean the system. They also locked it down remotely so it's protected if they try to reinfect it."

"So that means the phone lines inside are working again?" Sandra felt hope spark in her chest.

Luis smiled at her. "Absolutely."

"What about the surveillance system? We have eyes inside yet?" Kreiger asked Luis.

"Still working on that."

Sandra understood Kreiger's hunger for more, but she was happy with what she had just received. Phones meant a way inside. "Luis, I need the number for the nurses' station on the fourth floor."

"One second..." A moment later Luis was reading the number off to her from his laptop.

Sandra punched in each digit as he said it.

The line rang, and rang, and rang. Just when she didn't think anyone was going to answer, there was silence except for the sound of breathing. It was most likely the gunman. Anyone else would have rushed ahead asking for help. She pointed at her headset to signal to everyone that someone had picked up, though they were listening in. "This is Sandra with the FBI. Who am I talking to?"

"Mickey Mouse," a man said.

Presumably, he was the man from the walkie-talkie, so the fact he was employing a sense of humor was unsettling given Gail's statement of a shooting. "All right, Mickey, are you doing all right in there?"

"Peachy."

"Glad to hear it. What about everyone else? Are they okay?"

"Yes."

She prickled at the switch in his tone that went from light to dark. "Yes?" she parroted, hoping for an elaboration.

"That's what I said."

So much for that... "Maybe if I could talk to some of the people with you. Everyone must be scared in there."

"Everyone is fine so far, but if you don't leave me alone that will change."

Brice wrote, *Is he lying?*

"Why does it have to change? We're just talking."

"No, we're not! You need to leave me alone, or I will kill him, I promise you that."

Only her training and years of experience kept her calm. "You will kill who, Mickey?"

The man let out a roar. "Stop calling me that."

Sandra glanced over at Brice. It was the name he'd provided but the status quo had changed. If she were to guess, his threat toward her made the situation more real for him, possibly pushing him out of his comfort zone. But that was a dangerous assumption to make, as were any in the negotiation game. "My apologies. Who will you kill?"

"Jordon Maddox."

The line went dead.

The vehicle went silent.

She took her headset off and set it on her desk. Brice turned to her, taking off his headset too.

"The guy's a liar, and I can't believe him when he says everyone is fine," Kreiger said.

For once, she agreed with the lieutenant. There was something in the way Mickey articulated his threat. "'Or I will *kill* him.' That sounds as if he did shoot someone but they're not dead." She could be reaching but she trusted her years of experience in reading people, detecting nuances.

"Whatever the case, it doesn't sound good for Maddox," Neal put in.

"No, it doesn't," Sandra said, looking at Brice.

"We're going to have to tell Rowe," Brice said.

She nodded, not looking forward to that conversation with

her boss, but she needed to get in front of this in case things turned sideways. "If you'll excuse me." She got up and left the vehicle.

She found Luis out there with his laptop under an arm, his phone to his ear. She hadn't even noticed he'd stepped out to make a call. Based on what she overheard he was on with the hospital that had the donor heart.

Elwood's line was ringing in her ear by the time she hit the pavement. He picked up on the second one. "Tell me the nightmare is over."

She hesitated, considered sugarcoating things somehow, but settled on the cold reality. "The nightmare just got worse."

"Don't tell me it has anything to do with Maddox."

"I wish I could. The gunman on the fourth floor has him."

"Tell me you're kidding."

"He threatened to kill Maddox. So we assume he's still alive."

"Assume? Dear God."

"I couldn't get proof of life before the line went dead. But there was earlier gunfire, and it's possible someone else was injured."

"Or Maddox is dead already, and this guy is trying to extend his leverage."

"I don't think so. He referred to Maddox earlier as his *insurance*." The words were out before she caught her slip.

"You want to repeat that."

She really didn't. "We just need to watch our steps."

"Damn straight. From what you told me this hostage taker has shown himself capable of pulling the trigger. What's the next step?"

"This just happened, but I don't see how it changes our approach." Sandra brought him up to speed on the incident, realizing on the recap how little progress they had made. At least they had one man in custody for today's incident. There was no word from Eric about his interrogation with Stevie Cross. There must not be anything worth sharing.

"Well, I appreciate the heads-up. I will bring this to the attention of the FBI director, and he will make what he will of it." Elwood hung up on that ominous note.

Myron Hamilton wasn't a man who took things lightly or rolled with what came his way. It's how he made it to the top. Hamilton was a man of action with little patience for incompetence. Possibly little patience, period. That was the part that worried Sandra.

She was about to return inside, when Brice came out of the vehicle.

"How did he take that?" he asked her.

"It's not Elwood I worry about. But he was happy for the heads-up."

Brice nodded. "Helps us get a little ahead of the storm anyhow. Because you know there will be a storm."

"I hope you're wrong." She went back into the vehicle, determined to return to work.

"I really think we should consider moving in." Kreiger's suggestion came out flat, like he wasn't on board with it, but it was his comfortable fallback position.

"Absolutely not," she pushed out. "You do that, and you will sign Jordon Maddox's death warrant."

"The gunman isn't talking to you, and he made it clear he'd put a bullet in Maddox's head if you called again."

"Standard course for crisis negotiation. Lives are always threatened," Sandra said.

"Don't tell me you're taking this lightly?" Kreiger served back.

"Trust me. I take it very seriously." She made herself a coffee, with everyone watching her, and sat back at her workstation. "When Mickey, we'll call him that for the lack of something better, got on the walkie-talkie with his accomplice, she fired back with 'stick to the plan.' Mickey is going off-plan by taking Maddox. I suspect he was seen as an opportunity."

"Or as Mickey put it, *insurance*," Monica pitched in.

"Exactly. Leveraging Maddox wasn't today's goal. It was happenstance, a lucky turn of events for the gunman. He's unlikely to hurt him."

Kreiger took a deep breath, inflating his chest. *"Unlikely,"* he muttered.

"I believe Mickey acted on his own here," she said.

"So you believe this guy went off-plan? Then what's to say he won't go further off the path?" Kreiger raised his eyebrows.

Sandra didn't want to admit it was possible. Not out loud, especially to Kreiger, who seemed to be itching for a reason to move in.

"Well..." Kreiger prompted her.

"You want me to say something? I'm not a mind reader, never claimed to be. But I am pretty good at detecting underlying indicators. One of these tells me, he won't shoot Maddox."

"Agreed. He's a bargaining chip, as awful as that sounds," Brice wedged in.

Sandra wanted to get on the phone, but she needed time to consider a strategy before doing so. Luis was also still outside, and he could provide her with direct numbers for the nurses' stations. She'd use this time to further discuss what had just happened with Mickey. "There is always more that isn't being said. To start, what are the base emotional drivers at play here? We can dispute it all we want, but humans are emotional creatures. These emotions make us do things, so what made these people—three, that we know of—go into Founders Hospital with guns today?"

"Whatever it was, it required them to be left alone," Brice suggested. "The infected system, the jammer."

"They were buying time," Gibson said.

"Exactly, and I think it was Mickey's lack of control over

that timeline that had him take Maddox as *insurance*," Sandra put in.

"And I sense contention between Mickey and the woman," Monica said.

Sandra nodded. "She certainly wasn't pleased by the interruption or Mickey being on the walkie-talkie."

"She had to know we'd overhear the conversation," Brice began. "She feared it would jeopardize their goal."

"Yes, so she's hyper-focused, but Mickey is making impulsive decisions based on emotion," Sandra reasoned.

"Just what you want to hear when he's got Maddox within reach," Kreiger griped.

"The guy also has a bad sense of humor. Pulling out Mickey Mouse at a time like this. Despicable," Gibson said while scribbling the name on the markerboard.

"The humor could simply be a deflection," Monica reasoned. "He might not want to even be involved today."

"Yet he threatened a man's life, to a Fed, no less," Neal said. "It's too late to unring that bell."

"Not that we're disputing this, but we have more to support that Mickey isn't in charge," Brice said. "In his exchange with you, I noticed he stuck to the singular pronoun of I."

Sandra nodded. "I picked up on that too."

"Either of you want to elaborate?" Neal asked.

Brice gestured for Sandra to do so. "Shot callers generally use plural pronouns such as we, they, and them. Since this guy stuck to *I*, this tells us he has very little, if any, power over this situation."

"Hence, taking Maddox hostage would make him feel more powerful and in control," Neal said.

"Precisely." Sandra didn't say anything else because Luis came back into the vehicle.

He had everyone's attention as he sat back at the table and set his laptop down again. "So I called the donor coordinator..."

"What is it?" Sandra coaxed out of him.

"Bad news. The surgery is scheduled, and people are relying on other organs from that donor. It can't be pushed off."

"Son of a bitch," Kreiger muttered and slammed his fist into the palm of his other hand.

"Ah." Luis's cheeks flamed bright red. "And now they know about our situation, they are prepping the next heart recipient on the list for possible transplant."

"They're not even giving us a chance here?" Neal's voice was strained.

"They are, but if things aren't worked out here by nine PM, Phoebe Chapman's heart will go to someone else. But everything should be, uh, wrapped up by then, shouldn't it?" Luis looked at his wristwatch.

"These things take the time they take," Brice said solemnly. "And sometimes that's far longer than we'd like."

"Oh."

The tiny utterance from the emergency director's lips hit like an anvil tossed into water. The repercussions rippled out, reminding all of them of the stakes involved.

Sandra sat back in her chair, feeling like she'd been hit by a dump truck. Putting a clock on negotiations was never effective. Deadlines made for impulsive decisions. She watched Kreiger's face ball into an angry mask, and she feared he might do something rash. But storming into Founders wasn't the smart choice. Not with innocent lives on the line. "Luis, I need the direct lines for all the nurses' stations."

Luis rattled off the numbers while noting the floors they belonged to. Brice wrote them down, while Luis added, "I just wanted to point out the number I gave you for the eighth is for the main admin desk. No patients stay on that floor. It's mostly offices and labs."

Sandra put her headset on and placed the first call, starting with the sixth floor. Presumably, the man who had infected the server was there. And now the thought occurred to her, *What if he never left the server room?*

The line rang repeatedly before rolling over to an automated voicemail.

Next, she started on the main level and worked her way up, while skipping the fourth floor for now.

No luck until the eighth floor.

A woman answered. Her voice was sheepish. "Hello?"

Brice wrote, *an innocent?* on a piece of paper and pushed it over for her to see. Sandra shrugged. It might be the shot caller making herself seem guileless.

"I'm FBI Special Agent Sandra Vos."

"Thank God. Are you here to help us?"

"We're working on that. What's your name?"

"Janie DeSilva. I'm an endoscopy technician with the hospital. I didn't know the phones were back up, or I would have called nine-one-one again. I did this morning and got cut off."

Sandra glanced over at Brice. The woman she spoke to at the cordon line said her sister's name was Janie DeSilva. "Is it safe for you to talk with me?"

"Yes. I'm hiding beneath the desk, but I don't think she'll be back."

"Who is *she*, Janie?"

"I don't know who she is, but she had a gun on Pam. That's why I called before."

"Do you know what she wanted from Pam?" She'd get around to asking who she was.

"She was walking down the hall with her, and they pushed their way into the meeting."

"Can you describe this woman's looks?"

"Average, but she's very thin, Caucasian."

"Hair color?"

"Brown."

"Did you hear her speak? Does she have an accent?"

"I briefly overheard her talking to Pam, but I didn't detect an accent or anything that stood out."

Sandra was impressed by Janie's calm composure. It was adrenaline helping her keep a cool head, or Sandra was wrong about the woman on the other end of the line. It was possible she was talking to the shot caller, who was pretending to be an innocent. She could have provided the name off a badge. To confirm this woman's identity, Sandra needed to find out something personal that went beyond a name badge. "Do you have a loved one we can call to let them know you're okay?"

"My sister, Remy Bishop," the woman said without hesitation. "She was going to meet me at break this morning."

Sandra nodded at Brice and mouthed, "It's her." But what were the chances she'd be in contact with her sister? Slim to none, but life had a way of presenting these serendipities. "You mentioned the woman with the gun and Pam went into a meeting. What one?"

"It's for the board of directors."

"And who is Pam?"

"Pamela Cherry. She's Megan Beal's assistant."

"And Megan Beal?"

"The CEO of the hospital," Janie said at the same time, Luis said, "CEO."

Brice wrote, *Possible motive connected to board members?*

Sandra nodded. The HT would be in a room with the most powerful people in the hospital. She either wanted them to do something for her, or she planned on hurting one or more of them. Either way, it would seem she wanted uninterrupted time. "You've done great, Janie. Now I need you to find a safe place that's out of the way and preferably has a lock on the door. Don't be wandering the hallways, all right. Go find that spot now, and stay there until this is all over." She added the bit about wandering because Janie must have at least popped out to answer the phone. Her insight was valuable, but she'd risked her life to convey it.

"Okay, I'll go now."

The line went dead.

Sandra hated thinking of Janie being in there without having eyes on her. There was no way to know if she'd make it safely into a room or not. But Sandra had other things that required her focus. For one, Luis. She took her headset off and looked at him. "Luis, I appreciate your contributions today. You have proven yourself an asset, but when I'm on the phone, I ask that you stay quiet. No matter who I'm talking to." She didn't like being placed in a position where she had to verbalize this request. But if he pitched in while she was speaking with a hostage taker, it could distract her enough to jeopardize negotiations.

"Sorry about that. I got carried away. It won't happen again."

"Thanks."

"So I've pulled backgrounds on Janie DeSilva and Pamela Cherry. Nothing flags," Gibson said, and wheeled out of the way. Their pictures were side by side on his screen. Janie was in her thirties, and Pamela was in her late twenties. "Both are confirmed hospital employees. DeSilva has a sister, Remy Bishop, who is married."

Brice faced her. "Which we know. That's the woman you spoke to when we arrived?"

"Yes."

"You going to tell her about her sister?" Neal asked, having listened to the call along with everyone else except for Luis. He'd just overheard Sandra say Beal's name and jumped in.

"Not yet." She feared that by telling Remy her sister was okay, she'd somehow jinx things. And technically, Janie wasn't okay. She was on the eighth floor with an armed woman. It was best to focus on what they just learned. "Now we know the location of another armed assailant. She's likely the shot caller we heard on the walkie-talkie."

"All fine, but why is she interested in the board meeting?" Neal asked.

"The most powerful people in the hospital would be in one room," Sandra offered.

"Not just people with the hospital," Luis said, speaking up. He rattled off several names and followed up with, "These are founders and CEOs of large medical and pharmaceutical companies. But there's one more person in there you need to know about. The director is Valerie Cowan MD, head of cardiology. There's no one better qualified than Dr. Cowan to perform a heart transplant on a four-year-old."

The back of Sandra's neck tightened on that reveal.

"Shit," Kreiger said under his breath.

She didn't say as much out loud, but the coordinator wanted more information, and now he had some. Sandra stood and stretched her neck. "Nothing's changed." She looked at Kreiger, petitioning him to hear her out. "We just didn't know this moments ago. The situation was still there." *Just like it was with Phoebe Chapman...* Awareness didn't make something exist; it simply drew attention there. "We need to consider what could be gained by an audience with these people. Is the goal here to get something from them or target one or more of them for revenge?"

"Well, this woman held a gun on Beal's assistant," Gibson said. "She had her take her to the meeting room. Maybe Beal's the main target?"

Brice teetered his hand. "Hmm, she could be. But without assuming that, maybe the woman just used the assistant as a point of entry to get into the meeting." Brice turned to Luis. "Are these meetings held on a regular schedule, and are they public knowledge?"

"The middle of every month, but they aren't publicized."

Brice let out a small groan. "Then it's possible we're looking at someone else on the inside who knew about the regularity of these meetings, who may be behind this."

"It could have been Stevie Cross, for that matter," Sandra suggested.

"Speaking of Cross, I'd say he isn't talking, or Detective Birch would have reached out to tell us," Neal said.

Sandra wondered who Cross was protecting and why. It was unfortunate people couldn't be made to talk. "Luis, are the identities of the board members public knowledge?"

"They are listed on the hospital website."

Sandra met Brice's gaze. It sure seemed like getting to someone in that room was today's goal. The reason remained a mystery, but what concerned Sandra more was being too late to stop this before someone died.

The only sound in the woman's ears was the beating of her own heart. She'd laid out her case to those in the room, but they weren't talking. Just giving her blank stares. The more she yelled at them and waved her gun, the quieter and more withdrawn they became. She wished she could shake some sense into them. Couldn't they see no one was going anywhere until this matter was resolved? But they obstinately thought they could remain indifferent, that the police would move in and rescue them. For many people in this room, who saved lives for a living, she would bet they'd be willing to sacrifice hers if it meant their freedom. But these people scared her far less than the sketchy people in that dive bar where she'd sourced the guns for today.

"None of you are leaving until I say so. You hear me? I'm the one in charge." She flailed the gun around, prepared to use it if it came down to it. To prepare for today, she went to the shooting range a few times for lessons. The last thing she wanted to do was blow off her own foot in a gunfire mishap. No, if she pulled the trigger, she'd make sure the muzzle was pointed at her target and hold the gun steady and true in a two-handed grip.

"Just let us go." Beal, the CEO, was still seated on her throne at the head of the table.

"No one cares that you're even in here, don't you get that?" She'd seen the police move in hours ago, even caught a glimpse of the law enforcement circus that had grown outside the window. But thanks to disabled phone lines and the jammer, she had all the time she needed. Uninterrupted. And so what if they got eyes inside through security cameras? There were none in this room, and if they saw her, they wouldn't be able to identify her anyhow. "Not about me, and not about you," she added.

"That's where you're wr—"

She held up her hand to silence the woman. Her ears were picking up on something else. Another voice from the hallway.

"The police are going to come in here and shoot you," one of the men said in a bold demonstration of stupidity.

She was tempted to pop a bullet in his skull. She might have if she wasn't so focused on... someone talking? Maybe she was hearing things. But just as she thought that, there was the scant sound of footsteps.

The police, or someone intending to play hero?

She couldn't let it go, or she'd be taking a big chance all her hard work in getting this far would blow up in her face. "Everyone stay put, or I will start shooting." She opened the door. A shadow streaked across the end of the hall. "You! Get back here!"

She waited, and the shadow gained form. A young lab technician came back, with her arms in the air.

"Come here," she prompted her.

The tech slowly walked toward her. "I'm sorry..."

As she came closer, she recognized the young woman. She walked past her and Beal's assistant on the way to the boardroom. Cold fear shot through her. "Tell me why you're sorry."

The woman shook but said nothing.

"Speak!"

"The phones are back online, and I—"

"The lines are back?" What happened to the virus put on the system or the jammer, and why hadn't she heard any phones ringing? Though those in the room might have muted theirs for the meeting.

"Yes, and the police... they called the main admin desk. I... I answered."

"What did you tell them?"

The lab tech started crying.

She shook her. "What did you tell the police?"

"Just that... *that* a woman took Pamela into the board meeting."

"Yeah, well, you're going to join the party. Get inside the room." She gestured with her gun, and the lab tech wisely did as she was told.

Son of a bitch! The gunwoman wanted to scream that at the top of her lungs, but she couldn't let anyone see her crumbling apart. The last thing today's mission could withstand was them viewing her as weak. But the timeline had been irrevocably narrowed. How this would turn out depended on the people in this room.

She entered behind the tech and locked the door after them. As she did so, it wasn't missed that a few in the room passed this one woman with long brown hair a glance. And the CEO was acting shiftier than before. The gunwoman turned to their new honorary board member. "Hand me your cell phone," she said to the tech.

"I don't have it on me. It's in my locker."

She quickly patted her down. "Fine. Now, get over there and sit on the floor."

Again, the lab tech did as she was told.

"If only the rest of you were so obedient like Janie here."

The tech's mouth fell open.

"Yes, I know who you are." She wasn't surprised the tech didn't know her. She continued her way to the brunette, towered over her, and held the gun in her face. "What are you doing there?" The furtive glances told her that the woman was up to something. And with the phones back online, she had a good feeling what that might be.

"I'm not doing anything."

"Do you want 'Stubborn Bitch' on your headstone? Hand me the phone."

The brunette glanced at Beal.

"Don't look at her. Look at me." She grabbed the brunette's chin, and the woman shook her hand off. She stopped struggling when the gun was against her forehead. "Phone!"

The woman put the device in her hand.

There was a voice coming through from the other end.

"Dr. Cowan, are you still there?"

She ended the call and saw that it had originated from another hospital. Its name was frozen on the screen. She was having a hard time knowing what to make of this. "You weren't calling nine-one-one?"

"No," the woman pushed out, refusing to look her in the eye. "And why would I? The police are already here. It's only a matter of time before you'll be dragged out of here."

"I'm the one who says when it's time, and I have as long as it takes to get this resolved. The question is, do the rest of you?" She slid her gaze over all those in the room.

"I was on the phone about a heart," the brunette blurted out, when no one else said a word. "There's a little girl who is going to die."

Her heart pinched, but she said, "We all have to die."

"She's only four years old. You really can't be that much of a monster. To let a little girl die. Without that heart, she will."

An innocent child caught up in all of this. It was a scenario she should have prepared for. A hospital was full of the sick and dying. But *she* was the monster? If she was, the people in this room had turned her into one. "Her fate is up to you, now, isn't it?" She tossed the cell phone onto the pile with the rest and smashed the devices under her boots.

Sandra was mentally preparing herself to make a call to the boardroom. With the hospital phone lines restored, she had a link directly to the person they'd pegged as the shot caller. Her strategic position in the hospital seemed to confirm their earlier theory that she was in charge. There were the lives of eleven board members in this woman's hands, plus Beal's assistant and presumably another employee taking minutes from the meeting. It would be great to have eyes on that shot caller. "Luis, what's the ETA on the security video?"

"I was just going to give you the good news. I got an email that I should have a backdoor link within the hour."

"And that will give us the live feed and earlier video?" Sandra was curious if the footage would reveal whether the gunwoman approached Beal's assistant directly or simply used her to get into the meeting. It also wouldn't hurt to get some backstory on all the perps.

"It should offer both," Luis told her.

"So we have a room full of these powerful people," Neal began, "but we still don't know if this is about a request or revenge. Or both, I suppose. Should I get officers out talking to assistants and family to see if there are any threats against them on file?"

"Let me see if I can get anywhere before we go dispensing manpower on that," Sandra said. "I'm going to call the board-room. I assume there's a phone in there?" Sandra directed the question at Luis.

"There is." Luis got her the direct number and handed it to Sandra on a piece of paper.

"Thanks," she said as she put her headset on again.

Kreiger stood and left the vehicle without a word. She imag-ined he was going to inform ERT about the armed woman being in the boardroom. They'd no doubt study the hospital blue-prints and strategize a breach. They could technically use the stairwell to bypass the other levels where the gunmen were placed. If they shut down the shot caller, her partners might surrender. At least Sandra imagined that was Kreiger's think-ing. It could backfire, though. With the shot caller taken out, one of the others might assume the lead and become more of a threat. Sandra was thinking the man on the fourth wasn't likely to roll over. Not after he'd already shown independent thinking. She wondered what the shot caller would think of that. Sandra couldn't imagine she'd be pleased with a rogue partner who could jeopardize the entire mission. This didn't stop her from putting the call through. The line rang six times before it was answered.

"Leave us alone!" a woman barked. Definitely the woman from earlier over the walkie-talkie. *Stick to the plan.*

"Please. Let me help you." Sandra used a calm, soothing voice. "I'm Sandra with the FBI."

"I don't need any help from you. And wait. You said Sandra? Aren't you that lady who was on the walkie-talkie this morning? What do *you* want?"

"Honestly, I'd like this to end now."

"Well, that's not up to you."

"You're right. But you've been in there a while now. You must be hungry. Let me get you some food." She passed Brice a side-glance, and he shook his head.

"We're doing just fine in here."

Sandra debated whether she should mention what Mickey had done, but decided it was potentially volatile and didn't want to risk escalating things. Instead, she said, "Why don't you tell me what I can do for you, then?"

"You called this number, so you know about the board meeting, don't you?"

"I do. Are you looking to speak to someone in there?"

"What's the point? No one's listening." This confession was hurled out, full of disappointment and tainted with confusion.

Sandra still wasn't assured that taking a room full of hostages was simply about talking. She couldn't rule out that the woman might murder someone to get her way. She couldn't take the chance that the gun was purely a prop to encourage cooperation. "Listening to you about what?" Sandra mirrored.

"Why would we discuss this with you?" the woman said and hung up.

Monica finished typing the script of the conversation, while Gibson popped up and wrote the time of 1:15 PM and that contact with the shot caller was made.

If Sandra had any doubts before, they were gone with the woman's use of the plural pronouns. Her last statement should have easily been a first-person response. *Why would I discuss this with you?* Her refusal to lay out any demands to Sandra suggested this woman expected someone inside that room to make things right or to deliver on something. She saw her goal as something that Sandra and anyone out here could not help with. Sandra removed her headset. "She wants someone in that room to do something for her and her accomplices."

"I'm more concerned with what she's prepared to do if she doesn't get her way," Neal put in.

"If we take her at her word everyone is doing fine in there," Brice said, "it tells us a bit about her. She's been in there for hours, and if she had intentions to shoot anyone, that would have happened by now."

"You're assuming it hasn't. We don't know this woman. There's no trust there," Neal said.

"I'm with you there," Sandra said, siding with the team leader. "We can't assume she didn't shoot anyone or that she won't. The fact is she went in there with a gun."

"You'd think if she discharged her weapon, though, Janie would have mentioned hearing gunfire," Gibson pointed out.

"That doesn't mean this woman hasn't hurt someone without discharging her weapon," Sandra said. "I think we need to consider she believes someone in that room has the power to do what they want."

"It's also possible they want the hospital to do something that takes the approval of a committee, not just one person," Brice said.

"Sure, but we have nothing but theories." Sandra turned to Neal. "I'm with you. I think it's time we reach out to the assistants and family members of everyone in that room and see if any of them have had any threats made against them recently or if any complaints have been lodged against them. I'd put priority on Beal."

Neal was nodding. "I'll get officers dispatched to the offices and homes of these people ASAP."

"Dr. Beal's husband might be harder to pin down." Brice pointed at the screen of his laptop, where he had the background pulled on a Wyatt Beal, along with his driver's license photo. "He's a high-profile defense lawyer with a downtown firm."

He was a handsome man too, judging by what Sandra was

seeing. And the only reason he probably hadn't called in was because his work was keeping him busy and away from the news.

"Someone will track him down and have a chat," Neal said and took out his phone.

The door to the vehicle opened, and Kreiger came inside. "ERT has eyes on the boardroom windows, but all the blinds are shut. Snipers are on standby until we give our word."

What he meant was when he gave *his* word. The true lingo of a shot caller shining through.

"Vos got in touch with the armed woman from the eighth floor," Monica said.

Kreiger leveled his gaze at Sandra. "Did she agree to surrender?"

"She's talking," Sandra responded.

"That's a *no* to surrendering then." If Kreiger was going to say more, he was interrupted by the phone ringing at Gibson's workstation.

Kreiger walked over to Gibson just as the intelligence officer spun. The back of his chair banged against the lieutenant's side.

"Son of a— Watch what you're doing," Kreiger cussed.

Gibson snapped his mouth shut, grimaced, waited a few beats before speaking. "I just received a call from the on-duty supervisor with nine-one-one dispatch. We already knew that calls have been flooding in, but they've gathered some conclusive information. By piecing together all accounts, there are four assailants with one positioned on floors two, four, six, and eight. Two are men, and two are women."

"So why not every floor?" Brice asked, looking at Sandra.

It was a valid question, and without the ability to read minds it was impossible to know the answer. "I don't know. It could be they wanted to be spread out, but didn't have enough people to cover each floor."

"Or there's something special about those floors." Brice

narrowed his eyes as he asked this question, and then turned to Luis. "We know about the fourth and sixth."

Critical heart and brain patients on the fourth. The server room for the hospital system on the sixth...

"The second is orthopedics, spine and pain center, rehabilitation, and maternity," Luis said. "I already told you what's on the eighth."

"They picked these locations strategically," she concluded. "The eighth for the board meeting, the sixth for shutting down communication, and the second and fourth to use influence over us. With critical patients and newborns within reach, they'd feel untouchable."

"There was definitely a lot of planning put into today," Neal said. "Video surveillance was the only thing they seemed to have overlooked. They must not have known it was serviced outside of the hospital, or figured with the system virus, it would be knocked out."

Sandra could think of another reason. "Or they're not afraid of having their faces on camera."

"They don't have criminal records," Brice said, rounding out her thought. "They wouldn't be in any facial recognition database."

"Exactly," Sandra agreed. "I'd like to add that despite what they've done here, I don't think we're looking at professionals. There would be someone on each floor, maybe more than one in that case. It would guarantee full coverage. Honestly, I think the gunmen on the other floors are nothing but a distraction or insurance that the shot caller gets left alone in the boardroom."

"That could make sense," Monica piped up from her desk.

Sandra turned to look at her. "Then her cohorts raise the alarm after she's in that boardroom."

"All right, let's say all this is the case, how does any of this help us?" Kreiger added.

Faced with that direct question, Sandra had an immediate answer. "It tells me that the woman hostage taker in that boardroom isn't just the shot caller, but she's the most invested and has the most at stake. She's not letting anyone else take care of the main job. That makes the others more vulnerable."

"That guy you spoke to on the fourth didn't sound vulnerable to me." Kreiger perched his hands on his hips.

"Give me some time to see what I can do," Sandra said. "In fact, my plan is to get him on the phone again, and with any luck, talking."

"You sure you don't want to rethink that?" Neal raised his eyebrows. "He made it pretty clear the last time what he'd do if you called again."

"But he's not calling the shots here," she said.

Kreiger pressed his lips. "He kind of is."

"Um, excuse me." Luis held up a finger and continued speaking when everyone looked at him. "I've got access to live footage now."

"Great, show us the nurses' station on the fourth," Sandra requested.

"Coming right up. Huh. No one's around."

"Chapman mentioned the gunman was in the nurse break room," she said.

"And that's it right there." Luis pointed at his screen, indicating a door close to the nurses' station.

There wasn't anything to be gained from looking at a closed door. "Can you bring up old footage?"

"Anything you want. I have access to all of it," Luis said.

"Bring up the footage at that station starting at one o'clock." That was the time she'd spoken with Mickey.

"One minute." Luis pushed some buttons on his laptop.

Seconds later, the gunman from the fourth floor was on the screen. He was of average looks and size. What concerned her the most was his relaxed body posture. He had supposedly shot someone, had threatened a man's life, and he was slumped in a chair behind the desk and slowly swiveling while he was on the phone with her. It wasn't the image of a man full of remorse. It was that of a man without a conscience.

TWENTY

1:45 PM

Sandra was delayed calling the assailant on the fourth floor. She was distracted by the other progress being made. Thanks to Luis's help, they were able to grab pictures of three of the four armed assailants. Including footage of Cross letting a younger man into the server room. There were no cameras inside the boardroom, and earlier video just showed the woman approaching Pamela's desk, head down. The faces they had were being run through facial recognition databases, but no one was expecting any hits. Gibson printed the images and affixed them to the markerboard with small magnets. Neal made sure that the pictures were distributed to all the officers and detectives in the field, with the primary focus being Eric so he could show them to Stevie Cross for a reaction. He flagged the man with Cross.

"The man from the fourth has to be in his mid-to-late sixties," Sandra said. "He's older than I had imagined."

"And then you look at his friends. The woman on the second floor, maybe late thirties. The guy on the sixth only mid-twenties," Brice added.

"His age lends to him being good with computers and tech," Kreiger said.

"Maybe that's a little stereotypical, boss," Monica said.

"Yeah? Look at you."

"I'm flattered you think I'm in my twenties. I turned thirty-two last week."

Kreiger smiled. "Well, whatever. Stereotypes became that for a reason. They track."

"Okay, I'm going in again. I'll try to get through to the HTs on the second and sixth floors first. Then I'll try Mickey," Sandra said, putting her headset on. The rest of the team followed her lead.

"Maybe we could call him Perp Four," Gibson suggested. "You know, for being on the fourth floor." He turned around and faced his computer again when no one responded.

The rest could call him what they liked, but she'd think of him as Mickey until or unless he gave her a different name. She didn't need to inadvertently mess up when she was on the phone with him. "Luis, I'll let you know before I try each floor. If you could bring up the live feed for each nurses' station as I go, that would be great."

He tapped some keys and brought his laptop over, holding the screen for her. "Here's the second."

No one was within sight. She put the call through and listened to the line ring. Still no one. She hung up. "The sixth," she said to Luis, and he brought up that nurses' station there. Like with the second, not a person in view, and her call went unanswered. Luis brought up the nurses' station from the fourth without her asking.

Here goes... She punched in the numbers, and after the second ring, the door of the break room opened and Mickey entered the frame alone.

He leaned over the desk and grabbed the receiver. "Didn't I

tell you I would kill him if you called me again? I'll put a bullet in him, I swear."

More threats, but there was no sign of Maddox, and no accounting for the victim of the earlier gunfire. "Mickey, the guys out here found out a gun was fired. I'm doing my best to keep everyone at bay, but I need to know that everyone is all right."

Brief hesitation, then, "Everyone is fine."

"Could I speak to Jordon Maddox, just to see for myself that he's okay?"

"No."

Sandra bristled, but if she pushed to speak with Jordon, she'd put Mickey on the defensive. "But he is okay?"

"For now."

He didn't want her to forget he was the one in charge between them. "Is anyone else with you, Mickey?"

"Two nurses."

"Do you know their names, Mickey? I could tell their families they're okay." She wanted to humanize his hostages.

"Nah, I'm not going there."

"You and your friends want something, and I can help with that. Just let me know their names, and I'll fight for you."

The man scoffed. "No one fights for me. And friends? That's a joke."

"Then, please, tell me who they are, Mickey."

Silence.

"We know there are others. Let me help you out of there. Maybe none of this was even your idea."

"What do you know? You don't even know my real name. Also, I'm a grown-ass man, and I make my own decisions."

"Then tell me what *you* would like. I can guarantee your safety if you will surrender peacefully."

"I'm not giving up."

The terminology was noteworthy. "No one said anything about giving up. You would be making a choice to stand up for yourself and your future. Nothing's happened that you can't walk away from." A lie regardless of whether there were no injuries or a death at this man's hands. He'd know that in the back of his mind, but her assurance might help him forget that long enough to surrender.

"That's bull crap, and we both know it. I came into this hospital armed with a gun and fired it. *I* fired it!"

"It doesn't sound like that's what you wanted to do."

"None of this is playing out like I thought it would."

That ad lib was his first sign of weakness. "And how did you see it playing out?"

Mickey didn't respond to her, but he was rubbing his chin in thought. His face was downcast. The weight of what he had done and was doing seemed to set in.

"The longer this goes on, there's a better chance people will get hurt, Mickey. Some patients in there are dying or will without their medication." *A little girl will die without her new heart...* But she wasn't putting the pressure of a child's life on his shoulders. That could make him feel more powerless and have him acting out. "You can put an end to this," she added after allowing him time to speak.

"No. She wouldn't want that. Same with the others."

Up until now, he spoke as an individual. Now it was like he was remembering some bond or allegiance he had with the others. "Who is she, Mickey?" She tiptoed around because coming out and saying she heard the woman bark at him that morning would hurt the trust she was trying to establish. She had hijacked their radio frequency, so he could have even put it together. But if he did, he didn't let on.

"Nah, I'm not telling you that. You don't know who any of us are, do you?"

She couldn't lie or he'd see through her. This was an opportunity to learn more and build trust. "We know of four of you. Are there more?"

"No."

Brice nodded.

"The woman on the eighth floor has people holed up in the boardroom."

"Wait a minute, how do you know…?" On the laptop screen, Mickey was looking around. He smirked. "You're spying on us. Well, keep watching."

Mickey slammed the receiver down and left the nurses' station, slipping out of view into the nurse break room.

"What's he doing?" Monica asked.

Sandra didn't answer, and neither did anyone else. Everyone was captured by the screen on Luis's laptop.

Just seconds after he left, Mickey returned to the nurses' station. This time he wasn't alone. He had a hold on Jordon Maddox and a gun pointed at his head.

Eric took a deep dive into Stevie Cross's financials, and nothing there suggested a payoff. Whatever had Cross breaking the law, it wasn't about money. A search of his home hadn't yet turned up anything linked to today's events. His phone records were also clean. So what made a forty-something man with a decent job throw his life away? Was it linked to this mysterious man who infected the hospital's mainframe? And if so, what influence did this man have over Cross that he'd protect his identity? Was it fear or loyalty?

Eric pushed one of the pictures Neal had sent over across the table. And so much for it being some guy in his fifties. This kid in the picture was in his twenties. "Who is he, Mr. Cross?"

"I never got his name."

Eric could call bullshit on that response all day, but it wouldn't do any good. "You've got a chance to clean up your mess here, earn some credit, even get yourself a deal."

Cross knotted his arms and looked away.

Eric laid out the other two photos and met with the same response. He gathered them up again and pushed out from the table. "Suit yourself. I'll find that young man, and once I do, there's no room for a deal."

Cross remained stoic, and Eric left the room even more frustrated. But at least Eric would get a little break from Cross. When Neal sent the pictures, he also asked if Eric would have time to talk with Wyatt Beal. Eric said he'd make time. It was more productive than spinning out here, that was for sure. And having learned about a four-year-old girl who would die without her heart transplant was fueling him. Eric didn't have children of his own, but he didn't need to be a father to know that the world lost out when a child was taken.

Since Wyatt Beal was the managing partner at a prestigious law firm downtown, Eric headed straight to their offices.

Walking through the door, there was no mistaking the dense energy, not alleviated any by the decor. Dark wood, hunter green, and brass. It recalled images he'd seen of gentlemen's clubs from a bygone era.

"Good afternoon." The receptionist, a young woman in her mid-twenties, possibly thirties, was watching him from the front desk.

As he made his way through the sitting area, he considered a man like Wyatt could have plenty of enemies himself. It was possible someone with an issue against him was going at his wife. Eric shook the notion aside, blaming it on his overactive detective mind.

"How can I help you, sir?" the receptionist asked.

Eric held up his badge. "It's urgent that I speak with Wyatt Beal immediately. There is an issue involving his wife."

"Be that as it may, Mr. Beal isn't in the office at the moment."

"Then let me know where I can find him, and I'll go there. As I said, this is an urgent matter."

She looked from him to her monitor, to her phone, back to him. "Let me try to reach him." She picked up the phone and avoided eye contact while she waited for Wyatt to answer. Which he did not. Eric heard the ringing, followed by Wyatt's voicemail greeting. "He's not picking up." She slowly returned the receiver to its cradle.

"I need to know where he is. *Right now.*"

Her cheeks flushed. "Ricardo's."

Eric hustled from the firm, and seven minutes later was entering the upscale restaurant with its dark-wood tables and chairs and richly painted walls. *Beal knows what he likes...*

"Good afternoon. A table for one?" The young man at the host stand preemptively grabbed a menu from the holder.

"Actually, I'm not here to eat." Eric's stomach rumbled, betraying him. "I'm looking for one of your customers." He flashed his badge and stepped past the host to look around the restaurant.

"Sir, you can't just..." The host's words petered out, and when Eric glanced over his shoulder, the man was flailing his arm in the air.

Eric spotted Beal at a cozy corner table with a leggy blonde and headed over. He stood at the edge of the table for a good few seconds before Beal and his companion looked up. It was an intimate setting even if it included a battery-operated tealight in the centerpiece. There was a bottle of red and a wineglass in front of each of them. The two of them were holding hands across the table.

Wyatt turned to face him, annoyance carved into his scrunched facial expression. "Yes? Is there something I can do for you?"

Eric swept his jacket back to disclose his badge that was clipped to his waistband. "Detective Birch, Metropolitan PD. I need to talk with you about your wife, Megan."

At least the woman had the decency to blush at the mention of Megan and pull her hand back. "Wyatt, I'm just going to go freshen up," the blonde said, getting up.

"You bet, sweetheart. Take your time."

Not even hiding the affair... That is one approach. Eric took a seat where Wyatt's date had vacated. "You might have heard that Founders Hospital went into full lockdown this morning?"

"No, I've been busy. And Megan knows about Crystal. My wife and I have had an open relationship for years. We both have highly demanding careers. Heck, she's at the hospital more than she's home. What's going on?"

It was interesting Wyatt felt the need to justify himself and strange that he didn't put things together for himself. "Your wife is in danger," Eric said, spelling it out. "There was a meeting with the board of directors this morning, and she was in attendance. At some point, this meeting was interrupted by a woman with a gun."

"Dear Lord." Wyatt put a hand over his heart.

"We don't know why this woman is there or what she wants, but we need to know if anyone has threatened your wife recently."

"Meg gets... uh... threats all the time." For an experienced lawyer, Wyatt was stammering. All his composure was gone.

Eric noted how he referred to his wife less formally, suggesting affection and respect still existed. "Any recently?"

"I don't know. Nothing she mentioned to me. Actually..." Wyatt's eyes widened.

"Don't hold back now."

"I think I remember her saying something about being in fear of her life."

"That's something you *think* you remember?"

"I know that makes me sound horrible, but when we're home together, she's constantly yammering away. I'm doing good to catch half of what she says."

Yet, he probably heard every word out of his mistress's mouth. "Did she say why?"

"If she did..." He waved a hand, leaving the rest to be implied as him not listening.

"This being in fear of her life, this was recently?"

"Yes. I think so."

"Did she mention any names?"

"No, but she keeps copies of any written threats she receives in her home office."

"I'll need to see those immediately."

"Sure." Wyatt signaled a server to bring the check.

Eric had considered before coming here that if the lockdown was about revenge, such as harming or killing Megan Beal, there would certainly be a better place. His mind on that was changed. As Wyatt had said about Megan, "She's at the hospital more than she's home." The hospital CEO could very well be the target.

"Is he seriously going to shoot him right in front of us?" Kreiger was hovering behind Sandra's shoulder.

Sandra's stomach clenched as the seconds ticked off.

Mickey took the gun off Maddox and pointed it toward them. A second later, they lost video.

"Get it back," Kreiger roared at the emergency director.

"He can't get it back," Neal said. "You realize that man just shot the camera."

"It's okay, guys." Luis was surprisingly calm as he balanced his laptop in one hand and clicked away. "There's another camera just down the hall. Here we go."

It picked up just after the last one was terminated. Mickey was pushing Maddox back into the break room.

"Fuck." Kreiger raked a hand through his hair.

"Yeah, this guy isn't fooling around," Neal said. "Maybe we leave him alone?"

"He didn't shoot Maddox when he could have made a statement right in front of us." But was Sandra willing to bank that his reservation would hold out? Mickey could just be building his courage.

"Fair point. And the first time could have been a warning shot," Brice offered.

"Which could also explain the screams," Monica said.

The others in the vehicle didn't weigh in. Luis returned to the table with Kreiger and Neal. The three of them continued to watch the security video. Gibson got up from his chair and updated the markerboard.

Fourth floor male, "Mickey", confirmed he's involved of his own free will and fired his weapon.

After making his notations, Gibson returned to his workstation and from the look of it pulled some more backgrounds.

"When he said 'she wouldn't want that. Same with the others,' he sounds like today is happening outside of his control," Monica suggested. "He might even be afraid of her, the rest of them too for that matter."

Sandra thought back on the call and nodded. "Just what has him cooperating?"

"Love, fear, or money are the strongest motivators," Brice pitched in.

"But which of those gets us here?" she asked, not expecting any answers. She was thinking she was going to call the boardroom again when a familiar booming male voice hit her ears from outside the vehicle.

The door was swung open, and a man stepped inside. He latched his gaze with hers.

"FBI Director Hamilton," she said. "Welcome." It had taken him less than an hour after her call to Elwood to turn up. As if there wasn't already enough pressure with this incident. Now she had him to deal with face to face.

But just as Sandra thought he was the worst of it, she realized he wasn't alone. A woman stepped up behind him. In her late fifties, her hair was a silver blond—a cross between holding on to one's youth and accepting the grays. She was dressed in an expensive, tailored pantsuit, and her makeup was tastefully applied with a light brush, complementing the contours of her face.

"Everyone, this is Ilene Maddox," the director said. "She'd like to speak with you." Hamilton's gaze dipped over Sandra's shoulder to Brice.

Sandra and Brice excused themselves and stepped outside with Hamilton and Maddox.

Ilene fixed her jaw as she let her eyes roll over them. "Tell me what you're doing to save my boy."

Sandra recoiled at that, as if the other lives at stake meant nothing. At the same point, as a mother who came close to losing her daughter, she found empathy. "We are working to bring this situation to a peaceful resolution."

A tight smile, followed by a puff of air. "Please spare me the canned response, Agent Vos. Are you a mother?"

Sandra could argue that held no relevance, but no good would come from that. It was best to play along. "I am."

"Then you would do anything for your child?"

"I would."

"As will I. It's why I insisted on coming down here despite Myron's admonition that I stay away."

Myron? They are chummy!

Ilene went on. "I wanted to look into the eyes of the people responsible for shutting this down. So I will kindly ask again, what are you doing?"

Sandra glanced at Hamilton, but he gestured at Ilene. So much for hoping the director would come to her rescue. *Very well...* She shared their progress thus far, leaving out names. She included the latest scenario.

Ilene's hand fluttered over the lapels of her jacket. Just a brief movement that disclosed her anxiety.

"We can take some comfort in the fact he didn't shoot your son," Sandra assured in a calm voice.

Ilene turned to Hamilton. "You need to extract Jordon."

"Ma'am," Sandra petitioned, drawing the woman's assessing eye back on her. She let the heat in them defuse before speaking again. "If we were to go in there now, there's a greater likelihood that things could go sideways." Sandra was showing mercy by not providing details. "I ask that you trust me here." Sandra's heart ticked up speed. She always thought before she spoke, yet she'd gone ahead anyhow. Ilene Maddox would likely take her words as a promise. *Shit!*

"Agent Vos, I don't trust easily, let alone when it involves Jordon's well-being, but I don't suppose I'm given much choice." She shot Hamilton a hot glare. "But know this, I remember people who break their word to me." With that, Ilene turned and left.

"Shut this down as quickly as possible." Hamilton jabbed a pointed finger at the ground and hurried off to catch up with Ilene.

"Well, that was intense," Brice said.

Sandra faced him. "How was that intense for you? You lose your voice?"

"I was reading the room. Ilene Maddox wanted assurances from another woman." Brice went back inside the command vehicle.

Sandra stood there for a few moments. Was that all she had done? Offered assurance? Or had she made a promise?

TWENTY-THREE

1:50 PM

Don't think I won't shoot you... Easier the second time...

Jordon was sure the stranger was going to make good on his word when he dragged him out of the break room. He should just be grateful he was still in one piece, but he was having a tough time forgiving himself for not pulling the trigger when he had the chance. He tried to excuse his inaction as being noble, but the truly noble thing to have done would have been to shoot this man. He could have saved others from suffering and relieved Mahoney from his. So far, Mahoney was hanging in there, but that could change in a heartbeat.

When the gunman returned to the break room, he sat at the table going through their phones. Apparently confiscating them wasn't enough. The man wanted to further violate their human rights by having them provide him with their passcodes. But surely sitting around in a nurse break room couldn't have been the point of today. And from the sound of it, there were others. Plural. He also didn't talk like someone in charge. So was he just hanging around, biding time?

It fit with Jordon's image of the man. A subordinate. Also,

he suspected he wasn't a hardened criminal, or he would have shot him a moment ago.

Easier the second time...

He clearly hadn't shot someone before Mahoney. And Jordon wasn't sure it was something the man particularly enjoyed doing. But he could be wrong. He vividly recalled the cold, calculating look in the man's eyes when he gave his gun back. Still, he hadn't pulled the trigger. Was that a testament to the stranger's character? Jordon had a hard time accepting that. He had shot Mahoney and was putting countless other lives at risk for the duration of the lockdown. Had this gunman thought of all the repercussions? Maybe if Jordon pointed this out... "It's been hours. People will need their meds."

The gunman slowly raised his eyes from the screen of Jordon's phone, but he dipped them back down again without a word.

"He's a father," Leah Winters said about Mahoney. "I've got two little girls." She hadn't left her spot on the floor in favor of returning to the couch. "They need me. I need—"

"Cut that out. Right now," the man barked without prying his gaze from the phone's screen.

Jordon imagined that the nurse was trying to humanize them, but the endeavor was failing. He flipped the scenario around in his head, trying to see another angle. All he landed on was what he had tried before. "Let them go. Hold on to me." He was accustomed to being viewed as a commodity, with a target on his back for kidnapping and ransom. Being the only child of billionaires, he grew up with a bodyguard over his shoulder twenty-four hours a day.

"And why would I do that?"

"As long as you have me, the police won't touch you. You know who my mother is. Her philanthropic interests and my father's business have earned them friendships with powerful people in DC. If that's not enough, my family has a crapload of money. I'm talking more money than God." Jordon didn't enjoy touting his family wealth, and he hated how he sounded. *But if it works...*

"That's quite a claim, but what does it have to do with me?"

The man's reaction had Jordon faltering. "You're kidding, right? You let all of us go, I can make sure you're set for life."

"Yeah, right."

Jordon hadn't expected such a lukewarm reaction to his proposal. He might have to try another tack. "You told your partner I'm insurance. But what if..." Jordon slowly got up and walked to the utensil drawer. There, he pulled out a knife.

The man lunged across the room, while holding the gun on him. But he wouldn't shoot. *I'm insurance.*

The only way he could think of to gain control here was to threaten harm against himself. This stranger would have to know the police would blame him, not Jordon. He held the blade over his wrist.

"Get that blade away from your arm," the gunman hissed.

"Why should I?" Jordon got the steel closer to his flesh.

"Put the knife down. Now!"

Jordon said nothing as he poked the tip into his skin.

"Stop right now otherwise I'll kill your girlfriend."

Jordon's world became still and spun.

"That's right. I saw the pictures of you two. I even know who she is, and I'm quite sure I know where to find her." The stranger held eye contact. Seconds passed, stretching into what felt like minutes. "Put the knife down or I will leave this room, track her down, and put a bullet in her head."

Jordon set the knife down. "Please, leave her out of this."

"Hmm. I'm not so sure I can anymore." With that, the man rushed from the break room with Jordon on his heels.

What have I done?

TWENTY-FOUR

2:05 PM

Sandra had enough to balance without stressing about Ilene Maddox. Though her enclosed threat was hard to miss. *I remember people who don't keep their word.* It only stamped in how long they'd been on scene and how little progress they'd made. The silence was torturous when it came to the negotiations, just as it was with her mother's health. Sandra had her cell phone out, and Dana hadn't called again. No news, good news? It was hard to say, but she had to believe that to keep her focus.

In hostage situations, silence was double-edged. While it could lead hostage takers to impulsive action, it could also make them uncomfortable enough to surrender. That didn't make waiting any easier.

And in her position, every passing second was like barbed wire slicing into her flesh. Each stab was a reminder of how hundreds of people inside needed medical attention. Adding to the pain was the irony they were in the right place for that, just at the wrong time. And the clock was ticking for little Phoebe Chapman.

Brice, Monica, and Gibson were back to pulling more backgrounds on vehicle registrations. But the wisest thing she could do right now was get back on the phone with the woman in the boardroom. But as she went to tuck her phone away, the screen lit up.

"Dana," she answered, and everyone looked her way. "Just a personal call I need to take," she told them and left the vehicle.

"Dana, tell me there's some good news." As if the request could affect reality, bend it to her will. If only a wish made a dream come true.

"I just saw that you called a couple of hours ago. I'm sorry that I didn't see this until now. I've been by your mother's side and talking with her doctors."

"What are they saying?"

"Your mother's bloodwork has come back, but doctors are concerned because her iron levels are very low. She's anemic, actually. They believe that's what caused her to faint. A transfusion is being considered, but they haven't done that yet. There are more tests they'd like to run and can't have new blood providing false readings."

"Can't they just give her an iron pill?"

"If only it was that easy. But supplements take weeks to absorb into the body. Apparently, a transfusion is the fastest way to spike her levels. Please know, though, that she is stabilized and resting peacefully."

Hot tears flooded Sandra's eyes. Resting peacefully was also what dead people did. "Okay, well, that's good at least," she said, her throat tight.

"Please be assured, she's receiving the best care."

"Do the doctors have any idea why her iron is low?"

"If they suspect something specific, they're not saying."

Which, to Sandra, wasn't a good thing. They wouldn't want to share a dire prognosis for it to be proven false.

"I assume the tests they're going to run will give them some answers," Dana added. "And Ms. Vos, I know you're worried about your mother, but there's no need. Please, trust me. I'll call you should anything change or take a turn." Dana's soothing voice helped her words penetrate.

"I trust you with her life."

"Thank you, Ms. Vos. I will call when I have more."

"Thank you." Sandra hung up and swallowed back the fear that rose in her throat and returned to her workstation. Focusing on work would get her through.

She put her headset in place, and said, "I'm calling the boardroom."

The rest of the team got on their headsets and nodded when they were set. She made the call.

"What do you want?" the woman answered, tense and immediately on the defense.

It wasn't a good sign of what was transpiring in that room, but Sandra was calm when she replied. "This isn't about me. You can talk to me, and I will listen."

"You're just saying that. I need you to leave me alone so I can take care of what I need to."

People gasped in the background. One man said, "She's going to kill us."

"Shut up or I will, I swear," the woman threatened.

"Please," Sandra inserted. "There's nothing you can't still walk away from." Not entirely the truth, obviously, but it could get worse.

"Are you crazy? I'm not going anywhere until I get what I want."

Sandra sensed Brice looking at her profile, but didn't turn to him in fear of losing the thread with the HT. "And what do you want?"

"I want them to pay!"

Brice scribbled, *revenge or is this about money?*

"You're angry," Sandra empathized.

"Damn right, I'm angry. They don't care about people. That's a lie they sell to make money. They're fat cats lapping up the cream. All of them."

Brice scratched out *revenge*, but Sandra wasn't so sure. She shook her head but didn't make eye contact with him.

"'Lapping up the cream'?" she parroted back.

"Making themselves rich off people. People who have nothing to start with, not that they care."

"Help us!" someone screamed in the background.

"Shut up!" the hostage taker yelled back.

Sandra feared the situation in the room was escalating. If the woman's hostages didn't calm down, this wouldn't come to a good end. "They're scared, that's all. Just like you."

"I'm not scared."

"What you're doing today is extremely brave." Sandra fed the woman's ego, approaching things from the way she'd see her actions.

A few seconds, then, "If they'd just do as I ask, then maybe we could end this."

Brice wrote, *After something from them...*

"What do you need? Let me get it for you."

"You can't!" With that, the line went dead.

"I don't have a good feeling about this," Brice said. "She's sounding like she's being pressed against the wall."

Sandra was familiar with the feeling. "The clock doesn't stop ticking. All this time and she hasn't made progress toward her goal either. Meanwhile, the cops and feds are set up out here, essentially breathing down her neck. And the people in that room are terrified and feeling hopeless, but their panic is only adding to the shot caller's."

"Right, so what is so important that she's still in that room?"

Brice countered. "I don't believe she's hurt anyone yet, or someone would have chimed in with that."

"Agreed." There was hope in that because of the time that had passed. If she was bent toward violence, she would have made an example of someone by now. Just as Mickey had.

"I'm with you guys," Monica said, swiveling toward them. "But I think she's getting closer. You mentioned the pressure she must be feeling. What's to say she doesn't start shooting hostages soon?"

"Nothing, except one thing. She needs something from them," Brice said.

"But is it from the group or one person?" Monica volleyed back.

"Hmm. Good question, and I'm leaning toward the former. Let me see the script, Monica." The woman handed it over, and Sandra scanned down. "Yes, here it is. 'Fat cats lapping up cream', 'don't care about other people.' We've already mentioned how the people in that room are some of the most powerful and wealthy in medicine and pharmaceuticals."

"Which makes the possibilities for wrongdoings endless," Brice put in.

"This could be about money or a failed procedure that hurt someone this woman loves. Or a faulty medication produced by any of those companies owned by the people on the board," Sandra said. "Though I suspect this has a financial trigger."

Brice nodded. "Me too, with that 'fat cat' comment."

"You don't think Beal is the target then?" Neal asked, weighing in on the conversation from the other end of the vehicle. He was seated at the table, nursing a coffee, next to Luis and Kreiger.

"Oh, I never said that. Beal is the CEO, and this woman probably holds her ultimately responsible for whatever this is about, or needs her backing for what she's after."

"And how does that account for her accomplices? What's their stake in all this?" Gibson asked from in front of the markerboard where he made his latest notes.

Woman on eighth floor escalating, wants the board members to do something... Fat cats...

The vague summary painted a bleak picture. "They may be friends, or she could have hired them. Next time I get through to her, I'm going to try and find out more about her accomplices."

"Excuse me," Luis wedged in and continued when everyone turned his way. "You mentioned this might be about money, but none of the people in that room have anything to do with medical bills or collection."

"But the HT might see them as being able to do something about their debt or even hold them responsible for their financial burden," Sandra said. "Again, that's assuming this is about money."

"And there are surgeons in there," Brice said. "It's possible this woman is in debt for a costly procedure with no way to pay it off. Do you have access to see past due accounts?"

Luis shook his head. "That's one system I can't access. I have a contact, but I'd need names. I suspect there are several past due accounts."

"He's got a point," Kreiger put in.

Fat cats... making themselves rich... This thought gelled with her earlier statement about a botched procedure. "Do you know if any of the doctors in that room have open malpractice suits against them or even recent claims that were rejected?"

Luis pushed his glasses up his nose. "The most recent case was against Dr. Jessup, and it was dismissed."

"What were the details of the case?" Sandra asked.

"It was regarding a liver operation that Dr. Jessup performed. The plaintiff accused Jessup of coercing his brother into having the operation that ultimately resulted in his death. While the procedure was a common one, it went sideways. There was an excessive loss of blood. The deceased's brother claimed that Dr. Jessup failed to exercise care and precautions."

"And the doctor's defense?" Sandra asked.

"He did all he could, but there was unexpected bleeding during the re-section procedure. Even though he responded as per protocol and infused the patient with blood, it wasn't enough to save his life."

"We'll need the name of the plaintiff," Coleman said.

"Jamie Radcliffe," Luis told him.

"Is he one of them?" Monica pointed at the photos of the gunmen on the markerboard.

Brice clicked on his laptop and stopped shortly after, shook his head. "Radcliffe's driver's license looks nothing like either male hostage taker we're aware of. According to his background, Radcliffe is thirty-nine, single, and lives alone. No criminal record. One of the women could be connected to the case involving his brother. A girlfriend or wife of the brother?"

"The deceased's name?" Monica asked.

"Roger Radcliffe."

Monica tapped on her laptop and beat Brice to pulling the background this time. "He was unmarried at the time of death. The girlfriend bit could hold true, though."

Neal nodded. "I'll get an officer out to talk with Jamie Radcliffe to see what we can dig up there."

Our efforts must pay off eventually... Right? Sandra stared at the photographs of the three hostage takers. Just ordinary-looking people. Surely, something had to give soon. A piece of intel that could help her fashion a strategy that would get them to surrender. But short of that, she didn't want to dwell on all the ways the next hour could go wrong. Thoughts of that little girl and her medical crisis weren't far from mind. Neither was Jordon Maddox and the others in the hospital who might need medical attention. She recognized the fine balance between killing time and pushing things a little too far. The former got her brother killed. But she had a horrible feeling about what would happen if they rushed things.

TWENTY-FIVE
2:15 PM

Eric followed Wyatt inside a cream-colored home office and waited while he dug a file out of the desk drawer. He handed it over to Eric.

It was a good half inch thick. Eric set the file on the desk and snapped on a pair of gloves. "You mentioned a more recent one that had her spooked."

"Knowing Meg, it should be the one on top. Most recent, most readily available."

"All right." Eric grabbed the top sheet and noticed two things right away. This wasn't a copy of the threat, rather the original, and there was a sticky note stuck to the page. He read that first.

Celeste Barrington, failed as an intern, fired

The threat was typeset and printed.

I blame you for my life. My failure of a life. You never had anything nice to say, never had my back. All you had to do was show just a teeny amount of kindness, but no, you were too proud and arrogant for that. You never listen to my side. You bitch! I plan to make your life a living hell, and if you doubt I can get that close, think again.

Short and to the point, signed off with the initials CB. She wasn't exactly hiding her identity. Beal was clearly able to determine who she was by the letters and likely some wording in the message.

Eric was about to return the threat to the folder when he noticed an anomaly at the base of the page. The top layer of the paper had been lifted, the fibers frayed as if something sticky had been stuck there and peeled off. Eric pointed this out to Wyatt. "Do you know what was there?"

Wyatt came closer and leaned in, shook his head.

"And she never mentioned this to you?"

"I..." Wyatt looked away.

Right, you don't make a habit of listening to your wife when she talks... "Does your wife have any close friends who she might have confided in about this letter?"

"Phyllis Hudson. I have her number if you'd like that."

"Please. Does she work at the hospital?"

"No, she's with Child Services." Wyatt took his phone out of the interior pocket in his suit jacket and rattled off the number as Eric tapped it into the Notes app on his phone.

"Your wife noted this letter came from Celeste Barrington, a failed intern. Is your wife responsible for the fate of interns?"

"Not directly, but she can override the decision of their supervising doctor."

"Has she ever done that?"

"I don't see why. As a confident leader, she trusts the judgment of the doctors she puts in charge."

"That makes sense to me, but clearly there's something your wife must have done to make Celeste feel slighted by her." Though maybe not sticking up for her was enough. In that case,

Eric could see motive for Celeste to hate Megan Beal. Her career would be over before it began, and she'd be hundreds of thousands in debt from medical school with no way to pay it off. Eric pulled out his phone to show Wyatt the pictures of the three armed suspects. "Let me know if any of these people look familiar to you."

Wyatt leaned in toward the screen. "Nope."

Eric shuffled to the next and received another no, and the same for the third picture. He then pocketed his phone.

"Who are those people?" Wyatt asked.

"They are working with the woman who is holed up in the boardroom with your wife."

"Yeah, well, I swear, I've never seen any of them before. I can't even believe this is happening." Wyatt raked his hand through his hair.

"Well, it is, and I need to leave. But I'm taking this with me." Eric referred to all the threats, and he pulled an evidence bag from his back pocket that he'd grabbed before coming into the house.

"Sure, do whatever you need to do. Call when you know more."

Eric turned around in the doorway. "I will. You should clear your schedule until all this is over and keep your phone nearby."

Wyatt patted his hand over his suit jacket, indicating the interior pocket. "It's always right here."

Eric left the house and called Phyllis Hudson from the department car. The woman answered on the fourth ring, just when Eric thought he was destined for voicemail. "This is Detective Birch with the Metropolitan PD. I understand from Wyatt Beal that you are close friends with his wife, Megan."

"That's right." Leery, and Eric couldn't blame her.

"Do you know anything about a letter Celeste Barrington sent her?"

"Threat, you mean. And yes. What's going on? Is Meg okay?"

"There is a situation at the hospital, and it's on lockdown. An armed woman is in the boardroom with Ms. Beal."

"Oh my God. If it's Celeste, she's crazy, Detective. There's no telling what she can do."

"Did you see the threat from Celeste, or did Megan just tell you about it?"

"I didn't see it for myself, but Meg was shaken by it. Celeste sent clippings of Meg's hair with it."

Nothing creepy about that... "And she was sure it was hers?"

"I don't think she had it tested, but it was the right color, and she received the letter a day after a haircut."

Maybe Megan had submitted the hair for testing, and that's why it was no longer attached to the letter. "And that was when?"

"Toward the end of last week. Thursday."

"Was the letter sent to the hospital or her house?"

"The hospital. Left on her chair."

It sounded like Celeste was building up her nerve to confront Megan Beal face to face. "Why didn't Megan call the police?"

"Are you blaming the victim here?"

"Not at all. I was just curious."

"She might have thought you had better things to do," Phyllis added.

Nothing like brutal honesty... As a seasoned detective, Eric had encountered prejudice against the police before. He even understood why it existed and wasn't about to fault anyone for their opinions. "Before I go, Megan left a note on the threat that Celeste was a failed intern who was fired. Is that how you know it, or is there more you can tell me? The more details, the better."

"That's about right. She just couldn't hack the job or stay in her lane. She fainted at the sight of blood and advised the parents of a dying child against taking the advice of their doctor. That child died."

"Okay, thank you. All of this has been very helpful."

"Please don't let anything happen to Meg."

"Everyone is doing their best to ensure the safety of everyone in that hospital, ma'am." Eric ended the call and selected Lieutenant Coleman's number. Neal picked up on the second ring, and Eric announced himself. "It's Detective Birch."

There were a few seconds of silence, then, "What did you find out?"

"I have a potential lead."

"Great news. I'm putting you on speaker."

Eric gave it a few beats before he continued. He imagined Sandra sitting on the other end listening in, and just the thought brought him closer to her. "Beal received threats against her on what seems a regular basis. But the most recent one had her quite concerned, and it seems like for good reason." When he finished, there was silence while he assumed everyone was absorbing his message.

"A clipping of her hair? That's a little *Silence of the Lambs*," Brice piped up.

Eric wasn't going to correct the reference. There were no hair clippings in the movie, and there was no evidence Celeste was a cannibal.

"She could fit," Sandra said, and Eric picked up on the nuance in her tone.

"*Could* fit? Is there something I'm missing?"

"The woman in that boardroom feels unheard, and it also seems that this might be about money. But I hesitate for one reason, and it might be down to interpretation. It could also be the use of plural pronouns that is throwing me, but she made it sound like *no one* was listening or cooperating. I wonder if she is appealing to the group."

"Right," Eric said, though the change in direction made him feel like he may have wasted his time. But following leads to their conclusion was what investigations were about. Some panned out, while others smacked into a dead end.

"Again, I might also be wrong and reading it too literally," Sandra amended. "And regardless, even if this woman's issue is primarily with Beal, she could hold everyone in the room accountable."

"Then what do you think I should do? See if I can track this Celeste down? If I find her, she's obviously not in that boardroom. And if I can't find her, I can talk to her closest friends and family."

"Couldn't hurt," Sandra said. "And I can try to elicit a reaction by using her name."

"So what is it, Lieutenant Coleman?" Eric asked, eager to know his next steps.

"Go, see if you can track down Barrington. But I also have another lead for you to follow if that doesn't pan out."

"Name it."

As Coleman filled him in on Jamie Radcliffe, Eric couldn't ignore the negative voice in his head that said both these leads could turn to dust. Not putting them any further ahead. The fact he had Cross in custody was the only thing currently soothing his conscience. Even then, he still didn't know who Cross let into that server room. The ongoing search at his house hadn't turned up anything of value.

TWENTY-SIX

Sandra had worked crisis incidents like today's before, including a prison riot that had the inmates assuming control. That one lasted for thirty-six hours, and she and other negotiators were brought in on rotating shifts. Today's situation wouldn't be allowed to go on that long, not with so many innocent lives on the line. ERT would find justification and develop a strategy to breach. But, so far, their best lead came from Eric. Before his call, Neal had heard from officers who had visited the medical companies belonging to the CEOs on the hospital board. No one flagged.

"I think we've caught a break." Gibson's declaration had everyone in the vehicle turning in his direction. "One of these last vehicle registrations matches the photo we have of the HT from the second floor. Meet Carmen Feeney, thirty-seven. Single, no record."

She noticed Gibson had stepped in to help with the registrations after the officer dropped off the last batch. He still had an ear out and the radio scanner running in the background, but there hadn't been any activity.

"Can we connect her to Radcliffe, or is there any apparent motive?" Neal asked.

Gibson returned to his computer, and Brice started tapping on his laptop. Sandra watched as windows opened and layered over each other.

"Her credit score is bad," Brice said a moment later.

"I can't see a clear connection to Radcliffe," Gibson said.

Monica was busy on her computer too. "I've found Feeney's Facebook profile. It is rather inactive with the last post from nine months ago about some Pilates class she took. The pictures in her media library don't include any of the other HTs we know about. There is nothing noted for her relationship status."

Neal huffed in frustration. "Right, so assuming she's not some criminal mastermind who has skirted the law all this time, what makes a thirty-seven-year-old, who has been a law-abiding citizen all these years, take these drastic measures?"

His question was clearly rhetorical, but for one generalized thing. "Whatever she hopes to accomplish with this move today, it means more to her than her freedom."

"Same could well apply to the rest," Neal said. "If we can find out how they are connected and how they communicate, we might get our motive along with their identities."

Something occurred to Sandra while Neal was speaking. "Maybe it's not exactly one inciting incident, but an experience they all share? Something that hit close to home on a personal and emotional level could explain such a severe response. The last time I spoke to Mickey he made it clear he was a grown-ass man, making his own decisions."

"It's entirely possible," Neal said. "But we need more than that. I'll get Detective Birch to Feeney's house with a search warrant the second he's finished up with Radcliffe and Celeste. We need access to Feeney's call history in case Feeney spoke with her cohorts. Are we sure she's the only one who matches vehicle registrations?" He leveled this question at Gibson.

"Hers was the last one I had to run," Gibson said.

"And we've finished with ours," Brice said, after glancing at Monica's workstation.

"I'll get on her phone records, requesting a fast turnaround," Gibson said.

Neal nodded. "That would be great."

"I'll need Feeney's number, Gibson." When Sandra tried the nurses' station on the second floor, Feeney never answered. Receiving a call on her personal cell phone might make her more likely to pick up.

"Yes, ma'am." He tapped on the keyboard for a few seconds, then rattled it off while she grabbed a pen and notepad and scribbled it down.

"I'm going to give it a try," she announced, and everyone got ready to listen in.

The call was sent to voicemail after the second ring. Feeney had rejected it. Undeterred, Sandra tried again. This time, the call was answered, but Feeney didn't say a word.

"Carmen, this is Sandra with the FBI."

There were a few moments of silence, followed by a tentative, "FBI?"

"Yes, and I want to help you."

"How do you know my name?"

Sandra took some victory in having one of their hostage takers identified. It was certainly a move in the right direction. "We have our ways of finding things out, Carmen. What we can't wrap our minds around is what brought you here today. Could you tell us?"

Silence.

"Maybe what brought your friends here?"

There was a pause before she responded. "We're in this together."

"In this together with whom, Carmen?"

She ended the call.

Sandra tried her back but went straight to voicemail. "She's turned her phone off."

"'In this together.' Clearly, they have a shared goal, but I didn't get the feeling Carmen's friends with these people," Brice said. "So now we're left trying to figure out what brought these people together."

"And we will. It's just a matter of time." *And we're closer than we've ever been...* That's how Sandra had to think anyhow.

Gail's patience was running out, and her nerves were beyond frayed. There had been another gunshot down the hall not long ago. At least there were no screams. It sounded like the bullet had struck something, not *someone*, at least. But why was it taking the cops so long to come in here and rescue them? As time continued to pass, her hope was draining away. Not so much for her welfare, but her sweet baby girl. Would she get the surgery she needed? Gail wasn't under any illusions they'd hold the heart for her daughter beyond tonight.

Phoebe looked so small lying on the bed. It was like she was shrinking before Gail's eyes. The heart monitor showed a slightly erratic rhythm, but it was familiar. That still did little to settle Gail's nerves. And Nurse Torres had retreated inward after talking to the feds. Maybe even before that, she had been on edge.

Currently, she was tucked into the corner of the room, next to a window, with her phone in her hand. Since she received that text a while ago, she was often cradling the device.

"Hey, are you all right over there?"

The nurse sniffled and pushed her phone into the pocket of

her pants. "Yeah, fine." She resorted to hugging herself, telling Gail she was lying.

"We will get out of this alive." The words spilled from Gail's lips. The confidence surprised her, considering how despondent she felt.

"You can't know that. While we're talking, someone just down the hall may be fighting to stay alive."

There were likely many in the hospital struggling at this moment, but Gail sensed Torres's immediate concern was for the victim of that morning's shooting. "It's understandable you're worried about your colleagues."

Nurse Torres looked at Gail with wide, wet eyes.

The pain in them told Gail there must be more to this. "You can talk to me."

Tears spilled down Torres's cheeks at the invitation, and she put a hand over her stomach.

It was a move that Gail remembered doing too many times to count when she was expecting Phoebe. "You're pregnant."

Torres bit her bottom lip and nodded.

It didn't take long to figure out how that connected with someone in the nurse break room. "It's the father, isn't it? He's a nurse and out there? That's why you're so worried?"

"He's an attending, but yes, he's who I'm worried about. He was in the break room with me moments before the lockdown."

"He could have been gone before the gunman got there."

Fresh tears fell down the nurse's cheeks.

"What's his name?" Talking about him might help calm her down. After she'd saved Phoebe's life, it was the least she could do.

"Jordon. He's my soulmate." The nurse slipped her hand into her pants pocket, and Gail saw she wrapped her hand around her phone. The text must have been from him.

"How far along are you?"

"Five weeks." She offered a weak smile.

"Congratulations." Gail grinned, relishing the little escape into good news.

"Thanks. It was such a shock, unexpected."

Gail looked at Phoebe, recalling when she first realized she was pregnant. It had taken a morning of hugging a toilet. "It's the most exciting adventure you'll ever have." And Gail had started off meaning that, but as she took in her daughter, she felt a jab in her chest. That *adventure* was clouded by her sweet girl's defective heart. Still, she wouldn't change anything or go back. If only she could save Phoebe the pain, though. "How did Jordon take the news?"

"Like an idiot." Torres laughed, but more tears fell and had her palming her cheeks. "That's why he was in the break room, to apologize. I think we'll be just fine. We were going to talk more after our shifts ended."

Gail tried to muster a smile, but her story couldn't have been further from that. She'd done everything to set a romantic scene. She'd made her boyfriend's favorite meal and broken the news. He'd gotten defensive, *blamed* the pregnancy on her, accusing her she'd done it on purpose to trap him. He'd left right after that, and she never saw him again.

Torres continued. "He was only there because of me. I should have eased him into the news, or something. Then he wouldn't have been in that break room."

"You never could have expected a gunman."

"But what if he's seriously hurt? What then? What will I do?"

"As you know, Phoebe's had a weak heart from birth. I've spent many hours spiraling out with worry. And as hard as it was to do this, at some point I had to accept that I was doing all I could for her. The rest is in God's hands."

"I'm an atheist."

"Though I'm sure you believe in something. Ah, science?"

When Torres nodded, Gail continued. "Isn't the study of science all about facts?"

"Yes."

"But you don't have all the facts to base any reaction on." Gail sure hoped she was helping ease Torres's nerves.

"I guess, but I just couldn't handle it if he was shot... killed." Another batch of tears splashed on her cheeks. Again, she quickly swiped them away as if she were ashamed to show emotion. "Especially now."

Gail assumed she was referring to the baby until Torres pulled out her phone. When she didn't say anything, Gail spoke again. "I'm sure Jordon wasn't alone in that break room. Assuming he or someone else was injured, they could help that person."

"If the gunman allowed that. But this is all my fault. And while I appreciate you trying to cheer me up, a gunshot needs urgent medical attention." Torres looked at her phone and more tears fell.

"What is it, Nurse Torres?"

"Maria. Just call me Maria."

"Maria," Gail said, trying on the name.

"It's a text from Jordon."

Gail brightened at that. "Then he's okay."

She shook her head. "I can't know that. The text came through once the hospital system and cell phones came back online. He likely sent the message before the shooting." Maria held the phone for Gail to read the message.

Marry me?

It was short and sweet, and Gail would guess Jordon was crunched for time. The proposition had Gail's stomach souring. It could be a sincere proposal or one that was rushed out of fear for the future. He wanted to make sure that Maria knew he loved her and the baby in case he died. But Gail forced a smile. "Well, that's good, right?"

"I don't think it is. Jordon loves me, but he told me before that he wants to wait until he's chief of neurology."

"He could have changed his mind. Things have changed. He's going to be a father... And it's possible this situation has him thinking nothing can be taken for granted."

"That's what I'm afraid of. He'd need to be scared to send this message, which tells me he was in danger when he sent this. What if he is hurt?" Maria trembled, and Gail hugged her.

Their moment was interrupted by a loud banging on the door, followed by, "Open up!"

Maria hurried to the door and peeked through the slats of the blinds on the door. "It's the man with the gun."

Cold dread creeped down Gail's spine, and panic swarmed her vision with pinpricks of white. "Maybe if we ignore him, he'll go away."

He banged again. "Open up, or I will start shooting."

Gail glanced at her daughter, and rounded the bed, placing herself between the door and her daughter.

"Stop! You don't need to do this. Just leave her alone!" a man yelled out, and Maria threw the door open.

"Jordon?"

Maria was yanked into the hall. Gail couldn't see a lot from her vantage point, but a handsome young doctor was on the heels of the gunman.

"I told you to leave her alone!" the doctor cried out, just as he dashed toward the gunman's back.

The man spun, and the doctor grabbed for his gun. There was a struggle, and the gun went off.

Gail threw herself over her daughter. She was too terrified to scream, hardly able to breathe, let alone able to leave Phoebe's side to see the aftermath.

Now that they had the identity of one hostage taker, Sandra was planning to call the woman on the eighth again. She could use this knowledge as leverage. Her headset was on, and her fingers over the keypad of the phone.

"Get over here quick," Kreiger barked, and waved his arms.

She set her headset back on her desk, and so did Brice. They went over to where Kreiger was at the table with Neal and Luis.

"Look." He pointed at Luis's laptop.

Neal's expression was grim, and she understood why the moment she saw the screen.

Mickey stormed into a patient room, and a few moments later, he returned to the hall with a female nurse. He nudged her in front of him and was holding his gun to her back.

Her gaze was frozen on the screen, and her insides were slush. "Do you recognize that nurse?" she asked Luis.

"I think that's Maria Torres."

Torres... The name ricocheted around in her head like a metal ball. "I spoke to her. She was with Phoebe Chapman. That must be Phoebe's room." She wouldn't need to remind anyone here that Phoebe was the child awaiting a heart transplant. That fact would be fixed in all their minds. And if he took the nurse, what was the status on the girl and her mother? "I assume there aren't cameras in there?" she said to Luis.

"None in any patient rooms for privacy reasons."

On the screen, a doctor seemed to come out of nowhere, and he attacked the gunman. There was a brief struggle followed by a blast of light. The doctor went down. A pool of blood blossomed in the doctor's torso.

Torres pushed the gunman aside and ran to the fallen doctor. She took off her lab coat and wrapped it around the doctor's waist.

"Oh my God. Was he...? He was just... shot." Luis was stammering. No one else was saying a word.

Torres remained leaning over the doctor protectively, and he reached up and affectionately touched her face.

"The gunman's just standing there like he's in shock," Brice said.

But seconds later, he was ripping Torres away from the doctor. She was screaming and batting at his arms, but it wasn't enough to get him to release her. He hauled her back to the room she had come out of. Torres was resisting, dragging her legs behind her.

The door was slammed shut behind them, and the doctor was left in the hallway bleeding out.

The command vehicle was silent for several beats. It was like everyone was holding their breath.

"Can you zoom in on his face?" Brice asked Luis.

"Yes." A moment later, the doctor's face filled the screen.

Sandra was going to be sick. "Is that who I think it is?"

"That's Jordon Maddox," Luis confirmed.

She heard the emergency director, but she was numb, her mind immersed in the past. The images of Sam in his final moments, created by her imagination. She wasn't there. She didn't get the chance to say goodbye to her brother. But based on his injuries, he would have looked much the same as what appeared on the screen. Sam never received help in time. The negotiator had failed her brother by not talking down his shooter fast enough. She refused to fail Jordon Maddox any further, and not because he was Ilene Maddox's son and her influence with the director could cost Sandra her job. No, she'd save Jordon for Sam.

TWENTY-NINE

2:30 PM

The gunshot was so loud, Gail's ears were ringing. Instinct had her wanting to hide away someplace with her daughter, but she couldn't move her. She was trembling as she looked toward the empty doorway. Maybe if she could shut the door and flip the lock, they'd be safe. Though that hadn't stopped the gunman from demanding entry. And could Gail really abandon Maria and her unborn baby? Protect her own like a coward? She cast one more glance at Phoebe before leaving her side. She ran to the door and caught a glimpse of a man in doctor scrubs lying on the floor in a pool of blood.

Maria was hunched over him, wailing. "Hang in there, baby. Hang in there."

The gunman hustled over and yanked Maria away from the man. Then the gunman was beelining straight for Gail, dragging Maria with him.

Shit! Gail scrambled to shut the door, but the man pushed it inward and herded her back into the room. She took up position at her daughter's bedside again, placing herself in front of her daughter. "Leave us alone!"

The man came right over to her. He was so close that Gail

could smell his breath and feel its warmth on her face. "I'm the one who gives the orders, not you. See this right here?" He held the gun up, pressing the muzzle to her cheek.

She drew back with a yelp. It was still hot from being fired. Gail glanced around the gunman at Maria. She was facing the doorway, her eyes blank.

The man snatched Maria by the wrist. "Only God can help you if you go out that door."

"You fucking bastard! You didn't have to shoot him!" Maria was shaking, but her eyes were steel.

"Mommy?" The sound of Phoebe's cherubic voice stood in contrast to the hell in this room.

Gail took her daughter's hand. "It's all right, baby. Everything is going to be all right."

"I'll be the one who says what will be all right or not. You hear me?" the gunman hissed. "Son of a... Urr." He gripped at his hair.

The reading on Phoebe's heart monitor ticked up speed and became erratic.

Gail stepped forward, standing on her toes to put her eyes near level with his. Face to face, she buckled inwardly as it sank in that this man could end her life with a bullet, Phoebe's too. But to hell if she'd let him frighten her daughter to death. "You will back off. You hear *me*?"

"And why would I do that?"

Gail's eyes drifted briefly to Nurse Torres, who was slowly shaking her head. She proceeded anyhow. "You might be a shit, but you're hurting a little girl here. *My* little girl, and I won't stand for that. Am I understood?"

The man stared back at her, but she held her ground, stiffened and squared her shoulders.

"Am I understood?" she repeated, talking firmer than she imagined possible. Tremors danced through her body.

The man said nothing, didn't move, and Gail was just about

to scream out when someone spoke. It wasn't anyone in this room. Then she remembered she had found a lucid moment to call 911 between Maria being taken from the room and the gun going off.

"Who is that?" The man angled his head.

The voice sounded again.

"Where is that coming—" He met her eye. "It's you. You're on your phone?" He moved like he was going to search her, and the thought of his hands roaming her body had her gagging.

She was pinned in a corner in more ways than one. Squeezing past him was risky and would leave Phoebe completely exposed. If she denied his accusation that might anger him more than her trespass. She pulled her cell phone from her pocket and held the device in front of his face. "Say hi to the nine-one-one operator."

"You bitch!"

He slapped her across the face with such force that she lost her balance and toppled to the floor. Her phone went flying across the room. She instinctively cried out and silenced herself as her vision pinpricked and was bathed in white light.

There was a crunching noise, and she was quite certain he'd stomped on her phone, destroying it.

The heart monitor was beeping loudly. There was movement in the room and words spoken between the gunman and Nurse Torres. All while Gail lay helpless on the floor, her sweet, innocent daughter was going into cardiac arrest, and there was nothing she could do for her.

Everything in her world faded to black.

Eric double-checked the address, and this was the place. Celeste Barrington's house could handle a little TLC. He knocked on the door, in one way hoping no one would answer. That would strongly suggest that Barrington was the woman in the boardroom. He raised his hand to knock a second time, but the sound of footsteps stopped him.

The door swung open, and a man in his thirties stood there, looking like Eric had disturbed his afternoon nap.

Eric flashed his badge and tucked it away. "Detective Birch. I'm looking to speak with Celeste Barrington."

"She's not home." The guy pulled on the door to shut it again, but Eric stepped in to prevent that from happening.

"Unfortunately, it doesn't work that way. Where is she?"

The man held up a hand. "She said she had some job interviews today."

A lie to cover her real intention? "Your name and relationship with Celeste Barrington?"

"David Galvin, and I'm her boyfriend. What is this about?"

"Let's just say I'm not sure I buy that Celeste is on job interviews. When did you last see her?"

"Before I went to work last night, though I felt her get out of bed around eight AM."

That would have given her plenty of time to get to the hospital. "So you live here with Celeste?"

"That's right." Some people walked down the sidewalk, and it had David looking over Eric's shoulder at them.

"We might be best to continue our conversation inside," Eric suggested. "Less distractions."

David crossed his arms. "Not until you tell me what this is about."

"There's a situation underway at Founders Hospital as we speak. Megan Beal is shut up in a room with others by an armed woman, who we suspect is Celeste." Eric let that sit out there.

"What? There's no way."

"Celeste sent a written threat to Ms. Beal, including a clipping of her hair."

David gestured for Eric to come into the house and shut the door behind them.

"We could sit somewhere perhaps?" Eric asked when David didn't offer.

David gestured toward the front sitting room, but Eric insisted David lead the way. There were two ratty couches. David sat on one, and Eric the other.

"Did you know about the threat I mentioned?"

David shook his head.

"You ever hear Celeste mention Ms. Beal?"

"Celeste talks about her a lot. There are times she's going on so much about her I've told her to shut up. Still, though, it's hard to imagine her going to this extreme. And I haven't the foggiest clue where she would have gotten a gun."

"There are others with guns too." Eric took out his phone and brought up pictures of the three hostage takers. He showed each of them to David in turn. "Do you recognize any of these people?"

"I've never seen them."

Keys jangled in the front door, and then it opened. "You left the door unlocked. Again!" a woman yelled out.

"That's Celeste." David jumped up from the couch and hurried to the entry. "I'm so happy to see you."

"Okay," the woman dragged out.

"There's a detective here saying you threatened Megan Beal and that you had her and others at gunpoint inside Founders Hospital. *Celeste?*" The last bit was pushed out in clear confusion, and that had Eric springing to his feet. Call it cop's intuition, but seconds later it was confirmed spot-on. Celeste was blazing down the sidewalk.

Eric set out after her, bolting past David. He hit the sidewalk and yelled ahead of him, "Stop! MPD!" His heart pounded in his ears as he ran flat-out.

Celeste passed a woman and yanked on her arm. She fell to the ground, and Eric jumped over her. He glanced over his shoulder, his conscience weighing on him, and saw her getting to her feet. She should be fine.

Celeste turned right down a side street, and Eric made up some time. She looked back at him and barely missed smacking into a bicyclist. But the course correction had her arms pinwheeling to stay upright. She lost the fight and crumpled to the ground. She struggled to get her feet under her again, but it was too late.

Eric stood over her. "All right, we're going to have a little talk." She clearly wasn't in that boardroom, but he was going to get to the root of why she ran. Was it because of the written threat or something else?

Time had slowed down for Sandra since watching the shooting. She kept superimposing her brother's face on Maddox. But now wasn't the time to get lost in memories or guilt. The phone at Gibson's station rang. It didn't stop Kreiger from making a case for breaching.

"The guy on the fourth is clearly coming undone," Kreiger said.

"I don't think this shooting was intentional." She recalled the look on Mickey's face after Maddox went down. How he seemed frozen in shock. She didn't think it was just because he was disappointed to lose his *insurance*.

"I'm with Sandra," Brice said. "We all saw that Maddox rushed him, and the gun went off in their struggle."

"Intentional or not, that kid could bleed out right in front of us," Kreiger argued. "Is that what we want?"

"You know it's not." Her tone was sharper than she intended. She took pride in reining in her emotions, but she was scared for Maddox, Torres, and the Chapmans. "If ERT goes in, Jordon Maddox *might be* saved, but at what cost? How many casualties will result? That gunman is going to start by shooting the people in that room." Sandra pointed toward the screen, where Phoebe Chapman's door was shut.

No one said anything. No one wanted an innocent little girl to become collateral damage.

"Ah, guys." Gibson spun around in his chair. "That was nine-one-one dispatch. I guess Gail Chapman was on the line after the gunman dragged Torres from the room. The operator was still on the line when the gunman reentered the room. Soon after, the connection was lost. She said there was a crunching noise before the call was dropped."

"The gunman destroyed her phone," Neal put out in a hushed voice.

"Give me that cell number, Gibson." Sandra needed a break from the live feed of Jordon bleeding out anyhow. She walked back to her workstation, sat down, and called Gail. It rang directly to voicemail. She shook her head for the others. "It is down. I'll try the nurses' station, see if he hears it and answers. I'd like to see if I can lure him out of that room."

As she listened to the line at the nurses' station continually ring, her stomach was in her throat. Every second that went by lowered Jordon's chance of survival. After the line transferred to an automated voicemail, Sandra hung up. "He's not answering. Or he can't hear. I have no choice but to call the room. That number?" She turned to Luis, and he rattled it off.

There was no answer. *Now what?* "Do we have a number for Maria Torres, the nurse?"

Brice looked it up and passed it to her. Sandra landed in voicemail after several rings. "It could be on silent or not with her."

"Employees are encouraged to leave their phones in their lockers," Luis said. "It doesn't mean they do."

"Thanks, Luis," she told him. Being told that a few seconds earlier might have been more useful, though she doubted it would have stopped her from trying. She attempted to get through again. This time it went straight to voicemail. "Well, I suspect Torres has her phone on her. But it's off now." Sandra had another card to play with the shot caller. It would be nice to get her reaction to Carmen's name. But before she did, she wanted more information on the shot caller herself. "We have the archived video. Have we tried to see if we can spot the perps entering the hospital?"

"Nope." Neal gestured to Luis.

Sandra viewed it as a shot in the dark, but they sometimes paid off.

Luis worked the mouse, the pointer flying around the screen as he clicked here and there. "Thinking we'll start at nine thirty. I know the hospital's system went down at ten."

A view of the emergency room doors came up on Luis's laptop. Soon after, Carmen Feeney was walking in with the man they knew as Mickey.

"Just the two of them," Neal said. "But we know the other man was already upstairs at that time, being let into the server room. It doesn't look like another woman is with them or in the immediate area, for that matter."

Luis spanned out, placing several women in the frame, but they had no way of knowing who they were looking for.

"Can you bring up the video from the eighth floor, Luis? Say, around nine forty-five," she asked him. "We might get a look at our shot caller."

"One second..." Luis switched things over and brought up that footage.

The camera covered the elevator doors. At nine fifty-five, a few people walked off, including a woman in her late thirties, early forties. Plain, average height, brown shoulder-length hair. She was wearing a light jacket and sunglasses.

"Unless she just had eye surgery, that's rather strange," Neal said as the video continued to play.

No one responded, as it seemed his observation was a given. It was strange.

Luis seamlessly patched video footage from several cameras together to follow this woman down the hall. She walked up to a desk. There was a young woman sitting there.

"Who is that?" she asked Luis.

"Pamela, Dr. Beal's assistant."

Sandra made eye contact with Brice. "This has to be the shot caller, and she came for an audience with the CEO."

"Yet if she knew she'd be in the board meeting, why not just go right for the room?" Brice countered.

Luis hit pause while they spoke.

"Pamela could have simply been a tool to get her inside," Sandra suggested.

"A gun would do that," Kreiger inserted.

"And she probably didn't want the alarm raised too soon," Sandra said.

"Luis, could I get your help?" Brice began.

"Whatever you need," Luis said.

"Could you send the clippings of this video to the FBI's Science and Technology Branch? We'll see if they can enhance any images of this woman and run them through facial recognition databases."

"Sure, just give me their info," Luis said.

Brice rattled off Agent Lakisha Hester's contact details.

"Well, I wouldn't be holding my breath on this woman having a criminal past. The rest of them didn't," Kreiger said. "But now that we have the earlier video, run back through it and find out when she came into the hospital. From there, we can track her backward through CCTV in the area. It might lead us to her origin point and her identity."

"I'll let Agent Hester at Tech know to expect an email from Luis and ask about this at the same time," Brice volunteered.

"The MPD is fully capable of doing the same," he said. "But knock yourself out."

Sandra was on board with trying whatever they could to get this situation to end peacefully. But speaking of something that was guaranteed *not* to end that way... "If you will all excuse me, there's a call I need to make." Assistant Director Rowe was going to lose his shit when he heard Maddox was shot.

THIRTY-TWO
3:10 PM

Eric had the backup officer take Celeste Barrington in for uttering threats. Not particularly satisfying because it left the gunwoman in the boardroom unidentified. He called Lieutenant Coleman to inform him and was given a measure of good news. One of the hostage takers was ID'd as Carmen Feeney. Neal told Eric to bench a visit to Radcliffe and go to Feeney's residence immediately. He had provided the address and confirmed a search warrant for the house and one for Feeney's electronics were in place.

Eric rang the bell, and no one answered as expected. He pulled out his lock-picking kit and worked the lock. He was opening the door seconds later.

The place smelled of hickory bacon, and Eric realized he hadn't eaten much today with all the running around he'd been doing. From the front door, he could see most of the main level. The living room, kitchen, compact dining space, and a hallway that branched off to the right.

He looked down at the carpet and wiped the bottom of his shoes but kept them on. After locking the door behind him, he set out into the house.

Feeney was tidy but not excessively so. Some hair tumbleweeds drifted across the hardwood, and there was a dirty glass on an end table in the living room. The kitchen was clean aside from the frying pan used for the bacon sitting on the stovetop, the cooled grease white inside of it.

Her bed was made, and the top of her dresser was clear except for a picture frame, a navy-blue jewelry box, and a ballerina figurine. The latter didn't exactly speak of a person who would go into a hospital armed with a gun to terrorize people.

Eric inspected the photograph in the frame. It was of Carmen Feeney with a woman in her sixties. Eric would guess from the striking similarities between them, it was most likely Feeney's mother. Both were sitting on a bench smiling despite their sterile surroundings. The wall behind them was a dingy cream. It wasn't a selfie as their arms and hands were both visible in the shot. Someone had snapped this of them.

He finished up in a room being used as a home office. There was a small, round, pine dining table serving as the desk with two matching chairs around it. A bouquet was in a vase next to a laptop, and there was a stack of papers on the makeshift desk. A florist card poked out between a few orange lilies that had yet to open. They likely hadn't arrived more than a day or two before.

Eric plucked the florist's card to read the note and find out the name of the sender.

Hope these brighten your mood. Love, C.

"Huh." The message suggested Carmen had been feeling depressed or stressed out recently. Had that led to her walking into Founders Hospital with a gun? And who was C?

Eric gloved up and flipped through the papers on her desk. Most of them were collection notices, and those that weren't would be headed there soon judging by the *Past Due* stamps.

He drew his gaze to the floor where there was a round garbage bin. It was mostly full, but he knew from working crime scenes, next to a person's electronics, garbage was a treasure trove for investigators.

He lifted it up to the table and rooted through it. There were some tissues but most of it was paper, either bunched up or ripped apart. One torn piece had the Founders Hospital logo on it, and that had him hunting for the rest of the puzzle. He laid the fragments out on the table, and the entire picture emerged. Carmen Feeney owed the hospital a hundred thousand dollars, and her account was being forwarded to collections for nonpayment.

Had Carmen Feeney been ill at one time? But as he asked himself this, his mind flashed on that framed photograph.

He walked back to the bedroom and looked closer. An IV tube was feeding into the back of the older woman's hand. And there was just the edge of a mobile IV cart. She was unwell. But the statement was in Carmen Feeney's name...

Could it be that Feeney's mother had died, leaving her medical debt to her daughter? Based on all the outstanding bills, Feeney didn't have the money to pay it off.

Had her strained finances pushed Carmen Feeney into the hospital with a gun? But what did she hope to accomplish? And how did the others tie in?

He returned to the home office, but nothing else in the trash revealed anything. He opened the lid on the laptop, and the screen came alive and asked for a password.

Figures...

He closed the lid again and had plans of putting it into a collection bag and taking it to the techies to hack into. A knock on the front door stalled him and had him going to answer it.

A man's silhouette showed through the tinted glass window in the door. He was holding something in his hand, but it was hard to make out what.

"Who is it?" Eric called out.

"The landlord."

Eric opened the door with caution, half barricading himself behind the wood. Not that it would stop a bullet from doing serious damage. It should slow it down, though, and hopefully his vest would take care of the rest. It turned out the only thing he was holding was a piece of paper.

"Who are you?" the man asked. "I received a phone call from a neighbor that a man was seen breaking into this home."

"In that case, you should have called the police, sir."

The man blanched, a flicker of fear shadowing his eyes.

"But there's no need to be concerned. I am with the police." Eric stepped out from behind the door, not sensing any threat from the man. The man was easily in his sixties and carrying some extra weight. "Detective Birch, and I'm executing a search warrant on this residence."

"A search warrant? Whatever for? Carmen's in trouble with the police?"

She's inside Founders Hospital with a gun... "You could say that, sir."

"Oh my. That doesn't seem characteristic of her." The man's shoulders sagged.

Eric stepped back. "Why don't you step inside, and we'll talk in here?"

The man did so without a word.

"What is your name?" Eric asked him.

"Garth Deleon."

"And what's that you have there?" Eric pointed to the paper in the man's hand.

"Oh, this." He handed it over to Eric. "I don't want to do this, but I can't afford to have this property sitting here not making me money."

The words *EVICTION NOTICE* across the top of the page were impossible to miss. "You were evicting her? I believe evictions need to be handled through the US Marshals office."

"They do. This is just a letter from my lawyer's office threatening eviction. I was hoping that it would shake her up enough that she'd pay me."

"How far behind is she?"

"Six months. She wasn't taking my phone calls anymore or calling me back."

Eric's mind went to the pile of outstanding bills, and he could understand why Feeney had been avoiding her landlord. She had nothing to give him. "But she used to communicate with you?"

"Yes, she was always respectful and pleasant. That's why I handed over the keys to her, but she hasn't been the same in months. Would you, please, tell me what's going on here?"

"I'm not comfortable saying any more than I already have." *Not to her landlord...* "How well do you know Carmen?"

"Not terribly well. I live on the next block, and we don't talk much. Especially recently, as I told you. In the past, though, she's always been kind. Something changed her."

"Do you know what?"

"No."

Eric considered getting the picture to show Garth, but from his statement, he didn't know Feeney well. It was unlikely he'd be able to identify the older woman. Though, Eric asked, "She received flowers from someone with a name starting with C. Any idea who that might be?"

"Colton maybe?"

"And who is he?"

"Her boyfriend. He lives two doors down from me, and I've seen Carmen visiting. He's in the blue house."

"Do you know how long they've been involved?"

"I think I first saw her there at least a year ago. But you know how time goes. It could be longer."

Eric pulled out his phone and showed Garth pictures of both gunmen. One looked closer to Feeney's age while the other man looked as old as the landlord, but that didn't necessarily mean anything. "Are either of these men Colton?"

"No."

"And neither look familiar to you? They didn't come around here?"

"As I said, I don't live close enough to see all the comings and goings here, so I really couldn't say."

"Fair enough. Do you know Colton's last name?" Eric thought he'd ask even though Garth already told him where to find Colton.

"I couldn't tell you."

"Well, thank you for all your help."

"Uh-huh." Garth turned to leave, pivoted around again. "She is okay, though, right? She didn't get herself in so deep that there's no turning things back around?"

Eric couldn't assure that and settled on saying, "Time will tell."

Garth stood there for a few seconds, nodded, and then left.

Eric called Lieutenant Coleman. As he listened to it ring, the pieces were coming together. Feeney had to know she was getting close to being evicted. Had that been the final breaking point for her?

THIRTY-THREE
3:10 PM

Maria Torres kept seeing it over and over. Jordon flying backward to the floor with a piercing scream. The blood spraying from his body and how warm it was when she put her hand over the wound. She turned that hand over and looked at her stained palm. Jordon's blood.

She seethed, staring at the monster responsible across the room. He was in Gail's face, but Maria had never been so full of hatred in her life. He'd shot the man she loved right in front of her. Jordon was only trying to protect her. And she hadn't even much of a chance to assess the extent of Jordon's injuries before she was yanked away. But all that blood… It was all she could see. And he was struck in the lower waist to his left. The bullet could have pierced his intestines. If so, he was certain to die without immediate help. She couldn't even let herself think that could happen. As if by loving someone so much you could grant them immortality. But surely help had to be coming soon. Though maybe that was also wishful thinking. The earlier instances of gunfire hadn't brought the police running in. It felt like they were on their own.

She couldn't hear Jordon's cries in the hall anymore, and she feared the worst. That she had lost him.

"Hey, aren't you going to do anything?" The gunman was staring at her, but she didn't know what he was talking about.

Between thoughts of Jordon, she was too busy fantasizing about this man's demise. But if she hurled herself at the man, all nails and teeth, like a rabid animal, she'd likely get herself shot. And as long as Jordon possibly drew breath, she'd summon the courage to carry on for him and their baby.

"Hello?" The gunman sped across the room and stood inches in front of Maria and snapped his fingers in her face.

She was frozen. Numb. She took in the world around her. Gail on the floor, her face swelled, and her phone smashed next to her.

"Do something or she's going to die!" he yelled.

Then, it was as if she were awakened from a trance. A piercing noise struck her ears. The heart monitor was sending off an alarm. *Phoebe!*

The little girl was turning blue. She would die without Maria's help. She backed up, and her heels hit against the wheels on the defibrillator cart. *Do something!*

Maria quickly pushed the cart across the room to Phoebe's bedside. She primed the unit and readied herself with the paddles.

Do something... The words were haunting, tempting, and challenging.

She put the paddles on the child's chest. Once the charge built, she called out, "Clear!"

Phoebe's little body jolted from the bed. She was so fragile, her heart so weak that every time she had to be resuscitated her chances of survival diminished.

Do something...

Maria stepped back and watched as the girl's breathing

evened out. Maria set the paddles back onto the unit. One of the handles was smeared with blood. Jordon's blood.

Do something...

As a nurse, Maria never took the Hippocratic Oath to cause no harm, but she recited the Florence Nightingale Pledge upon graduation from nursing college. *Before God... to practice my profession faithfully...*

Do something...

There must be allowable loopholes to the pledge, a way of working around or through. Exceptions could be argued. Like this piece of trash holding the gun. The man who had shot the man she loved, who may have stolen her baby's father.

Do something...

She hesitated for a few seconds, and her phone rang in her pocket.

"What the hell? Give me that," the gunman barked at her. "Now!"

She gave him her phone and watched him turn it off and push it into his pocket.

Do something...

With the man distracted, she grabbed the defibrillator paddles and charged them again.

"What are you doing?" The man was standing close behind her.

She turned. His arms were down at his sides, with the muzzle of his gun facing the floor. Even if he fired the weapon, it was of no threat to those beneath them. The levels were separated by concrete.

Maria pushed the charged paddles against the man's chest.

Elwood's swearing was still pounding in Sandra's head. To say he hadn't taken the news about Jordon Maddox being shot well was an understatement. Elwood confided in her he had no intention of sharing this with the FBI director unless the situation became fatal. She appreciated that but didn't relish being part of the conspiracy. The truth had a way of getting out, and if Maddox died, the director would be out for heads. She imagined Ilene Maddox spearheading the campaign. *I remember people who break their word...* Sandra tried calling the boardroom a few times, but the shot caller let it ring. The silence was unsettling, and that might be why Sandra jumped when Neal's phone rang.

"It's Detective Birch," he told everyone, and put the call on speaker. "Everyone's here, Detective," he told Eric. "Hit us with some good news, please. We're in desperate need of some."

"I've got an update on Feeney that you'll want to hear. I'll leave it up to you to decide just how good it is." Eric laid everything out, and as good as it felt to hear his voice, Sandra wished he was coming to them with more. As if he heard her thoughts, he added, "I wish I had more."

"It's a start," Neal said. "It will be good to know what the boyfriend has to say, and get that laptop over, Eric. Or I can send a unit for it."

"The department's already spread thin. I'll bring it over as soon as I can."

Neal thanked him and ended the call. At least Sandra had one thing to look forward to. Seeing Eric's face.

"Feeney has money problems and owes a large sum to Founders. That doesn't seem to be inconsequential considering where we're at today," Sandra said. "Is this all about money?"

"I'd say there's a good chance," Brice said. "The statement about 'fat cats lapping up the cream.' Now we know one of the four perps owes the hospital, maybe the rest do too."

"But without knowing who she is, anything we talk about is theory and best guess," Sandra said. Brice had given them bad news before Eric's call. Lakisha Hester from the FBI Science and Technology Branch couldn't clear up any shots of the mystery woman to run through databases. A look at CCTV didn't get them anywhere either.

"Even if this was motivated by money, they've already shown themselves capable of violence." Kreiger gestured toward Luis's laptop. "And how many people has he shot at this point? Did he hit someone in that room earlier? He's obviously capable."

Sandra couldn't dispute that. No one could.

"But if this is about money, how does it pertain to Megan Beal, the CEO?" Neal asked. "What do they expect her to do for them?"

"The question of the day," Gibson chimed in.

"And if we're wrong and this is personal toward Beal, why target her at the time of a meeting? Though, that's assuming the shot caller was aware she'd be in one," Neal said.

Those were all good questions, and Sandra could land on

one possibility. "Maybe she needs all the hospital power players to fulfill her request."

"To pardon the debt owed to the hospital," Monica said.

"Is that something they could do?" Sandra asked Luis.

"Technically I suppose so, but they wouldn't or it would open the hospital up to this type of terrorism all the time."

They all fell silent at the emergency director's words. As much as the policy was valid, it didn't help the situation.

This may be what the shot caller meant when she said they weren't listening to her. "We still need more information. I'm going to try the shot caller again."

"Hold up," Kreiger said, stopping Sandra's steps and causing her to turn around. "Didn't she tell you the last time that if you called again she'd shoot someone? Maybe you're pushing it here."

"I need to speak to her if we're going to shut this thing down." Sandra resumed walking to her workstation. She couldn't allow the team coordinator to get into her head. Hostage takers said a lot of things and followed through on less. But she had something she could work with. Carmen Feeney.

Sandra called the phone in the boardroom and waited anxiously as it rang. Just when she thought it was going to hit voicemail, there was an answer.

"Let me guess, this is Sandra with the FBI." It was the shot caller.

A man yelled out in the background, "Help us."

"Shut up!" the shot caller roared.

Even with a gun, she was still losing control of the people in that room. "Please, you obviously came here today for a reason. Maybe this is about money. One of your friends who is there with you today, Carmen Feeney, owes the hospital a lot."

After a few beats, she said, "How do you know about Carmen?"

"We were able to identify her." That was all that Sandra

was disclosing. To tell her that a detective was rooting through Feeney's life to find a connection to the rest of them wouldn't be a smart move.

"I told you I'd shoot someone if you called again."

"You told me you're prepared to do what you have to do, but killing someone? I'm not so sure. Your friends aren't bad people." Carmen had said she wasn't friends with her fellow accomplices, but Sandra hadn't tried this approach yet with this woman. They knew for sure that Carmen Feeney didn't have a criminal record, and it was likely the same carried over for the rest.

The woman remained mute.

Sandra continued. "You can tell a lot about a person by the company they keep, their friends."

"Who said we're friends?"

It was a weak protest at best. "You came here today with her. You must trust her and the others."

Silence.

"Your one friend isn't so good, though." Sandra let that dangle there, deciding it was finally an advantageous time to disclose Mickey's actions.

"What are you talking about?" the woman eventually asked.

"He shot a doctor on the fourth floor. This person is bleeding out and needs treatment." Sandra held back Maddox's name intentionally, and she never mentioned the young girl in need of a new heart. She couldn't know how this woman would respond. In a way, the child's fate was out of her hands, out of her control. But one of her "friends" had shot someone. Possibly more than one, another tidbit Sandra didn't share.

There was ruffling on the other end of the line and sniffling.

Brice wrote on a note, *Sounds distressed by this news.*

"That wasn't part of the plan, was it? Someone getting hurt," Sandra said.

"No. But I told you we would do what we must."

"Well, he didn't need to do that. And what he did doesn't need to affect you. You can still walk away from this."

"No. I'm not ready to let them off that easy. They need to start listening to me, but it's like I'm invisible. They don't see me. I don't matter to them. Fat cats." She spat the condemnation.

And that term reared up again. It almost sounded like she'd been brainwashed. "You don't matter to them?"

"No, I'm just a number like everyone else that comes through those doors."

"Well, I'm listening to you. Who are you talking to in there? Can you tell me their names?"

"I don't know all of them. Just Megan Beal and Murray Berkshire."

Sandra remembered the name from Luis's recap of the board of directors, but she looked at Gibson. He nodded, seeming to have received the unspoken request she'd want information when she got off the phone. "Could you find out the names of the others in the room?"

"Why?"

"I'd be able to let their families know they are okay. Can I do that?"

"Everyone's fine. And okay. Say your name, one at a time. You start first," the woman told those in the room, and Sandra imagined her pointing someone out.

Every name felt like a victory. "That was great..." She allowed time for the woman to volunteer her name, but she didn't, and Sandra didn't think it was wise to push her. "You can trust that I'm going to bat for you, but I'm not going to lie. Since your friend shot that doctor, it's getting more difficult to hold ERT back from storming in there. Can I tell them you're willing to surrender and come out peacefully?"

"Pfft. No way. Not until we get what we want." With that, she hung up.

Sandra had pushed too hard, and it blew up in her face.

"You did your best," Brice assured her.

"We all know who Megan Beal is, but Murray Berkshire is the CEO of Bright Future LLC," Gibson said. "The company specializes in oncology drugs, including, but not limited to, chemotherapy drugs." Gibson updated the board with key takeaways from the call.

Hostages ID'd in boardroom, eighth floor

Special interest in Beal and Berkshire?

HT not confirming nor denying friendships with conspirators, seems to be about money

Sandra was fixated on the two names. "We might have been wrong earlier to think this was only about Megan Beal. The shot caller was ready with Murray Berkshire's name just as quickly. Maybe her goal was to get into that boardroom with the two of them. She would know they'd be there because, as Luis told us, the members are listed on the hospital's website."

"Okay, and those two people could make sense if the shot caller also owes money to the hospital, say, for cancer treatment," Brice suggested. "She might think Beal can write off her debt while Murray might absorb costs."

"So she's running her own negotiation in that boardroom," Neal said.

"That seems possible," Sandra admitted. "We all know that chemotherapy isn't cheap. And we could be looking at someone who had cancer or still does."

"If that's the case, she has nothing to lose," Gibson said.

"Or it's a relative whose debt passed on to her, as we suspect was the case for Feeney," Brice inserted.

"So we have a bunch of broke and desperate people in

there." Kreiger pounced to his feet. "None of this has me feeling warm and fuzzy. That woman's a loose cannon just like the rest of them."

"We can't judge the entire lot based on that man on the fourth floor," Brice pointed out.

"While we're on the subject..." Sandra returned to Luis. "Is Dr. Maddox still...?" She couldn't bring herself to finish the question.

One corner of Luis's laptop screen showed Jordon Maddox lying on the floor. Luis expanded that window to full-size.

The blood pool around Maddox wasn't getting any bigger, so the tourniquet must be doing its job. That wasn't enough to ease Sandra's concern.

Please hang in there a little bit longer...

Eric knocked after ringing the doorbell hadn't worked. That brought a man in his late thirties to the door. Eric held up his badge. "Detective Birch. Are you Colton?"

"I am."

"And your last name?"

"McGill. What's this about?" Colton's brows pressed downward.

"Carmen Feeney is your girlfriend, right?"

"Correct, and now you're scaring me."

Eric would wager by this guy's reaction and rigid demeanor he had no clue what Carmen was involved with. "Mr. McGill, could I come in for a moment, please?"

"Ah, sure." The guy backed up, allowing room for Eric to join him in the house's entry. "Did you want to sit down or is here fine?" Colton asked him.

"Sitting down would probably be best." It wasn't for Eric's comfort but for Colton's. Eric suspected when he heard his girlfriend was of interest to the police, it might take the strength from his legs.

Colton took Eric to the living room, where they sat down.

Eric broke the silence. "Carmen is involved with an ongoing situation at Founders Hospital." He paused there to let that sink in. Then, he added, "She went in there with a gun and three other people, who are armed as well."

"She did... *what?*" Colton's eyes became round.

"I see this comes as a shock to you. We don't understand all of it yet either, but Carmen was identified from video inside the hospital, and we're trying to figure out what she's after. I conducted a legal search of her residence and found that she owes the hospital a lot of money. Do you know anything about that?"

"Ah"—Colton wrung his hands as he spoke—"I know about the debt, and that she tried to work out a payment arrangement with them. She told me they wouldn't work with her. They didn't believe that she didn't have more money to pull from. But she was already spread thin. I gave her props for even trying to make good on the debt. But that's Carmen. She never liked to be outstanding with anything, and the hospital put her in a very tough spot."

His statement backed up the overdue bills and collection notices. "You two must be close for you to know so much about her finances. Do you know why she owes the hospital money?"

"Her mother came down with horrible pneumonia and required a hospital stay. That would have been fine except she contracted a bacterial infection while she was there. Doctors couldn't figure out the strain or how to effectively treat it. She ended up dying soon after."

The mother's fate was as Eric had suspected. "So the bill racked up because of an extended stay and different tests?"

"That's right. And the mother's medical insurance wasn't that great. It was pretty much useless, honestly. Carmen wanted to sue the hospital, but she was so distraught. She and her mother were close, so I took it upon myself to speak to a lawyer on her behalf. They told me the case against the hospital wouldn't go anywhere. But clearly, their protocols or whatever weren't up to snuff."

People always wanted someone to blame after losing a loved one. Was today about Carmen holding Founders Hospital accountable? "When did she lose her mother?"

"Ten months ago. When Carmen realized she'd have to pay her mother's bill, she had a massive panic attack, and her mental state and outlook haven't improved much since."

"That's why you sent her flowers recently?"

Colton smiled. "I wanted to cheer her up, if only a little. I still can't believe she got a gun and is in that hospital. Does she really expect them to respond to that? To wipe out her debt?"

"As I said, we're still figuring things out." Eric took out his phone and showed Colton the pictures of the two men. "Do you recognize either of them?"

"Nah. I wish I could say I did."

So do I...

THIRTY-SIX

4:00 PM

Maria had jumped back after striking the man. He cried out and jolted backward. His gun fell from his hand and dropped to the floor. With it, the balance of power shifted to her. She knew the charge from the paddles wasn't likely to kill him but would shock him enough to give her a chance to assume control. It might cause him to lose consciousness. It only took him a few moments to recover.

He came at her, nostrils flaring. "You stupid bitch!"

She reached back and charged the paddles and stepped toward him again.

He jumped out of the way, this time foreseeing her plan. He swatted out, and she let go of the paddles. Their cords allowed them to reach the floor, and it drew her gaze down.

The gun...

She rushed for the weapon, and he must have had the same idea because he went for the gun at the same time. Their heads bumped and sent them both backward from the hit. It only stunned them for a second, though, and they were both back in a race to assume control of the gun.

Her fingers danced over the handle. She reached out

farther, her fingertips searching for the edge to get a firm hold. Just as she was about there, she heard it. The charge of the defibrillator.

There was only one reason that she'd been able to get so close to the gun. He'd allowed her to. The man was getting ready to repay her "kindness." She saw the shadow of him before the actual man himself. If she got shocked by the machine, she was likely to live, but it would probably kill her baby. He was blocking her path to the gun now. She rolled to the left, putting even more distance between herself and the weapon.

He trailed her as she squirmed across the floor. There was nowhere for her to go but into a corner. But if she was down here, she was safer. Instinct had her wanting to cocoon, to make herself small. Less of a target. She tucked into the corner, drawing her knees to her chest. He wrestled with her, trying to expose her chest. While he might have shot the man she loved, there was no way she'd let him hurt the baby inside of her. She pushed out her legs as hard and as fast as she could, aiming as high on his body as she could. Her kick impacted him in the crotch, causing him to scream, and sent him stumbling backward. But the strike didn't set him back for long. He came at her again. The paddles still very much a threat.

She dropped lower, crawling across the floor toward the gun. But it was gone.

Where the...

"Leave her alone, you shit!" Gail was back on her feet, swaying, the gun in her hand.

The man roared, "I'm getting sick of you two!"

"The feeling's mutual." Maria grabbed the defibrillator itself. Its weight of less than twenty pounds made that possible, while it should also be enough to cause some damage if wielded just right.

He was mid-turn when she raised it and smashed it into the side of his head.

One yelp, and he was a heap on the floor.

The cords on the paddles had them springing back toward the unit.

Maria stood there in silence, as did Gail across the room. The only noise was their deep breathing and the hum of the heart monitor tracking Phoebe's heart rate.

"You saved my baby." Gail took a step toward the bed and swooned, reaching for the rails with her free hand.

"Be careful." Maria jogged to her side to steady her balance and took the gun from her hand. She set it in the waistband of her pants. "You might have a concussion from your fall. Let me see your eyes."

Gail faced her, and Maria did a brief test.

"You're going to be fine," Maria told her and pocketed her penlight. "But you took a nasty fall."

Gail touched her jaw. "Not to mention that man smacked my jaw."

"Okay, but it's not broken or there's no way you could stomach talking right now. You will be all right."

"He shot your baby's father."

Maria met Gail's gaze, not sure what her goal had been in making that declaration. The effect had Maria running cold. "And I will get to him, but first we need to do something with *him* so he's no longer a threat." She nudged her head toward the gunman.

"He's not dead?" Gail whimpered.

His chest was still rising and falling. "He's just out cold." Not that she trusted he'd stay down for long.

Gail rubbed her arms as she stared at him. "But he can't hurt us anymore."

Maria could see that Gail was in shock, likely still reeling from her fall. Even Maria was uneasy having been terrorized by this man. To see him inert was almost difficult for her mind to accept. Still a voice of caution told her she had to snap out of it. "We need to move him."

Gail looked at her, rubbing her throat. "Move him? Move him where?"

It was a good question, but Maria had one idea. "There's a storage closet down the hall. It locks from the outside."

Gail licked her lips. "So if he, uh, comes to then he can't get out?"

There was a release latch inside if one knew where to look. Maria wasn't going to obsess about that right now. Besides, they'd have his gun. "Just help me, Gail, please!" She desperately wanted to get this man dealt with so she could get back to Jordon.

Both went over to the man, and they each hooked an arm under one of his and tugged. The man barely budged.

"He's so heavy," Gail said, straightening out, and she put a hand to her forehead.

Maria studied the woman. She was still recovering from her fall, and her left cheek and eye where she was struck were swollen and turning purple. There was no way she could physically drag this man down the hall. Maria pressed the gun back into Gail's palm. "If he moves..." She didn't want to put the rest into words as if that made her thoughts more an intention and a sin.

Gail licked her lips and nodded. "I know what to do."

"I'm going to find a wheelchair to bring back here. We'll load him on it, and use it to get him to the storage room."

Maria left the room without looking back. Her heart was pulling her toward Jordon, and she couldn't resist checking on him. She was going toward the nurses' station that way anyhow.

"J," she said, sinking down to the floor at his side.

He groaned, and his eyelashes fluttered. "My sweetheart," he said.

Hot tears blazed trails down her cheeks. "You must hang in there, okay? You will be all right." *You have to be!* She checked him over, and the external bleeding had been staunched. But she remained concerned about internal damage, possible bleeding, and infection. His face was pale. "I'll get you help soon. I swear I will." She went to get up, but he grabbed her arm, stopping her.

"In my pants pocket... get it. I want you to have it."

She did as he requested and found a small box. Her heart fluttered. "What is this?"

"My great-great-grandmother's ring. Will you..." Jordon winced. "Marry me?"

She opened the lid. A gold band with a marquise-shaped diamond. Fresh tears spilled down Maria's cheeks. She'd been prepared to reason with him, assuming his text was sent out of desperation, as if he expected he would die today. But he had the ring in his pocket. He'd come to work prepared. Was he intending to ask her today anyhow, maybe after work?

Jordon squeezed her leg, and she took the ring from the box and slipped it on her ring finger. "Yes, Jordon Maddox, I will be your wife." She leaned over and kissed him. "I'm sorry, though, I must go. But I'll be quick." She tapped another kiss to his lips, but forced herself to move before her emotions paralyzed her any further. She was torn between her charge, that of Gail and Phoebe Chapman, and the man she loved. But as long as the gunman was breathing, he remained a threat. He'd have come with friends too, who might want revenge.

She ran toward the first wheelchair she could see and marched with it down the hall to Phoebe's room. Her heart was pounding as she rounded the doorway. Her fears had her imagining the man was back on his feet and that he'd overpowered Gail and held the gun again.

Maria entered the room. The man was still on the floor where he was when she'd left.

Gail ran over to Maria, and the two of them worked to hoist the man's dead weight off the floor into the wheelchair. It was intensive labor, and even Maria was heaving for breath. Her job as a nurse had made her strong, conditioning her to lift a patient's weight. She suspected this scenario had more to do with the risk and her innate fears. Jordon was so pale, and he was drifting. She spun the ring on her finger. Was she going to get the chance to walk down the aisle and marry the man she loved? Or was the bright future they had planned going to combust to ash?

Sandra was gathered with Brice, Kreiger, and Neal around Luis and his laptop. Live video from the fourth floor was playing out on the screen. Nurse Torres had just come out of the Chapman room and was hustling toward Jordon Maddox. She kept giving furtive looks over her shoulder.

"Where's the gunman?" Brice asked. "Did you see him leave the Chapman room earlier?"

Luis shook his head. "No one has come or gone from that room since we all watched them go in there. That is, until now."

Sandra kept her gaze on the screen.

"What does she think she's doing?" Kreiger asked.

Sandra was wondering what had happened in that room that allowed Torres the freedom to go to Maddox's side.

Nurse Torres sat on the floor next to him, and the two had what appeared to be a tender exchange. She then took something from his pocket. A small box?

"He's proposing," Sandra said, stunned.

"From the looks of it, she accepted," Brice said.

But the engagement glow didn't last for long. Torres got up

and grabbed a wheelchair. But instead of loading up Maddox, she pushed it back into the Chapman room.

"What the... I thought she was going to move Maddox," Neal said.

"This ought to be interesting." Kreiger crossed his arms and leaned forward, concentrating on the screen.

Nothing happened for several minutes.

When it did, everyone pulled back. Torres was wheeling the gunman out of Chapman's room. His head was slumped to the side, suggesting he was unconscious. The fact Torres left Maddox suggested the gunman was still alive and a potential threat.

Torres went out of sight of the camera, but Luis was quick about transitioning to another one.

"Any idea where she might be taking him?" Neal looked at Luis.

"Not a clue."

Meanwhile on the screen, Torres stopped in front of a door and pressed in a code on a keypad. She left the gunman in place while she propped something against the door to keep it open. Then she wheeled the gunman inside and shut the door.

"What is that room?" Kreiger asked.

"A supplies storage room, some stationery, but also medical supplies such as gloves, needles, and bandages. It locks automatically when it's shut. There is a release switch inside, though, if one knows where to look."

"Guess the nurse just did our jobs for us and cleared the fourth floor," Kreiger said.

Sandra feared he might be getting ahead of things. "Just one floor," she stressed.

"We still have Feeney armed on the second," Brice pointed out.

"And I haven't seen her in a while," Luis said. "She went into a restroom hours ago, and hasn't come back out."

"Then we have two of four taken care of," Kreiger said. "We move in, while someone continues to monitor the live feed to alert us if she comes out. What about the guy on the sixth floor?"

Luis clicked some buttons, but the screen was blacked out.

"What's going on? Fix it." Kreiger thrust a pointed finger toward the screen.

Luis brought up older footage, and they discovered the origin of the problem. They watched as the gunman went around and disabled the cameras.

"Yeah, there's nothing I can do about that," Luis said.

"We thought this guy was a techie, given how he disabled the hospital's phone system," Brice said. "But there's nothing that *techie* about unplugging the cameras or slicing the wires."

On the screen, the man had acquired a ladder and was pushing up near the cameras. He was likely lifting the ceiling tiles to get to the wires. But for every two steps he took up the ladder, he stepped back one, until he got all the way up.

"Well, it seems he has a type of compulsion disorder." Sandra shared what she observed with the others, not sure how to use it with negotiations, though. She couldn't even get him on the phone.

Luis switched the feed to the coverage of the fourth floor.

Torres was back at Maddox's side, and there was another doctor with them. She must have gone to get a doctor for him. Sandra hoped it would be enough to give Maddox the chance of pulling through this.

There was a knock on the door, and Sandra answered to find Eric standing there with two evidence bags in hand.

"Delivering Feeney's laptop, as promised."

She took the computer from him as he stepped inside, and she handed it over to Brice. He took it to his station and got to work.

"And what's that in there?" Sandra asked, gesturing toward the other bag.

"I was just going to get to that. So a chat with Feeney's boyfriend was enlightening." Eric told them the story of Feeney's mother, and Sandra was feverish by the time he'd finished. Feeney's mother had checked into the hospital for standard treatment but left in a body bag. Losing her mother that way would have been devastating. It was so random, there would be no preparation. Heartbreaking.

Margo, I need you to be all right...

"I found this on Feeney's dresser." Eric handed Sandra a framed photograph. "It's Feeney with her mother."

Sandra's heart pinched looking at the image of the smiling women. Their body language confirmed they were close. The way they had their heads resting against each other. But there was pain in both women's eyes. This picture was probably taken before the unknown bacterial infection devastated her body.

"As if losing her mother wasn't enough, Feeney was saddled with the medical debt from her mother's treatment," Eric said.

"That would be enough to trigger anyone," Sandra said. "And earlier you mentioned she was being evicted from her house."

"Lots of bad luck hitting all within a short time," Eric said.

Neal shook his head. "Like a line of dominoes falling over."

"I feel for the woman," Kreiger wedged in, "but we all fall on rough times in life. Most of us don't storm into a hospital with a gun."

Brice said, "Desperate times call for—"

"Please don't say it." Kreiger leveled Brice with a hard glare.

"Well, that's about it for now," Eric said, turning to leave.

"Hold up. Any more on Cross? The search of his house turn up anything?" Neal asked.

"Not yet, but I'm going to pop over and see how things are coming along." Eric shot her a look before he left the vehicle, and she debated whether she should follow and have a word with him or not. She decided she would and set the framed photograph on the table before following him.

"Eric? Hold up a minute." Sandra hurried after him.

He turned around and closed the distance between them. "What's going on? Are you all right?"

She uncrossed her arms, realizing she'd been hugging herself, and she pinched her St. Michael pendant. When his eyes fell to her hands, she let them fall by her sides.

"What is it?" He stepped within a few inches of her and peered into her eyes.

Sandra licked her lips and shook her head. Tears filled her vision.

He cupped her elbows with his hands. "Talk to me."

"It's Mom." Just two words, but the pain they carried spliced through her. She appreciated he held the silence, letting her pace herself for when and how she continued. "She was taken to Howard University Hospital this morning."

"Oh, Sandra, I'm sorry. I hope it's nothing serious."

His calm energy soothed her. He must have assumed nothing bad because she was still here. "She fainted, and the doctors are running tests. Dana assured me she's being well looked after, but I worry that..."

He moved like he was going to hug her, but he stopped short. He was aware how she felt about public displays of affection, and this showed he respected her viewpoint. "You can leave, Sandra. Someone else could step up in your place. Heck, Brice is already here."

"No. Besides, Dana said the doctors there are taking good care of her. I'd just be sitting there when I can be helpful here." As she recapped this, she questioned if she was barricading behind her fears by staying put.

"I get that. Do they know what caused her to faint?"

"Not exactly. All they know is her iron levels are so low,

she's anemic." She'd checked her phone quickly just before Eric had shown up.

"I'm sorry this is happening, Sandra."

She scanned his eyes. "Could you go over there? Maybe just pop by and check in with Dana? I mean if you have a minute."

"I've never met them before."

He was right, but somehow, she'd forgotten about that. Making this request of him felt natural. "Maybe it's time that changes."

"All right. Leave it with me. I'll head over there when I have a minute."

She'd love to kiss him and fall into his arms, but now wasn't the time. "Thank you."

"No need to thank me."

She stood there, watching him walk away, thinking she was lucky to have him in her life. It might be time to discuss taking their relationship to the next level. But that was a conversation for another day. Right now, she had a job to do.

THIRTY-EIGHT

4:30 PM

Sandra sent Dana a quick text to expect a friend of hers to show up. She told her he was a Metropolitan PD detective by the name of Eric Birch. Dana fired back a quick response.

Okay, all is moving along over here. Not to worry.

Sandra returned inside the vehicle. She wanted to try reaching the hostage takers again, but just calling for the sake of calling wouldn't move things along either. It was always best to be armed with an edge.

"I've got something." Brice sat back and pointed at Feeney's laptop in front of him.

"Already?" She failed to keep the skepticism out of her voice.

"I'm a miracle worker. What can I say?" Brice boasted.

"With a little help from over there." Monica smiled and pointed at Luis.

"Hey, don't give my secret weapon away," Brice said. "But, yeah, Luis got the laptop unlocked."

Sandra looked at Luis. "Well done."

Luis shrugged. "I took some computer training."

"Just say it how it is, you're a hacker," Kreiger said with a smile.

It was a pleasant switch to see Kreiger happy.

"A novice white hat at best, but I only use my powers for good." Luis blushed at his self-praise.

"Happy you're on our side. All right, so what did you find?" She gestured toward her colleague.

"Feeney bookmarked a website called Fat Cats. It's a forum with chat rooms for people to voice their complaints against big companies, corporate America," Brice said.

"It sounds like less of a coincidence that our shot caller referred to the people in the boardroom as 'fat cats licking up cream,'" Sandra said.

"Agreed. One of the chat rooms is specifically for people who owe money to Founders Hospital. Feeney has an account with the site, the logon parameters autofill in, and her handle is Drained Dry. She interacted with three other members in this chat room, responding to their comments, and they hers. Their handles are Alaya Princess, Broken Bridge, and Angry1111."

It didn't take effort to do the math on that. "Four people. That can't be a coincidence either."

Neal shook his head. "And that first one you mentioned, Brice, would likely be a woman. By process of elimination, Alaya Princess could be who is holed up in that boardroom."

"I can get a warrant rolling and submit the request to the website to release their information," Gibson volunteered.

Kreiger pointed at Gibson. "Get on that ASAP."

The information officer got on the phone.

"I don't like the sound of Broken Bridge, as in there's no going back," Monica weighed in. "Does he plan on walking away from today?"

Sandra kept her thoughts to herself, as it was far too early to voice her theory. But to her that sounded like a name a mature man would give himself, rather than a twentysomething. The rash action taken by the man on the fourth floor could support what Monica just suggested.

"Let's hope they all do," Neal said. "We don't need anyone going out in a blaze of glory and taking people with them."

Brice glanced at Sandra, and she caught the message in his eyes. He wasn't one for hyperbole. "Going back to the website, from the look of it, private messaging isn't an option."

"So we still don't know how they conspired today," Sandra said. "Assuming these four are the ones inside."

"Which I'd say the chances of are pretty good," Neal offered.

Sandra nodded.

"Right, so this leaves us to figure out how they communicated," Brice began. "Now, there is one concerning comment in the forum from Alaya Princess. 'Someone needs to take a stand. Who's with me?'"

"It's a call to action. She's looking for help," Sandra said. "It also explains why Carmen Feeney and the shot caller didn't admit to being friends with the others. They were people brought together by a shared purpose."

"We're still waiting on Feeney's phone records, but what about email on her laptop?" Monica asked. "Any stand out?"

"Nope, I looked in there first," Brice said.

"They could have been deleted, and they started communicating over the phone." Sandra turned to Neal. "Speaking of, where are we with Feeney's phone records?"

"I'll follow up on that," Neal told her and pulled out his phone to put the call through.

"Save yourself the trouble," Gibson blurted out, just after ending his call to a judge about the website. "The report for Feeney's call history just came in. Give me a few minutes to look it over..."

Everyone in the vehicle remained silent, and Sandra

debated contacting the shot caller and using the name Alaya. But until she had proof that she was the woman in that room, it was best not to go that route.

"All right. We might have something," Gibson said. "Obviously, I can't see the content, but Feeney had a conversation with three other people. Let me see if I can find out who the numbers are registered to." He typed on his computer. A few moments later, he was saying, "Shane Perkins, Tom Sparling, and a third number that's a burner. Doesn't appear to be in service now."

Sandra would wager it belonged to the shot caller on the eighth floor.

"Perkins is twenty-six, single, works for a dot com company," Gibson said.

"That confirms what we thought. He's a techie," Brice said.

"Next of kin?" Neal asked. "Possibly someone who died recently?"

"Looks like his mother is still alive, and he has, or I should say *had*, a brother but he's showing as deceased nine months ago," Gibson said.

"That could be where his motive started, but what's his recent trigger?" Monica asked.

"Assuming he's one of the people from that Fat Cats forum, he could have gone there already angry and hurt, only to have his feelings validated," Sandra began. "This empowered him and incited him to act."

"Well, the site does seem to radicalize people," Brice said. "One chat room on there is called 'What you'd like to do...', and it encourages people to share revenge schemes."

"Then it needs to be shut down. It preys on vulnerable people, and instead of giving them a healthy environment to heal and find belonging, it fosters violence," Sandra said.

Brice bobbed his head. "I'll see what I can do."

"So what's the story on this Sparling fella?" Neal asked Gibson.

He punched on the keyboard again. "Fifty-six, widower. It looks like he lost his wife, Mable, of thirty years, eight months ago."

"That's three of the four who have lost someone they loved and who blame Founders Hospital," Sandra summarized.

"Like I said before. We've all lost people, but it doesn't give anyone the right to do what they're doing," Kreiger said.

"On that point we agree, but grief can outweigh logic. Then add financial stress..." Sandra was curious if Kreiger had ever lost someone he'd truly cared about, though. It took away reason and rationale. It might have been between eight and ten months since the hostage takers lost their loved ones, but those wounds would still be fresh. Anyone forced to carry on without their person could testify to that. "Any next of kin for Sparling?"

"It looks like his wife had a daughter when she was a teenager. Her name's Trudy Hall, currently thirty-five," Gibson said.

"And her birth father?" Neal asked.

"Deceased," Gibson shared stoically.

"Well, I'll get search warrants in place and have officers dispatched to the homes of Perkins and Sparling, also have them talk with family and friends," Neal said. "Gibson, let me know the minute we have access to the website. We need the shot caller's identity and background ASAP."

"I'm going to try Perkins's cell phone," Sandra said and got in position to do that. She listened to the line ring several times before her call was flipped to voicemail with a generalized robotic greeting. She hung up and tried him again. This time it went right to voicemail. "He just turned his phone off."

"Then we're three for three, four really considering the woman on the eighth floor isn't talkative," Kreiger said.

Sandra could feel the team coordinator was getting restless.

If she couldn't get someone inside to talk soon and surrender, things were bound to get worse before they got better. At least she had an edge to work with the shot caller. She had the names for her three buddies now. Whether or not the woman knew their real names didn't matter. But there were two sides to sharing that information. It might make the shot caller feel they were moving in on her, and push her to do something drastic. Or it would help her see that there was no way out of this but to surrender. It wouldn't be long before they knew all about her too. Sandra would give the strategy some more thought before she did anything.

Eric had popped by Howard University Hospital before heading over to Stevie Cross's residence. While his relationship with Sandra was serious enough, it felt past time to be meeting the woman who meant so much to her. He'd heard the stories about how Margo and her husband adopted Sandra and her twin brother when they were twelve years old. Before that the children had spent two years of bouncing around in various foster homes. Margo had been a huge help for Sandra through the loss of her brother.

Dana had been expecting him and said it was lovely to meet a friend of Sandra's. Dana introduced him to Margo Davenport as a friend of hers. This was something she'd prepared Eric for before entering Margo's room. She didn't want to confuse Margo by mentioning Sandra in case she didn't know who she was at that moment. Eric had known before from Sandra that Margo had Alzheimer's, but he wasn't prepared for what he saw.

Doctors had run their battery of tests, and they had visibly taken their toll. The results still weren't in, and that fact twisted a knot in Eric's stomach. Sometimes delays could result from backlogs in the lab. It could also be that the results were clear, and doctors were left scrambling to figure out what to suggest for treatment. But it was the third possibility he could conceive that filled him with dread. They had found something and were delaying with the dispensing of that news until Sandra was present. When this long day ended and reality sank in, he'd be there for Sandra.

Eric was thinking back on all this as he walked into Cross's home. Officer Bingham came over with something in his hands and passed it off to Eric. It was a memorial card with the photo of a young man in his twenties. His name was Sullivan Perkins, and the service was held nine months ago. Not a son of Cross's or he'd have the surname. "Where did you find this?"

"Stuffed into the back of a desk drawer in the home office."

"Great find. This could be the lead we've been looking for." It was the first personal connection for Cross they'd uncovered that held promise.

Bingham dipped his head and returned to the deeper parts of the house, while Eric went to his car. He keyed *Sullivan Perkins* into the onboard computer. The results weren't enlightening on their own, but he clicked on his mother's name to bring up her background. Her maiden name was Cross.

Bingo! Eric pulled his phone as it started to ring. "Birch here," he answered, briefly catching *Lieutenant Coleman* on the caller ID. "You're just the person I was about to call."

"Oh, yeah? Well, me first. Feeney's laptop gave us the identities of two more hostage takers, leaving us only needing to find out the woman's name in the boardroom. I'll get another officer to Tom Sparling's house, but I need you to check on Shane Perkins."

Eric stiffened. "You said Perkins?"

"Yes."

"Huh. Small world. I just found out that Stevie Cross would be Shane Perkins's uncle."

Neal was silent for a few beats. "Mind bringing me up to speed on how you got there?"

Eric did so, and when he finished, Neal said, "Then let me get this straight. Stevie Cross let his nephew into the server room at Founders?"

"Sounds like it, which would explain why Cross tried to mislead us by providing a false description of this person's looks and then giving us Hartley's name."

"He didn't want to betray his nephew."

"Yep. Well, I'll get right over to Shane's house. Address?"

Neal provided it to him and an overview of what they knew about Shane, which wasn't much. Twenty-five and a graduate of MIT.

"Consider me there already." Eric ended the call and got on the road.

Soon after, he was parking in the lot for Perkins's apartment building. After clearing his presence with the building manager and getting the key, he let himself into unit 215.

The place smelled strongly of lemon cleaner, making Eric draw another breath in the hallway before stepping inside. After shutting the door, he turned around and got his first look at the unit. The rather open-concept layout allowed Eric to see the living room, past it to the kitchen and a small dining area all from the door. All that was out of view was where the hallway led to off on the right.

Eric set out, and nothing flagged. Unless one counted the orderliness. Though maybe Eric was influenced by the fact as a young man, he was never this meticulous.

He found a few photographs of Perkins with his late brother. The two had looked like they were close.

Eric returned to the living room, eyeing a bookshelf that was organized alphabetically by author. A chair next to it with an overhanging floor lamp and a side table completed the picture of a perfect reading nook.

A hardcover textbook on tax law sat on the table. A strange reading choice for a tech major. Eric picked it up with gloved hands. There was no bookmark slipped between the pages, so had Perkins yet to start reading? Or had he finished? And did it even matter to the ongoing incident? Eric wasn't sure it did and went to return it to the table. As he did, he caught the edge of the book and lost his grip on it. The textbook fell to the floor and splayed open, facing down.

Eric picked it up and noticed a checkout envelope at the back. This was taken from a library outside of Perkins's neighborhood. Maybe it was closer to where Perkins worked. But the fall had knocked out something else. A piece of paper was poking out from the front top corner.

What the...

He opened the cover and discovered it was tucked between the inner lining and the hardshell of the book. Someone had deliberately separated them. He pulled the piece of paper out and read the handwriting.

This is the last communication. We'll be doing it Monday, May 5th.—Alaya Princess

Good to go.—Broken Bridge

Ready to do this.—Drained Dry

May fifth was today, and these names struck him as usernames. Possibly the same ones used on that website forum that Neal had mentioned. Time to call this in.

Sandra was at her workstation as Brice, Monica, and Gibson were at theirs. Luis was with Neal and Kreiger at the table. They had just watched Nurse Torres fetch two doctors. One went into the nurse break room, while the other tended to Maddox. Torres was still at his side when Sandra left the table. She called the nurses' station.

"She's going to answer," Luis said from the table, still watching the live feed.

"Hello," Torres answered.

"It's Sandra," she told the nurse.

In the background, someone spoke to Torres. "One minute," she replied.

"Tell me what's going on, Maria."

"It's..." Sniffles traveled the line. "He's my everything. We can't move him to surgery right now, but he can't die."

Sandra's past loomed on the horizon like a hurricane. She needed to buckle down before its gale-force winds reached her. This situation was about Maria and Jordon, not Sandra and her brother. "We can see that he's getting care from you and a doctor."

"Yes. Dr. Bell, but Jordon has lost a lot of blood. Dr. Bell has staunched the flow and believes he can keep him stable for a while longer."

"Not guaranteed," a man called out, presumably Dr. Bell.

"What happened with the gunman?" Sandra asked Torres.

"Gail and I got the upper hand on him. I didn't want to hurt him, but he left me no choice."

"Is he still alive?" It seemed likely since she'd locked him in the storage room. A dead man wasn't a threat.

"He's only been knocked out. I locked him in a storage room where he shouldn't bother anyone."

"And his phone?" He might have an active number for the shot caller on the eighth floor.

There were a few seconds of silence. "Oh, God. It's on him. I should have taken it from him, shouldn't I? If he comes to, he can call his friends and—"

"Maria." Sandra spoke in a smooth, comforting tone to stop the woman from spiraling out. She couldn't ask Maria to risk her life trying to retrieve it. "You did a good job getting him locked away. Just remember regrets and worrying about things do nothing but rob you of your energy. All right?"

"Yeah, but it's hard not to worry. If Jordon's going to survive, he will need surgery to remove the bullet and stitch up the damage it caused. The elevators are locked, and the operating room he needs is on the first floor."

Sandra glanced over at Luis. He told them he could remotely activate the elevators, but doing so would potentially put other lives at risk. People on them might unload onto the second, sixth, and eighth floors where perps with guns were still roaming. They couldn't count on Feeney, on the second floor, staying in the restroom forever.

Neal's phone rang, and he answered quietly before stepping out of the command vehicle.

"Sandra?" Maria said. "Please help him. He means everything to me." Maria started crying, and Sandra's heart felt like it had been stabbed through with a stake.

"I'm sorry that you're going through this, that Jordon is, and while it might seem like this is taking a long time, we are doing everything we can out here to bring this lockdown to a safe and peaceful resolution." Sandra heard her words as they cycled back to her ears. All the plural pronouns boiled down to one thing. She assumed the outcome on her shoulders, be that good or bad. With that weight, her thoughts went to Gail and Phoebe Chapman. "You said Gail helped you subdue the man. Did you take his gun from him?"

"Yes, I have it on me."

"Okay, and how are Gail and Phoebe?"

"I had to resuscitate Phoebe a second time, but she's resting now. The man knocked Gail to the floor too. She took a solid hit, but she'll be okay. I don't see evidence she's concussed. She's with her daughter, where I told her to stay."

"We saw that another doctor went into the nurse break room. Is someone else hurt in there?"

"Nurse Mahoney. He was shot in the arm."

"And his current condition?"

"Stable."

That only had Sandra breathing moderately easier. "Do you still have my number, Maria?"

"No, I..."

"It's okay. I'm going to give it to you again. Do you have a piece of paper to write it down?"

A few seconds, then, "Yes, go ahead."

Sandra rattled off her number. "Did you get that? I can repeat it again."

Maria read it back to Sandra. "That right?"

"Yes. Call me if things change on your end."

"Will do."

"And, Maria, you've done a great job so far, but please, don't play the hero. Help is coming."

"Thank you." Maria disconnected the call.

Sandra looked over at the table where Luis was hunched over his laptop. "Luis," she said.

He turned toward her. "Yeah?"

"You're doing great too," she told him. "Keep watching the video, switching between all the floors, and let me know if you see anything we should know about."

"Happy to help any way I can."

Neal came back into the vehicle, and his face was pale. "That was Detective Birch with an update on his finding at Perkins's apartment."

Everyone listened intently as the lieutenant filled them in.

"So they're communicating through notes tucked into a library book," Monica said. "That's rather clever and keeps their conspiracy offline."

"And he's sure about the names?" Gibson said from the end of the vehicle at his workstation.

"Yes. They are the same as the usernames we flagged from the forum. I've sent Detective Birch to the library to see what more he can find out. If another woman checked out the book, we might finally get the shot caller's identity."

Alaya Princess... "It's time for me to try her again." It had been a matter Sandra had given a lot of thought. She pushed the digits for the boardroom, and the woman answered. She said nothing. Sandra let the silence ride for a few moments before speaking. "Alaya, let me help you." Sandra felt far more comfortable pulling out this name now.

"Then you know."

"Not everything. Talk to me."

"I just have nothing left to lose."

"You sound sad, Alaya."

"No, I'm angry. I should just pull the trigger and—"

People in the room collectively cried out.

"Has anyone been hurt?"

"Not yet."

Sandra wasn't sure whether to be assured by that response or not. There was more chaotic noise in the background. "Alaya," Sandra said, a little louder to get her attention, "you say you have nothing to lose, but you came here today wanting something. Maybe it's time to walk out, let this end. Do you want to surrender peacefully? I can run you through all of it, how it would work, and I'd be here for you when you come out. What do you say, Alaya?"

"I'm not ready yet. Even if I'd like the nightmare to end."

Sandra didn't like the tone of her voice more than her words. Was she talking about her own life? And earlier when she mentioned pulling the trigger, had she meant on herself? Assumptions were fatal in negotiations. "What nightmare?"

"This one. Being here with these people, with police outside."

"We can end this right now. You just have to say the word." Sandra waited as the seconds ticked off. She was prepared to hold the silence until Alaya broke it.

"I'm not going to let everyone down."

"Your friends Carmen, Tom, and Shane?" Sandra wedged their names in there, and asking this might also reveal if the woman was concerned about anyone else.

"They're not my friends. But you must know about the forum. You're calling me Alaya."

"We do. Fat Cats."

"Then you know that this hospital has destroyed our lives," she spat with venom.

"How did it destroy *your* lives?" Crippling debt and the loss of loved ones, or was there something Sandra didn't know about yet?

"You wouldn't understand!"

The line went dead.

Sandra sat back, a little shaken by the shot caller's reveals. *The hospital has destroyed our lives...* "I think motive here is twofold. This is about money and retribution."

"Which is a scary thought," Neal began. "They don't get the money, they're prepared for the other."

Sandra nodded, recalling the shot caller's repeated claim that she was prepared to do what she must.

"There was something in the heat of her voice when she said *our* lives that made me feel she wasn't necessarily referring to her accomplices. I also got the feeling this destruction cuts real close for her personally," Brice said.

"Me too. Possibly a loss very close to home. A spouse like Sparling, or a child?" Sandra said. "Since it seems today may have been motivated by medical debt, she likely owes the hospital money too."

Gibson returned to his chair. "I've searched the system in the DC area for Alaya, but the results are overwhelming. I tried narrowing it down by referencing the vehicle registrations we looked at. No Alaya."

"Maybe Alaya isn't her real name," Brice suggested.

"She answered to it without hesitation," Sandra volleyed back.

Brice shrugged. "It's her online name."

"Which suggests even if Alaya is an alias, it must mean something to her for her to choose it. I've also been thinking more about her 'destroying *our* lives' comment. It's possible someone else is burdened by her situation. Maybe she was sick...?" It was just the glimpse of a possibility, but no one in the vehicle could answer that question at this point. Not without a name, and even with one, Luis couldn't disclose patient records without violating HIPAA. The act was put in place by Congress to protect a patient's privacy. A court order could overcome that barrier, but for right now, they were in limbo.

Eric grabbed the door for a woman leaving the library and hurried inside with the textbook from Shane Perkins's apartment. It was in a clear, plastic evidence bag, and the librarian at the checkout desk narrowed her eyes when he set it on the counter.

"Can I help you?"

He fussed with his jacket and cleared the way to his badge. "Detective Eric Birch."

"What can I do for you, Detective?"

"This book was signed out from your library by Shane Perkins, and I need to know who took it out before him."

"You want the entire borrow history?"

"That would be great."

"Do you have a warrant?"

"Is that really necessary? Let me show you something." Eric put on gloves and opened the book.

The librarian gasped when she saw the damaged interior. "If you did that, you'll need to reimburse the library for the book."

"There was a note stuck in there that is a key piece of

evidence in an active crisis situation. Your cooperation would be appreciated." Eric could say *crucial*, but he didn't want to put too much pressure on the woman.

She pinched her lips. "Fine. One minute." She positioned herself behind the computer and tapped on the keyboard.

As Eric waited, he hoped this would be what netted that fourth perp's identity. He suspected it wasn't the plan for Perkins to hang on to the book. That led to the question of why he had.

"All right, here we go," the librarian said. "Before Shane Perkins, it was checked out by Carmen Feeney. Do you want her number and address?"

"No, that's fine."

"Before her, Tom Sparling. Need his information?"

Eric shook his head, recalling Neal mentioning that name and that another officer would be checking out his home. "And the person before that?" He reined in his excitement that so far the people who had withdrawn this book matched the names the team had already uncovered. If this track record held that meant the next name would be the person behind the username Alaya Princess.

"Mindy Ashmore. That line up with what you were thinking?" The librarian stood back and studied Eric.

Alaya/Mindy... not really. "Did anyone check this book out before her?"

The librarian looked at the screen. "The last time someone took that book out was eight months prior."

That suggested that Mindy Ashmore had, in fact, assumed the username Alaya Princess, but he had to be sure. And if the foursome communicated once through a book, they had likely done it before. "Do these four people share a history with any other books in recent months?" He doubted their conspiracy went back further than that.

"Let me see." The librarian returned to the computer and

confirmed the four of them held two other books in common. Both on tax law, and they dated before the one Eric had found in Perkins's apartment.

"Could I see them?"

"Sure. They're all here."

A handful of minutes later, Eric was thumbing through the books. They held more in common than their topic. The interior lining had been compromised in both. This more than cemented things for Eric. He had the identity of their shot caller.

FORTY-TWO

5:40 PM

Sandra was considering trying to reach Alaya again when Neal came into the vehicle holding his phone and looking victorious. He'd stepped out for some fresh air, and he must have gotten a good call.

"Detective Birch is on speaker. Go ahead," Neal told Eric.

"The shot caller is Mindy Ashmore, thirty-seven, married to Dylan Ashmore, forty-one. The four accomplices have been passing notes in books for a few months now."

"The same book?" Brice asked.

"No, there were three total. I couldn't recover any of the other notes, though."

Gibson pecking away on his keyboard was slightly distracting, but Sandra shut him out. "Perkins was probably responsible for destroying them."

"He just never got around to the latest one?" Eric tossed back, and it had her thinking.

"His holding on to it might have been intentional," she said. "He must have figured the police would be led to his home at some point. This could be something he planned to hand over to make a deal for himself?"

"Possible, I suppose," Eric consented.

"Ah"—Gibson spun around—"there's no one close to Mindy Ashmore marked as deceased."

"Lieutenant Coleman, anything else I can do for you?" Eric asked.

"Someone needs to talk to Mindy's husband," she said, and quickly felt that she'd crossed the line with Neal. "It could be insightful. We still don't have a clear picture of her motive here, but if I can get her to surrender, the rest will likely follow her lead."

"You assume that, though Tom Sparling was following his own agenda when he shot two people," Gibson pointed out.

Sandra considered. It might not hurt to have Sparling's daughter and Perkins's mother on standby either. She shared as much with the team.

Neal eventually nodded. "I agree. Detective Birch, please go have a chat with Tom's daughter. I'll get other officers on the rest."

"Sure thing," Eric told him and ended the call.

"Actually," Sandra said, gaining Neal's gaze. "Maybe we should have Dylan Ashmore brought here." There were times involving a close relative of a hostage taker worked against peaceful resolution, but with Mindy seemingly at the root of today's incident she wanted him on hand to make that determination. He could also provide insight into her health without making a warrant for her medical records necessary.

"Should we round up Sparling's daughter and Perkins's mother too?" Brice asked.

"We're going to need a bigger vehicle," Gibson quipped.

"I think as long as they are on standby, that's good enough," Neal said. "But I agree that Dylan Ashmore needs to be brought here. I'll get an officer to bring him in."

Sandra only hoped what Mindy's husband had to say would help end this thing once and for all. She turned to the emergency director and said, "Luis, now that we have names, can you find out from the billing department if our perps owed the hospital and for how much? Not for what, just dollars and cents."

"Yeah, I should be able to do that."

FORTY-THREE
6:00 PM

Eric knocked on the door for Trudy Hall, Sparling's daughter. A brief background showed she was thirty-five, single, and living in this house by herself. On that latter point, he'd been surprised before, so he was prepared for anything.

Footsteps padded toward the door, and it cracked open. A woman stood there, keeping a hold on the door, as if bracing to slam it shut and throw the lock.

He was quick to hold up his badge. "Ma'am, I'm Detective Birch."

She relinquished her firm grip on the door, but her body language remained rigid. "Okay, what do you want?"

"Just to confirm, you are Trudy Hall?"

"Yes, that's me." She accompanied her words with a nod, as if that added further proof of her identity.

"I need to talk with you about your father, Tom Sparling."

"He's not exactly my father, but is he okay?" She flung the door open all the way. "I've tried reaching out to him, but it's like he just disappeared from the face of the Earth."

Eric got stuck on the first point. "I'm going to need you to back up here. What do you mean he's not *exactly* your father?"

"Maybe you better come in." She retreated into the entry and gestured for Eric to follow her. She shut the door behind them. "Tom was married to my birth mother, but she died eight months ago now. I only met them both about five years ago when I tracked her down."

Trudy was thirty-five, so she would have been a full-fledged adult five years ago too. "Then you were placed for adoption?"

"That's right. At birth. My mother was just a girl herself when she had me. And it might have been best if I'd left things as they were."

"Why would you say that?"

"Tom didn't know about me, and I'm pretty sure my turning up caused some upset in their lives. But I backed out and told them I wasn't after anything from them. It was just about meeting the woman who gave birth to me. I'm just happy that I got to meet her before she passed. Before then, though, Tom and I had grown to be relatively close. What is it that brings you here about Tom?"

"Maybe we should find a place to sit for this conversation." He phrased it like a suggestion, but it was his recommendation.

Trudy gestured toward a sitting room off the entry. "Make yourself comfortable wherever." She dropped onto a gray chair, and he sat on the couch.

Eric told her the situation, after which Trudy didn't respond, didn't move, and didn't blink for several seconds.

"Ms. Hall?" Eric prompted her.

"Yes, I heard you. I'm just assimilating it."

"We believe that his wife's death might have prompted his actions today. Is there anything you can tell me about him that might help us?"

"Well, I haven't seen him in a few months."

"Not long after Mable's death then?"

"That's right. I've tried calling him and leaving messages many times as recently as last month. That's when I found out his number was out of service. So I went over to the house only to find out that he'd moved. To where, I don't know. I suspect he must have gotten a new number too, but he's never reached out to me."

"Any idea why he'd cut you off?"

"Not really. Though, I know he was utterly heartbroken when his wife, my birth mother, died. For me, it's been like I've lost Tom too, ya know?" Her voice turned gravelly.

"How did she die?"

"Tragic story, really. Mable went in for an undiagnosed illness. Her doctor at Founders convinced them she needed brain surgery. She died due to complications."

"So Tom holds Founders responsible?"

She nodded. "After the autopsy, he tried to hire a lawyer, but they told him a misdiagnosis wasn't malpractice. You see, if the doctors had thought about running a certain test, they would have seen her illness and could have treated it with a common run of antibiotics. But as the lawyer put it, the doctor had acted in what he felt was in the best interests of the patient. It dragged on for a few months, but it came down to the fact she was gone, and there was nothing he or anyone could do about it. I still can't believe it's come to this. Storming into Founders with a gun."

"Was Tom burdened by medical debt from this?" Eric was searching for all the reoccurring themes he could find among the hostage takers.

"Oh, yeah. They only had basic medical coverage and had leveraged all they had for the surgery. They thought it would be worth it if she got better. He just never expected…"

For her to die. Eric filled in the rest. Tom Sparling was deep in debt with nothing left to live for. He'd already shot two people. Would it end there?

FORTY-FOUR

6:00 PM

The picture was getting clearer by the update. A flood of information seemed to hit all at once, and Sandra wished it had only come sooner.

Sandra had tried seven times in the last hour to reach Ashmore and the two of her collaborators who were still conscious, without luck. None of them were answering her calls whether it be through the hospital lines or trying their personal cell phone numbers.

Now that they knew Mindy Ashmore's identity, they had her active cell number. It wasn't doing Sandra any good either. If she didn't get someone inside to talk to her soon, she expected more pressure to come from Kreiger about moving in. Something had to give, that much she knew.

Neal pocketed his phone. He'd taken a few back-to-back calls from officers he had out in the field. "All right, people, I've got more news. Officer Moore had a talk with Perkins's mother, and we gained valuable information about the brother and insight into Shane himself. The brother ultimately died of a drug-induced stroke. Efforts made by the doctors at Founders Hospital failed, and the treatments resulted in significant debt to the family. The mother, who assumed financial responsibility, is struggling to keep her head above water. And that's working two jobs."

"Let me guess. Shane's reeling from the loss of his brother and can't take watching his mother run herself into the ground," Monica said.

"Bingo." Neal pointed his finger at her. "It also wouldn't help that Shane was diagnosed with OCD."

"Which would explain his ladder routine of two steps up, one back," Sandra worked in.

"It would," Neal agreed. "But due to the OCD, he likes order and calm. According to his mother, losing his brother only intensified his condition. He wanted to fix everything, but he's not in any position to do that either. She blames herself for not wanting to let go of her son when it was already clear he was brain-dead, and only machines were keeping him alive."

"I can't even imagine making that call," Brice put in, and Sandra shook her head.

"And that's what you meant by *ultimately* died from the stroke?" Sandra asked Neal.

"That's right. And the second call was from Detective Birch," Neal said.

Just hearing his name had Sandra sitting up straighter.

"He's spoken with Tom's daughter." Neal filled them in on his findings.

"That confirms that three out of the four hostage takers inside owe great sums of money to the hospital. How much do you want to bet the same applies to Mindy Ashmore?" Brice said.

"Not only that," Sandra began, "but three out of four lost a loved one in this hospital."

"Ah, I just received an email from my contact in the billing department," Luis said. He picked up when everyone fell silent. "Feeney, we know about. An account for Perkins owes a hundred grand, Sparling owes one hundred and seventy-five K, and Mindy Ashmore owes two hundred and fifty thousand. All the accounts have now been forwarded to a collection agency."

"Holy hell." Brice whistled.

"And where do the Ashmores work?" Sandra looked at Gibson.

"Nothing that would make them that much money a year combined. Gross," he said. "She's in admin for an office supply company, and he works at a garage."

There was a knock on the door, and Brice answered as he was the closest.

"Officer Hernandez. I'm here with Dylan Ashmore."

"Yes, please come in." Brice stepped back, and a man entered the vehicle. "Thank you for coming, Mr. Ashmore."

The man's gaze darted around the vehicle at all of them. "Sure, but I don't understand why I'm here."

Sandra glanced at Neal. He must have told Hernandez to just bring him back here without providing a reason. "Mr. Ashmore, I'm Special Agent Sandra Vos." Then she introduced Brice and the rest of them. "It might be best if you sat down."

"Here. Have my seat." Neal got up and walked down the vehicle toward the alcove with the coffee.

Dylan took Neal's spot at the table, looking at Luis several times. His gaze drifted to the laptop's screen, and then he scanned more of the vehicle and landed on the markerboard. Gibson had pinned photographs of the four perps on there with magnets. Even if Mindy's face was obscured.

"Why is Mindy's picture up there?" Dylan made eye contact with Sandra.

Gibson had swiveled in his chair when Sandra had introduced him, but he grabbed a notebook and a pen. As the information officer, gathering intel primarily fell under his purview. The circumstances made this a little unorthodox, but it wasn't unheard of in a crisis incident.

"There's an ongoing situation inside Founders Hospital, and your wife is involved," Sandra began, dispensing with an appetizer of what was to be a heavy main course.

"In what, exactly?" Dylan's posture was stiff and closed off.

"This won't be easy to hear, but she has a gun and is working with three other people."

"The other photos on the board there?"

"Yes. Do any of them look familiar to you?" They hadn't uncovered any trail that would make Sandra think he would recognize them, but she had to ask.

Dylan looked past her toward the markerboard. "I've never seen them before." Meeting her gaze again, he added, "This isn't making sense. Why would Mindy go in there with a gun, with those people? Strangers? They must be forcing her into this."

Sandra appreciated why he'd want to believe that. It would certainly go down a lot easier than what she had to tell him. "Actually, Mr. Ashmore, it seems your wife orchestrated today's events."

Dylan wiped his face and shook his head. "I... I don't know what to say to that. But Mindy is a kind person, and she wouldn't hurt anyone."

Sandra could point out that people, even the ones closest to us, were capable of far more than we could imagine. Though if his assessment of his wife held merit, it made it less likely that she would shoot anyone. So far, she'd threatened, spoke of doing what she must, but there was nothing to indicate that she'd followed through and hurt anyone. Or worse. "We're aware that you owe Founders Hospital quite a bit of money. Would you tell us why?"

"Mindy was diagnosed with breast cancer three years ago. It made us realize how life can change in an instant. But she recovered and went into full remission. She rang the bell in the cancer ward. We thought it was behind us." He licked his lips, as his eyes filled with tears, and his chin quivered.

"It came back," Brice said, in a near whisper.

"Yes. Six months ago. Neither of us were prepared for that."

"Financially?" Sandra asked.

"In all ways." He wiped his cheeks. "Emotionally, mentally. We barely got through it the first time the cancer hit."

Brice angled his head. "Your marriage was affected?"

"Yes and no. Not like you might think. It brought us closer together. We were partners in this battle."

Except for now it seemed Mindy was taking matters into her own hands. "Then, you've been able to handle a payment plan?"

Dylan let out a long, jagged breath. "Not at all. Mindy lost her job through all this. We could fight that, of course, unlawful termination, but with what? We don't have money to hire a lawyer. Her boss replaced her. He wrote her dismissal off as poor job performance. Absolute bullshit. She's been picking up temp office jobs here and there, but nothing steady or reliable. And she's getting weaker."

"She hasn't begun treatment?" Sandra asked.

"With what? We don't have any money, and our medical insurance is tapped out."

"I can only imagine how hard the last year or so has been for you." Sandra's heart went out to this man and Mindy. She might be holding a roomful of people hostage, but part of being a good negotiator was relating to the person with the gun. Roles reversed, same triggers initiated, same baggage, any human being could be in Mindy's place.

"Unbearable for the most part. The only light was that brief time when the cancer was gone. We were thinking positively and glimpsed a bright future." His eyes glazed over. "We celebrated our fifteenth wedding anniversary the week before the diagnosis came in that the cancer had returned." Dylan picked mindlessly at his fingernails, seemingly retreating inward. Likely wishing he were anywhere else.

"Do you have any idea what she might hope to accomplish in there?" Sandra asked.

Dylan's chin quivered again, and a few tears fell. Everyone let him have this time without speaking. Eventually, Dylan spoke. "We still owe two hundred and fifty thousand from her first fight against cancer. Neither of us had any idea how we'd pay it off in our lifetimes let alone face more, possibly the same amount, again. That's if they'll even treat her."

"Is the hospital refusing to do so?" Sandra was disgusted by the extent of humankind's greed. She knew the justification would be the hospital was independently owned and a business like any other that focused on profit.

"Founders is, and since they ruined our credit rating by sending our account to collections, we can't get a loan and go to another hospital. But I told her we'd figure it out. She told me I would be better off if she was dead." Tears dripped off his chin as he lifted his gaze to Sandra's.

This hospital destroyed our lives... Mindy's words ricocheted in her head, along with so much else that Dylan had revealed. Mindy sounded suicidal and truly felt she had nothing to lose. "Did she talk about Founders Hospital, maybe Bright Future LLC?" Sandra recalled the only other person Mindy said she knew was the owner of the pharmaceutical company.

"We both talked about the hospital. It still doesn't make sense she'd go in there with a gun, and with strangers. But that company sounds familiar, though I'm not sure why."

"They make chemo medication," Sandra told him.

"That's why, then. I must have seen the name somewhere during her treatment."

"But Mindy never said anything about them to you?" Sandra asked.

"Nothing about storming in with a gun, if that's what you're getting at."

"She's holding members of the hospital board in a boardroom. One of those people is the CEO of Bright Future."

"I don't understand."

"Then she never expressed any malice toward them or the hospital? Or people who worked for them?" Sandra just wanted as much information as she could before getting back on the phone with Mindy. Assuming she'd answer her call. But she thought of a workaround for that when the time came.

"She'd get frustrated at times, yeah. Like how much money they were making from inflating the cost of medication and treatment. How they should be ashamed of themselves."

"Besides talking about suicide," Sandra said, putting extra care into saying that last word gently, "was your wife acting differently in the last few months?" That would account for when she'd got online with Fat Cats and found like-minded people in Feeney, Sparling, and Perkins.

"She was quieter, but I thought that had to do with her depression."

"Which it could, but it would seem there was more to it." Sandra told him about the website and the forum. "Did she ever mention it to you?"

"No. I'm starting to think I haven't known my wife these last few months. I thought she might be getting better. Now this. What does she expect to accomplish? That they're just going to wipe out our debt?"

"It is our belief she feels the people in that boardroom can do that."

"I told her we would figure it out. She just had to focus on getting better." Dylan shook his head. "Now, she'll spend the rest of her life in prison."

Where she will receive free treatment... The thought fired through Sandra's mind. But prisons were only required to provide very basic medical care to inmates under the US Constitution. "Your wife isn't thinking rationally right now. She probably isn't even concerned about that."

"She must be in a darker place than I thought," Dylan said. "I should have seen this coming."

"There was no way that you could have seen this." Sandra felt confident in offering that assurance. From what he'd told them, Mindy had essentially shut herself off from him, her true feelings, her plans...

"Is she going to be all right? Can I talk to her? Maybe if I do, she'll see she's made a huge mistake."

It could also trigger her to do worse. So far no one was hurt in that room that they knew about. "I don't think that's a good idea at this point."

"But there is a way that she can walk away from this, right?" Dylan looked around anxiously. "I saw those ERT guys out there. They look ready for war."

"No one is moving in." Sandra was quick to quell the man's panic. There would be no advantage to telling him there were two shootings that would reflect on her. "On that site I mentioned, Fat Cats, she used the handle Alaya Princess. Do you know why?"

"Yeah. When Mindy was at her lowest during chemo, she took up meditation. In this guided one she was encouraged to ask the name of her higher self."

Sandra didn't miss Brice's tense facial expression. He clearly wasn't a fan of new-age spirituality. She had a tolerance for it, appreciating there was more to the universe than could be explained with science. But running was her god. She hadn't found a better way of purging her demons and glimpsing peace of mind. After consideration, the fact Mindy allowed Sandra to call her by that name could be something she used to her advantage when she spoke to her next. "What did you think your wife was doing today?"

"She told me she was going to shop for flowers for the back-yard." He pinched the bridge of his nose. "All a lie."

"You couldn't have known, and none of this is on you," Sandra assured him. "And I will do my absolute best to get your wife out of that hospital safe and sound."

"But she'll still go to prison?"

"I'm sorry, but there's nothing I can do about that."

"You can talk for her, maybe lessen her sentence."

"It's possible, but there are no promises in this. Your wife's responses in the next while will determine where we end up." She kept her tone firm, level, and confident while exuding genuine empathy.

"I guess that's the most I can ask. Are you sure you don't want me talking to her? I might be able to help."

Sandra shook her head. "We all appreciate your willingness to do that, but if you were to talk to her, it could have detrimental effects on how things play out."

"I don't understand. Clearly, she's doing this for me. She's given up hope, right? She doesn't want me saddled with enormous debt. She's trying to get the people in there to write it all off and treat her again. I can help her see that we'll both be fine."

"But your wife is a smart woman?"

"Yeah."

"Then she'll see through that. Despite best intentions and plans, tomorrow is never guaranteed. Your desire to help things could easily backfire and escalate things." She watched as shadows passed over his face. "For that reason, I need to ask that you don't try contacting her on your own. If you do, it could be considered as interfering in an active crisis incident." She let the rest go unsaid, trusting that her full message got across. He'd be in trouble with the law. "Actually, I'd like to borrow your phone," she added.

"You're going to use it to call her."

"I am."

Dylan handed his phone over to her.

"Thank you."

"Come on, Mr. Ashmore. I'm going to have an officer take you home." Neal left the alcove and escorted Dylan from the vehicle. "We'll get your phone back to you later."

When Neal returned, Sandra was going to share her thinking with him. She would be using everything she learned about Mindy Ashmore and convince her to surrender peacefully. What she'd just discovered gave her an edge.

Sandra had her strategy mapped out in her head but didn't attach herself to how it would pan out in its minutiae. It was certainly unorthodox from one standpoint, but negotiation always had to take into consideration what was important to the hostage taker. "I'm going to call Mindy using her husband's cell phone, and I'll do it on speaker." She'd given that part some thought. At least others could weigh in afterward if they picked up on something she might miss.

"So hush, everyone," Neal told the group.

She nudged her head toward Brice and called Mindy's cell phone number. Mindy answered on the second ring.

"Dylan?"

"It's actually Sandra Vos."

"I have nothing to say to you."

"Alaya is such a beautiful name," Sandra said, the intent at this point to throw her off again.

"Ah, thank you."

It worked... "It almost sounds ethereal and magical."

"What does that matter? That's not who I am."

"Not who you are?"

"No, I'm dying, which you must know if you have Dylan's phone. You spoke with him."

"We did."

"Then you know I'm dying."

"There are treatment options."

"For the rich, or if I was magical..."

"What would you do if you were magical?"

There was silence.

Sandra was quick to step in. "You seem magical to me, Alaya. You beat cancer, and that makes you a survivor. That's *magical*," she stressed.

"But it's back. I can't fight anymore. I just can't. And Dyl and I... we can't afford it. We have no more money to give these leeches!" she roared.

There was no sound in the room behind her, which concerned Sandra, but she had to stay the course. Using a soft voice, she said, "Your husband loves you, Alaya. He says you'll figure things out."

"He's naive. He's always been a pie-in-the-sky dreamer. There's no way we can *figure* this out. We don't have money trees in the backyard. My husband and I are one buck away from claiming bankruptcy. I told him he's better off without me. He just needs to move on and forget all about me."

"You sound desperate and like you can't see a way out."

"I don't."

"Let me help you see there is one. Just surrender peacefully. No one else needs to get hurt."

"No, I can't. Dylan needs me to do this."

"He loves you and said you can work this out," Sandra repeated.

"It's too late. Look where I am, what I've done."

"There's nothing you can't walk away from, Alaya."

"Stop calling me that."

"It sounded to me like you chose that name for yourself. You don't want me to call you that anymore?"

"No."

"Meditation is soothing to the mind, body, and spirit." Again, Sandra veered some. "Do you still enjoy it?"

"Yeah, sure."

"After learning how you chose the name, I looked up the meaning of Alaya." She did this quickly while preparing for the phone call. "Did you know its origins are in ancient Sanskrit meaning 'abode' and 'dwell' but that it also has a connection to a Buddhist term that means 'storehouse consciousness.' Or where higher consciousness or *universal* wisdom dwells? That just blows me away. And you chose that name. Magical."

"It came to me."

Brice nodded at Sandra.

"Again, just wow. How transcendent and spiritual."

There were a few beats of silence. "This isn't who I am normally. A person who holds people at gunpoint and makes demands."

Sandra's posture relaxed, feeling like she'd finally broken through the woman's barricade. She'd shown that she was tuned into her real person. She'd listened to her and molded the conversation to fit her. "It sounds like life has just been rough lately."

"Try for the last few years, but I'm doing this for a higher purpose. For Dyl. I want these fat cats to write off my medical debt. I don't even care about future treatment. I can't go through it again. I just want to die in peace."

Kreiger scowled, and Sandra felt he was willing to honor her request.

"Is that what Alaya wants for you?" Sandra had managed a lot of negotiations, and this wasn't the first time spiritual things came up.

Silence.

"Dylan doesn't want to lose you," Sandra said. "He wants you to come out safe and sound so that you can face the future together."

"What future? Even if I got more treatment and beat the cancer, we can't afford a roof over our heads."

"Your higher self, Alaya, knows that you will always be provided for." Sandra debated whether to further point out that higher-self thinking wasn't rooted in or concerned with matters in the material world such as money. She decided against pushing it.

"Haven't you read any of those books on the Law of Attraction and manifestation? You can't just sit back and wait for things to magically fall into your lap. You must *do* something, take action. And that's what I'm trying to do, but they refuse to write off my debt. I tell you what... You get me two hundred and fifty thousand, and I'll walk away. Surrender peacefully."

Sandra glanced at Brice, who was looking back at her. That amount just covered her debt, not what the others owed, and there wasn't an allowance for her future treatment. She either figured the government would cover it while she was in prison, or she planned to die. "Is that all?"

"Yes, and make it quick. One hour from now, and you bring me that money yourself."

Face-to-face negotiations statistically ended badly. "What about a money transfer? I'm sure there's a computer in there? You can log on to your banking and see it there?"

"No way. You act like you're on my side, but you put the money in there, I see it, I surrender, and then you take the money back. The only way I'm coming out is when you hand me cold, hard cash and I give it to these fat cats."

"Let me see what I can do, Alaya—"

"Stop calling me that!"

Any leverage Sandra had from the spiritual angle was over. "All right, Mindy. But you will need to do something for me. A sign of good faith. Otherwise I can tell you right now my boss won't go for it." One of the first laws in negotiation was there had to be a give and take to balance the scales.

"Okay, what?"

"Two people were shot on the fourth floor and need surgery. You want the money, then you need to work with me." Sandra left it there, the silence making the earlier implication clear.

"Tell me what to do."

"Are you still in contact with your team? Maybe through the walkie-talkies?" That would be the only way they could communicate as the others weren't answering their cell phones or picking up at the nurses' stations. Tom Sparling couldn't answer, but Mindy didn't know that.

"We still have them."

"Good. You're going to tell them to surrender, that you've worked out a deal."

Silence for a few beats. "Though you know, don't you? That the two hundred and fifty thousand is just what I owe. That's why you asked if I wanted more. I just want Dyl to be okay. They'll think I'm getting all our debts forgiven."

"What you tell them is up to you." Sandra couldn't condone the fact that Mindy had no intention of following through on the team's original plan. If she said something like *the others don't need to know*, it would paint her as disingenuous and untrustworthy in Mindy's eyes. That was the last thing she needed.

"Okay."

"Now, the elevators and stairs are locked down, so they can't just see themselves out of the hospital. You need to tell them that officers will be coming to them, and they are to surrender peacefully. You understand all that?"

"Yeah."

"Okay, great. I'll need the frequency so I can hear you tell them this, so we know when it's safe to move in."

A few seconds and then Mindy shared that frequency. "But what if they want proof the money is also coming through for them?"

"I'm not sure what you expect me to do about that." Sandra flipped this problem back to Mindy for her to solve. Often it worked for the person requesting something to see their demand wasn't feasible.

"What do I...? I don't know."

"Just tell them you made a deal. They came here with you today, so they obviously trust you."

"Okay, fine, I'll do it."

"Good."

"One hour from now. I won't forget or lose track of time."

"Neither will I." Sandra set a timer on her phone. "But I'll call you once I've heard the others agree to surrender and have the money. I'll be calling from my phone."

"Okay." With that, Mindy clicked off.

"Holy hell." Brice rubbed his forehead and bulged his eyes. "Great job, but I'm sure you considered that Tom Sparling is likely still out cold. And if he isn't, he's going to tell her he's locked in a storage room."

"I'm counting on the guy still being down for the count," Sandra admitted. "Gibson?"

"On it, don't you worry." He fiddled around with the radio scanner.

Sandra continued. "Hopefully, 'keeping the chatter to a minimum' will prevent her from freaking out when Tom Sparling doesn't respond to the request to surrender."

"Let's hope so. I'm guessing you have the rest of this worked out too?" Brice asked her.

"You know me so well." Which was only true more recently. Before Olivia's kidnapping, Sandra kept her walls up.

Gibson stood to make some notes on the markerboard, and Monica was finishing up the transcript.

"Gibson, did the Fat Cats site ever respond to the warrant for their user info?" she asked him.

"No, they're delaying and hiding behind their lawyers," Gibson said. "But we have our hostage takers' names so I haven't pushed it."

Sandra turned to Brice. "And your efforts to shut them down? They clearly radicalize their members the way Mindy keeps dispensing with 'fat cats' all the time. It's almost like she's giving them credit."

"I'll see this through, don't you worry," Brice told her. "You know these things don't happen quickly, though."

Which is too bad...

Monica looked up from her work. "I need to say something, or it will gnaw on me. Mindy said you can't just sit back and wait for the universe to deliver. I agree you need to work toward your goals, sure, but it's not anyone's job to figure out *how* everything comes together. The universe decides that."

Gibson groaned. Brice took his headset off, not giving any impression he'd heard Monica. Neal brewed himself a cup of coffee.

"I heard that." Sandra offered Monica a kind smile.

"Okay, so let's say Mindy convinces the others to surrender," Neal started, after stirring a sugar packet into his cup. "Where are you getting two hundred and fifty grand in cash?"

"Leave that with me." She'd be going to her boss, AD Elwood Rowe.

"Gladly." Neal tossed the stir stick and sipped his coffee.

Now Sandra's mind was working to untangle what Mindy would do once the money was handed to her. The million ways walking in there with a load of cash could go wrong...

"And she's only out for herself," Gibson put in. "I'm sure none of you missed that."

"She just used the others to get herself in the door," Neal said.

"More like to cover her ass." Brice got up and made himself a coffee.

The door swung open, and Kreiger came inside. He jacked a thumb over his shoulder. "Did I just see the shot caller's husband being escorted away with an officer? Shouldn't you get him on the phone?"

"It's not the best move in this case," Brice told him.

Kreiger massaged his forehead and squinted like he had a headache. "I'm going to need more."

"She's doing all of this for him," Sandra began. "So even if he told her not to, she's in too deep and she knows it. This would only have her feeling more desperate, and we all know what people do when they feel desperate."

"This." Kreiger flailed an arm. "Storm into a hospital with guns. But I suppose you're telling me we're just going to keep standing around?"

Sandra smiled at Kreiger, more than happy to reveal her plan. "Not exactly."

Sandra and the team filled Kreiger in on the last call with Mindy Ashmore.

"I have so many questions, I'm not sure where to start," Kreiger said.

"At the beginning, boss," Gibson said and laughed.

Sandra smiled, and so did Brice, Monica, and Neal, but after all the hours that passed with little to show for them, this arrangement was the light they needed. A relief to the palpable tension.

Kreiger shot Gibson a glare and mumbled, "Smart-ass. All right, lay out what you're thinking."

"ERT goes in and clears each floor one by one." That was the simple overview.

"Whoa, okay, now I need to sit down." Kreiger had Luis squeeze over to make room, and then Kreiger looked at Sandra once he got comfortable. "Am I hearing you right? You want ERT to move in? I never would have expected this turn of events."

"Don't get carried away there, big fella," Brice said with a smirk.

"Special Agent Sutton is right," Sandra cut in. "ERT needs to move in strategically."

"The only way they know how," Kreiger said drily.

Sandra wasn't doing him the favor of responding to that. She could point out what he seemed to miss was that in this situation, there were advantages to brains and brawn working together. "No one moves in until Mindy Ashmore has contacted her teammates."

"How much longer could that take?"

"I wouldn't think long," Sandra said. "I told her I wouldn't get the money together until she told them to surrender. She knows I'm listening in." She pointed at the walkie-talkie, that so far was silent.

"So now we just sit around and wait? It seems more attractive to just move in, call it for what it is. No need to get any money together for that."

"Are you forgetting about the boardroom full of innocent people?" Brice popped his eyes, and it had his brows shooting up.

"I'm not, but..."

A strange energy emanated from him, and Sandra read it as judgment. As if he didn't view those on the board as *innocent*. And maybe it was her perception of what he left unsaid, but her intuition was typically spot-on. It was a stereotype that the rich had a shady side, and some people in that room might have done things, but no one out here was qualified to stand in for judge and jury. Regardless of any transgression, those people must possess goodness or they wouldn't have gone into healthcare and medicine. Her thoughts briefly switched to Dr. Cowan specifically, who was scheduled to perform a heart transplant on a little girl in a handful of hours. There was no way she'd fail her. She nudged out her chin. "Our job is to protect people, save lives, prevent injury and death. No matter who they are, what they've done, what they plan to do. Do you see it differently?"

Kreiger didn't touch her question. "Where are you getting the money? And she wants you to go with the cash? And you said you would?"

"I did."

"I can't condone that."

She could argue it wasn't his decision to make, but as team coordinator it technically was. To respond by telling him she'd go over his head to the FBI wouldn't be conducive to a good working relationship. "I can appreciate there are risks involved."

"Too many. Just get the husband on the phone to tell his wife he has the money."

Brice was shaking his head. "It's not that easy."

"He's right," Sandra added. "She'll see right through that. And she's made it clear she wants cold hard cash put into her hand."

"And then what?"

"She said she'd walk away."

"Nah, I don't like this. Surely, she'd believe her own husband."

It took a lot to rile her, but this man was well on his way to doing just that. "They've been married fifteen years, and you don't think she could tell if he was lying? She detects that, feels his betrayal on top of everything else, and you can bet everyone in that room is dead."

Voices came from the radio scanner through the speakers in Gibson's computer.

"I've secured a deal," Mindy said over the airwaves. "This ends now. Police will be coming to help you get safely out of the building. Cooperate with them."

"You're sure this isn't a trick?" Carmen asked.

"I'm sure. The FBI is bringing these fat cats their money, so we'll be free."

"Okay, then," Carmen Feeney said.

"All right, I'll surrender," Shane Perkins said.

A few seconds of silence before Mindy spoke again.

"Broken Bridge, do you copy?"

"Shit, that's Tom Sparling," Brice said. "What's going to happen if he doesn't respond?"

"Or if he does and tells her he was knocked on the head and locked in a room?" Gibson said.

A collective hush came over the vehicle as seconds ticked off.

"Broken Bridge, do you copy?" Mindy repeated.

The walkie-talkie crackled.

"Copy, over," Tom Sparling said. "As long as you're sure you can trust them."

Brice faced Sandra. "Sparling's conscious."

She expected Sparling to tell Mindy what he'd been through and where he was, but there was nothing more. The frequency went dead. Sandra had a horrible feeling. The release switch inside the storage room. Had he regained consciousness and let himself out? If so, he was roaming the fourth floor again. She turned to Luis. "Can you switch the view so we can see the storage room where Nurse Torres put Tom Sparling?"

Luis did as she asked and gestured at the screen. "Nothing looks any different."

"Can you back up the footage and see if he came out?"

What they saw from one hour ago sent chills through Sandra and had her feeling it was all her fault.

Maria never would have left Jordon's side if it wasn't for Sandra's words running on a spool in her mind. *Don't play the hero…* But being a hero was in her DNA. She didn't fight injustice on the streets like a cop, but she did her part to save lives inside this hospital. Being placed in such a position where her hands were tied by a man who saw fit to storm in here with a gun was infuriating. And watching Jordon in so much pain had her feeling powerless.

She also felt lost without the freedom to conduct her rounds and check in on her patients. They would need her by now. And even if they didn't, this had dragged on for hours, and they'd be hungry. She'd do what she could.

Dr. Bell tried to discourage her from leaving, and so had Jordon. His pleas had been the hardest to overlook. What if he wasn't alive when she returned?

But, no, she couldn't think that way. No good would come from that.

She'd start by checking in on Gail and Phoebe Chapman, but she'd hit the vending machine first. After using change from her pockets and getting two bags of chips, she headed to their room.

She tried the handle and found it was locked. "Gail? It's me, Nurse Torres. Maria."

Silence. When they'd parted ways, she told Gail not to answer the door under any circumstances. Maria knocked softly and announced herself again.

This time, the blinds on the door were lifted. Gail peeked through.

Maria tucked inside the room and locked the door behind her. "How are you two?"

Gail looked over her shoulder at her daughter, who was sleeping. "We're doing all right. Why did you lock the door again? That gunman can't hurt us now, right?"

"Just extra precaution. And you don't want to be roaming the halls when the police come in."

"Have you heard something about that yet?"

"No. But here. I thought you might be hungry." She handed the chips to Gail, knowing that Phoebe wasn't to eat this close to her heart transplant. She had to believe the operation was still happening. "I know Phoebe needs to fast."

"Thank you." She popped a bag open and took out a chip but didn't put it into her mouth. "But that's only if she's getting the surgery." Gail's voice cracked on that, and Maria touched her hand.

"Let's keep positive, okay?"

"I'm trying. How is your boyfriend?" Gail crunched down on the chip, and Maria realized how hungry she was.

"Would you mind if I...?" She pointed at the unopened bag in Gail's hand.

"Not at all." Gail handed the bag over with a smile, which faded fast. "But you never said how your boyfriend is doing."

Maria didn't want to give too much thought to his condition.

He was stable, but that could change in an instant. She took out a few chips and munched them down. Then licked her lips of the crumbs. "A doctor is with him, but he needs surgery."

"Let's hope he gets it." Gail put a hand over her chest. "When I saw you, I thought maybe he was already..."

Maria shook her head.

"Good, but I just don't understand why the police haven't stormed in here yet."

Maria struggled with the same question, but it came down to one thing. "There are a lot of lives on the line in here. And there are other gunmen."

"What?"

"It's not just the people on this floor in danger. Dr. Bell told me he heard about one on the second and sixth floors before the phones went down. There could be more."

"And you never shared this with me?"

"I didn't want to scare you any more than you already were."

"But Phoebe..."

"She's fine, and so are you. And you will be as long as you stay in this room."

"And what about you?" Gail looked Maria up and down. "I get the sense you're not staying."

"I'm not."

"At least leave me the gun in case another gunman comes."

"The ones from the other floors can't get to here. The elevators and the doors on the stairs are locked. The man from this floor is locked in the storage room."

"Why are you holding on to the gun?" Gail's eyes were wide, and fear was etched into her facial expression.

"Just in case..." Maria took a deep breath and put a hand over her stomach, her thoughts drifting to the child she was carrying.

"I don't understand."

"Other patients could need my help. This has been going on for hours. I'm going to get more food from the vending machine and do whatever I can to make this easier on everyone until the police shut this down."

Gail greedily ate the chips and quickly polished off the bag.

"Here, finish mine." Maria gave what was left of her chips to Gail.

"No, you don't have to do that."

"I want to. They really aren't doing anything for me."

Gail smiled at her. "Okay. I'll happily eat them."

Maria couldn't think about taking one more bite. It wasn't the chips that were the problem, but her clenched stomach. She just had this horrible premonition in the pit of her gut. It was unclear if it was uncertainty about Jordon or more than that. "I'm going to go now. Lock the door behind me." She left and ducked into the hall. Before moving on, she waited to hear the lock engage.

Maria didn't know why she was so anxious. That man was secured in a locked room. The other gunmen couldn't get to this floor. She went over all these details and facts repeatedly in her mind, but there was still this niggling feeling in her gut. *It's just my imagination... all those drama shows on TV...*

She hit the vending machine again, this time feeding every cent and buck she had into the thing. She used her credit card when that ran out. Armed with a cart full of chips, chocolate bars, and nuts, she carried out her rounds, checking on her patients. Surprisingly she found most of them in good spirits, considering. Those who weren't holed away with nursing staff or doctors didn't know much of what was going on, just that the hospital was in lockdown. They were terrified when she knocked on their doors, and at first, she wondered if she was doing more harm than good. But when she let them select a snack and saw the smiles on their faces, she felt better.

After making her last stop, she found herself across from the storage room where she'd locked up that man. She wondered if he was still out cold, or if he'd come to and was disoriented in the dark. Then she remembered he wouldn't need to be for long. She'd left his phone on his person. He'd just need to fish it out of his pocket and turn on the flashlight. Would he find the release switch? That was a strong fear.

She went to move on, but found her steps were leaden. That FBI agent had asked about his phone, and she'd only do that if it might serve a purpose. Possibly it would shut down communication between him and the others, destroy chances of him coordinating his moves with theirs.

Don't play the hero...

The haunting words cycled back. She had hit him hard, and it was quite possible he was still out cold. She could get in, grab his phone, get out. Easy peasy.

Don't play the hero...

Instead of pushing her away, the advice was urging her forward. As she thought earlier, she *was* a hero. Wasn't that what her patients thought when they saw her? Getting his phone might help the FBI and police bring this all to an end sooner. Jordon would get the surgery he desperately needed. The bad guys would be taken away, and the patients would be safe again. Her baby would be safe.

She inched up to the storage room and leaned her ear to the door. Silence. If he was awake, he would most likely be moving around in there trying to figure a way out.

This was it. She was going to do this. She'd make it quick. In and out, then call Sandra.

She entered the code to unlock the door, and slowly opened it. The lights automatically engaged.

The man was still in the wheelchair. His head was slumped forward, just the way she'd left him.

Get his phone, call Sandra. You're a hero, Maria! Her inner cheerleader spurned her on.

She quickly reached him and rooted through both his pockets at once to save time. What she didn't count on was for him to wake up, wrap his arms around her middle, and pull the gun from her waistband.

Watching Nurse Torres go into that supply room made Sandra sick. She was playing the hero just as she told her not to do. But seeing her come out with that man was even worse. He had a gun on her. She must have gone in there with his, but he got the upper hand.

"Why would she go back in there? It makes no sense," Brice said.

"I think she was trying to get Sparling's phone." Sandra shared her suspicion.

"Why would she do that?" Kreiger leveled a glare at her with the enclosed accusation.

"I just asked if she knew where his phone was." Sandra could say she cautioned her, but what difference had that made?

"Brave or stupid, take your pick," Neal said.

Sandra couldn't argue, as it surely appeared that way. Luis switched from one camera to another as Sparling nudged Maria around the fourth level back to Phoebe Chapman's room, where they went inside. He didn't seem to pay Maddox any attention, and somehow Dr. Bell must have been alerted because he'd left Maddox's side.

Sandra wanted to call Sparling right away, but she had to call Mindy first to honor their deal.

Mindy answered after the first ring. "You heard everyone agree to surrender?"

"I did, and I'll work on arranging the money."

"Call me before you head in."

"I will." Sandra ended the call and ran to her workstation. "I'm trying Sparling's cell phone," she told everyone.

Brice got into position and so did the others.

"What do you want? I'm not in any mood to talk," Sparling answered.

"You've been through a lot in the last eight months. I'm sorry for the loss of your wife."

There was a moment of silence.

"You didn't even know her," he spat out.

"No, but I know what it's like to lose someone." As she said this, she instinctively pinched the St. Michael pendant hanging from a chain around her neck. "You lose your mind for a minute or two, maybe more. But that's no reason to hurt other people, Tom. *Innocent* people who have done nothing to you."

"You don't know anything!"

"You think that Founders Hospital killed your wife."

"They did."

"The doctors might have failed her, but the little girl in that room, she hasn't hurt you. Her name is Phoebe. She's four years old and scheduled for a heart transplant tonight." Sandra could only hope that humanity and empathy still lived within the man.

"The hospital will be to blame for whatever happens." His voice trembled.

"Haven't you heard, though, Tom? This is over. Mindy worked out a deal."

"Good for her. Maybe I don't want to surrender."

His words were ominous, but his tone disheartening, belonging to a broken man with nothing to live for. "It sounds like you don't know what the future holds from here, but it's up to you."

"I'll tell you when it's over."

Either Maria or Gail screamed in the background, and the line went dead.

"That's it. We're moving in. Money or no money." Kreiger lunged for the door.

Sandra ran after him, pulled back on his arm. "As we discussed before. Just skip the fourth floor for now. Let me work on him."

"What you need to work on is getting your hands on that cash because ERT's going in with or without you. It's up to you to decide if you're working with them or against them."

"What the hell is that supposed to mean?" The question was out before Sandra got a leash on her anger.

"You're about talking. Fine. But at some point, when that's not working, more persuasive measures are needed."

"So after all this time you're going to sanction ERT going in there and risking lives?" Her heart was slamming against her ribcage.

"No one said anything about risking lives. We will proceed as discussed. You, should you decide to, will go in with ERT. You will be accompanied by two officers up to the eighth floor through the stairwell, where you'll be prepared to hand over the money to Mindy Ashmore."

"As long as ERT stays out of Ashmore's sightline. We can't risk scaring her."

"Fine, but they'll be hanging right outside the door, ready to move in if the need arises. That is my offer, take it or leave it. You preach about risking people's lives. Well, Special Agent Vos, I'm not risking yours. Capiche?"

Anger was boiling in her veins, and her cheeks were on fire. She pushed past him. "I'll get the money and let you know when I'm ready." She flung the vehicle door open and stepped into the evening air.

She heard Kreiger come out behind her, but he carried on to the ERT tactical sergeant while she rounded the corner of the command vehicle and pulled out her phone to call Elwood Rowe.

She caught the remaining time on her phone. Thirty minutes.

When Elwood answered, she laid out the details in record time and finished with, "So I need two hundred and fifty K, in cash, delivered ASAP."

Two seconds, then, "I'll need more than that."

"This is how we end this thing before anyone else is hurt."

"So you plan to hand cash over in person?"

She knew he was trying to stress the risk involved with doing that. She could argue that she'd pulled it off in the past, but realized that was the exception not the standard. "I'll do what needs to be done." As she said this, maybe Kreiger had a point. She was so concerned about the lives of others, but where did her own safety weigh in?

"I don't think I can justify that."

"And how do you think it will go over when you tell Director Hamilton that Jordon Maddox died because we didn't stick to the deal?"

"A deal you never should have made."

"But I did." She batted away at all the bitter frustration bubbling up inside her. "I realize this isn't standard procedure."

"No, it's a desperate measure."

"Under extreme circumstances." She paused for a few seconds. "Let me end this."

"Fine," Elwood huffed out, "but you better hope this turns up roses. You'll see the money within fifteen minutes."

Leaving fifteen and cutting it close... "Thanks."

Elwood ended the call, and she looked up at the sky. It was a clear night, and soon the stars would be shining brightly, indifferent to the chaos down here.

She took a few deep breaths. A run along the Potomac was the balm she needed right now, but it wasn't an option, and it wouldn't wash away reality. Over a thousand lives were on the line, and her mother was fifteen minutes down the street facing her own health scare. Sandra took the time to try Dana. When she answered, Sandra got to the point. "How is Mom? What are the doctors saying?"

"Are you finished with your job for the day, Sandra?" Dana said, destabilizing Sandra's emotions. It was unlike Dana to respond to a question with one.

"I'm not."

"Well, there is news, Sandra."

Just that much soured her stomach. "Tell me."

"The doctor wants to wait until you get here."

Sandra's eyes filled with hot tears. The world around her felt like it was spinning. It was never good when one had to hear the diagnosis in person. "Ah, okay."

"She's resting right now, so don't worry yourself, please. There is nothing you could do if you were here. Your job is important."

Sandra sniffled, thanked Dana, and hung up. She continued to grip on to her phone. The results must be life-changing, possibly life-*threatening* for the doctor to hold off.

"Sandra?" Brice's voice reached her before he did. She had just enough time to wipe her eyes and pocket her phone.

"Elwood's getting the money over. Should be here in fifteen minutes."

"Good. Are you okay?" He angled his head, peering into her eyes.

"Yeah, I'm fine. Why?" The question was a challenge. She

could hear her stuffy nose, and in the light, he probably saw that her eyes were wet.

He pointed at her. "That right there."

"What, right where?" She made a show of looking around her.

"You're not as good at hiding your personal shit as you think you are."

"You say that because you saw me at my worst." Having Olivia kidnapped certainly qualified as that.

"If you don't want to tell me, that's fine. I understand. It's best we keep some mystery about ourselves." Brice turned to walk back to the vehicle door.

"It's Margo, my mom."

He pivoted back but didn't speak, leaving the space open for her to continue.

"Something's wrong with her." She gave him the highlights. "I guess the doctor has some answers, but I'll need to wait until this is all over. Apparently, it's news best delivered face to face."

"Oh, Sandra. I'm sorry to hear that. You should go to her. I can handle this and step up as lead." He put the latter out there with a bit of a smirk, as if teasing with her.

"Wouldn't you like that?" she volleyed back, trying to muster some frivolity. "No, in all seriousness, my leaving wouldn't change things anyway. I'm seeing this through. We're close now. We've got to be, and Mindy Ashmore is used to dealing with me."

"All right, but if you change your mind..."

She shook her head. "Thanks, but I won't."

"Ah, you might like to know something else."

Sandra braced herself.

"A bit of Kreiger's mystery has been unraveled. After you both left, Neal told me Kreiger's haunted by a past incident when he held off from sending ERT in. The gunman killed a family of four, including a six-year-old boy."

Sandra assimilated that. She thought back to earlier when she'd mistaken his abandoned sentence for judgment. *I'm not, but...* It came after Brice pointed out the innocent lives at stake in that boardroom. She'd assumed Kreiger didn't see them that way. She was wrong and couldn't have been further from the truth. After Kreiger's experience, he'd always consider the innocent, the ones in danger. He wanted a peaceful resolution like she did, but life told him that came from action, not talking. "Thank you for telling me."

FORTY-NINE

7:05 PM

There was fifteen minutes on the clock when Sandra was standing outside the hospital's main doors with ERT at her side. They had her in a vest and armed with a hidden mic, but she refused to carry a weapon. If Mindy searched her and found a weapon it could be seen as a threat and turn things sideways in a flash. That didn't stop Sandra from wishing for a gun in an ankle holster. Olivia's father, like a real-life Rambo, never left home without one.

Luis provided them with override codes for the stairwells, which they were going to use instead of the elevators. It would be far easier to contain risk that way. If the elevators started operating before the perps were disarmed, then people could unload and potentially find themselves in the crossfire.

An agent from the Washington Field Office delivered the cash in a backpack and left.

Sandra had called Mindy to let her know she was coming in with the money and to have her team position themselves at the stairwell doors for apprehension. Mindy's request came over the walkie-talkies a moment later. She received agreement from everyone, including Tom Sparling. But Luis confirmed through security video that everyone was in position but Tom Sparling. They were still going to move ahead with their plan.

The ERT officer, a man named Albert Willis, turned to her. "Just remember, do whatever you can to get the blinds open in that boardroom. If we need to, we'll handle the rest."

She nodded, knowing how they'd *handle* things. It would be through a sniper's rifle. The thought of facilitating Mindy Ashmore's execution didn't sit well. "Let's hope it doesn't come to that."

"Just do your job, and we'll do ours."

The ERT unit commander made a motion with his arm, and the officers moved inside the hospital. The one in the lead swiped the keycard to unlock the main doors, and they flocked to the stairwell.

After getting there, the group made their way up. Three officers branched off on the second floor and took Carmen Feeney into custody. Three ERT officers walked out on the fourth against her judgment. From the last update before they left, Sparling was still in Phoebe Chapman's room. Kreiger's argument was the possibility for casualties was contained, and it was his call. While two would position themselves down the hall from Chapman's room, the third would accompany Dr. Bell with Jordon Maddox and Nurse Mahoney to the main floor for surgery. They would use the elevator reserved for doctors to transport patients to surgery rooms. Those on it would be staff with the hospital and know the procedure during lockdown. Again, less risk.

The process repeated on the sixth, where two more ERT officers took to the hallways to bring down Shane Perkins.

This left Sandra with ERT Officers Willis and Kemp as they continued to the eighth floor.

"If you need to stop and rest, we can do that." He glanced over his shoulder at her.

"I'm fine." Her regular jogging gave her incredible cardio

health, and it took a lot for her to get winded. The fact she was carrying two hundred and fifty K in a backpack wasn't enough to tax her heart. And she had her mind set. Phoebe Chapman was getting her life-saving surgery.

"Suit yourself."

Two more series of stairs, and they were at the door with 8 on a sign next to it.

"This is us." Willis paused by the door and adjusted his vest, then turned to her. "You ready?"

"I am." She let go of the straps on the backpack, preferring her hands free if they were needed.

Willis unlocked the door with a code, and the three of them stepped into the hallway. It was shadowed like the stairwell with only emergency lighting in effect. Maybe she had made a huge mistake coming here, deciding to face Mindy Ashmore in person. Had she let her past successes with in-person negotiations affect her decision?

Willis led the way down the hall, with Kemp walking behind her. Both were wearing helmets with a flashlight attached to them. Ahead of her, Willis's beam cut across the darkened hallways, giving Sandra an eerie feeling.

She remembered where the boardroom was located from the blueprints she'd peeked at before entry, and she stayed in step with Willis. He stopped walking three doors down and motioned for her to tuck against the wall.

"You know what you're supposed to do?"

"Yes."

"Amuse me."

"Announce myself, knock on the door, step off to the side, and go in when it feels safe."

"Yes. Now, go."

Sandra wondered if they were just planning to take Mindy down with force. And if so, why had they bothered letting her haul the money up the stairs? She walked toward the board-room, noting there were a few windows facing the hallway too. The blinds in them were closed.

This is it...

"FBI Special Agent Sandra Vos," she called out. "Mindy, I'm here with your money." She reached out and knocked on the door. Stepped off to the side.

Willis nodded at her, the beam from his headlamp moving with his head arching from the floor to the ceiling and back.

The door opened slowly, and Pamela put her head through. "Come in." Her voice was tiny and scared.

Sandra resisted the urge to look back at Willis. "Pamela, I have the cash for Mindy."

"Bring it to me," Mindy called out from inside the room.

Sandra subtly shook her head, the motion for Willis, though he would have heard everything.

"I'm coming in, Mindy."

She stepped into the room. Mindy was standing in a corner holding a gun on the doorway. Her hair was standing up and frizzy around her face. Her skin was pale against her brown hair. Sandra scanned the faces of the hostages. There was one she hadn't expected to see and was now happy that she hadn't called her sister. Janie DeSilva.

The fate of everyone here was in Sandra's hands. What happened in the next few seconds would decide life and death.

Pamela was quick to move behind her and lock the door again.

"Unload the money on the table," Mindy told her without moving from her position.

"It's all here." Sandra slowly took the backpack and unzipped it.

"No funny business or I will shoot her." In a flash, Mindy had moved behind Pamela and was holding a gun to her head.

"If you don't trust me, you can get the money out," Sandra told her. If Mindy took her up on the offer, it would allow Sandra time to assume control of the room. She could overpower Mindy and take her gun. That was her Rambo ex-boyfriend talking in her head.

"I trust you." Mindy strengthened her grip on Pamela, now wrapping an arm around her collarbone.

Sandra slowly unloaded the stacks of cash onto the table. "You can count it."

Mindy shook her head. "Again, not necessary. I trust you."

If she wasn't going to let her guard down for a second, it was going to be harder to assume control physically. "All right. And I came in here trusting your word. The deal was the cash, and you would surrender peacefully and let these people go." Sandra barely took her gaze off Mindy.

"You're not going to let me just walk out of here. Why should I let you?"

"You sound like you don't trust me again," Sandra said softly. "We had a deal, and I held up my end. Now, it's your turn."

"Deals change all the time!" Mindy roared and turned around to take in the room. "Why should I trust anyone when money is everyone's god?"

While Mindy's back was to Sandra, there was an opening to act. But if Sandra didn't execute it perfectly, there could be fatal consequences.

"Please, Mindy, think about what you're doing. You have your money. Please, let these people go."

Mindy turned on her. "Do you have the others?"

"ERT officers are securing them now." Her mind distracted her briefly with thoughts about Tom Sparling, who was the anomaly. *Remain present, Sandra...*

"Good. Then I've held up my end of the bargain too. Here,

take the money," Mindy hissed and threw some cash in Megan Beal's face. "Choke on it!" Mindy raised her gun on Beal, and before Sandra had a second to think of doing something, saying something, the gun went off.

Deafening silence followed.

Gail didn't understand why this man couldn't just disappear already and was trying to piece together how it had even come to this. But he was back in this room with her and her daughter. Nurse Torres was apologizing and sobbing in the corner of the room. The man had tied her with the phone cord to a chair there. Then he paced the room and alternated the aim of his gun from one of them to the other. Even her little girl. "Get that thing away from her!"

"I'll do whatever I like. Other people do."

"What do you want from us?" She'd heard him on the phone with Sandra earlier, and she'd watched a wildfire light in his eyes. That heat was back with more intensity.

"I want everyone to suffer like I have." He rushed to Phoebe's bedside. "What is wrong with her anyway?"

"It's none of your—" Her arrogance was silenced when he lifted the gun on her. "It's her heart."

"She doesn't have long to live."

Gail was livid listening to this man talk about her baby. He had no right to come in here and do this. None. She also hated how he hadn't phrased his words as a question. It was an observation he'd made, something everyone around could see except for Gail. She refused to let go and would continue to hold on to hope, to her daughter's survival until it was indisputable. To that point, she would fight with all she had and encourage her daughter to do the same. "She's going to live longer than you."

"Are you seriously threatening a man with a gun right now?"

"I'm telling you. This isn't going to end well for you. But my girl, she's going to survive this." Tears burned in her eyes.

"Tom Sparling!" a man yelled from the hallway. "Metropolitan PD! Kick your gun out the door, and come out with your hands up in the air."

This monster's name is Tom? Like my uncle?

"Shit." Tom rushed around the bed toward the door.

"Help us!" Gail shouted.

"Shut up!" Tom roared at her, and she trembled.

"He's got a gun, and he's tied up Nurse Torres. He's threatening my daughter!"

"Shut up!" Tom came over to her and grabbed her by the hair. "Get away from this room, or I will kill everyone in here. Even the little girl!"

Gail gasped and struggled against him, but he was stronger than he looked. "Help us!"

FIFTY-ONE

7:45 PM

The boardroom had fallen silent after the gun went off. Sandra's mind was working on how to turn this around. She half expected ERT officers to storm into the room. Surprisingly, they hadn't, but this situation was spiraling out of control.

Mindy was staring at Megan Beal, while still holding her gun up. Her arms were shaking, though.

Blood was pouring out of the CEO's side, and her eyes were glassy. She pushed her hand to her wound, and blood seeped between her fingers.

Sandra motioned for everyone to move to the opposite end of the room near the door, and they complied. Mindy didn't seem to notice. Sandra then waved for them to go into the hall. One by one they started filtering out.

"I can't believe you shot me," Beal said, her voice small.

"You... you brought this on yourself." Mindy was quaking, and it appeared that holding the gun up was becoming a more difficult challenge by the second.

Someone bumped into the doorframe on the way out, and the sound had Mindy turning.

"Stop right there!" she roared. "Shut that door, and get back in here."

Four hostages returned into the room. Pamela shut the door.

"Please, Mindy," Sandra petitioned. "Stop this. Please surrender. The hospital has their money. Your husband's future is secured."

Mindy turned around. "You lie. You will take that money back."

"Take it back? It's cash." Sandra had worked on becoming a convincing liar for the job. In truth, once Mindy was secured, the money would be returned to the FBI.

Mindy came toward Sandra. What neither of them counted on was Pamela wedging in there and kicking out her leg. She hooked her foot around Mindy's ankle, causing Mindy to trip and lurch forward.

Sandra rushed out of the way, ducking under the conference table. All she could envision was the gun going off, missing her vest, and hitting her in the head. Maybe it was time to accept that Mindy had no plans of surrendering. But one more try. She rose to her feet with her arms in the air. Mindy had gotten herself up. They were face to face, only a table between them.

"Please, Mindy. Let's end this," Sandra petitioned.

Mindy's eyes narrowed. In that moment, Sandra saw what she had refused to accept. Mindy was a sick woman without hope. The money wasn't going to solve her deeper issue. She couldn't face another fight against cancer.

"I can understand why you might feel there's no hope," Sandra said, slicing into the stretched silence. "Cancer's a killer. But you survived it once. You can do it again."

Mindy's face softened, just a fraction, and her mouth twitched. "Nah. I just don't have it in me." She raised her gun to her head.

"No," Sandra said. "Don't do that. Not to Dylan. It will destroy him."

Tears were falling down Mindy's face. "I just don't have the strength to..." She sobbed.

"I will stand by you, Mindy. Please just hand me your gun and surrender peacefully." Sandra spotted Pamela moving and shook her head.

"Come on, Mindy, I'm here for you," Sandra said. "You said that you trust me. Here's your chance to prove it."

"Okay."

Sandra slowly walked around to Mindy. They were standing mere feet apart when Mindy extended her gun to Sandra.

"Actually, please set it on the tab—"

The next few seconds moved in slow motion.

There was a deafening crack as the glass in the conference window shattered.

But Mindy didn't have a split second to react. Her blood and brain matter splattered across Sandra's face, clung to her eyelashes, and some went into her mouth.

The gun in Mindy's hand dropped to the floor.

Mindy crumpled down beside it, a lifeless puppet.

Pamela was crying, and Megan Beal was staring wide-eyed toward the window. Pamela had opened the blinds, allowing ERT a line of sight.

Sandra looked back to where Megan was sitting and now saw there was a bullet hole in the wall behind her. The CEO had merely been grazed.

What the hell just happened? Sandra put a hand on her stomach and stared down at Mindy's lifeless body. All those hours, all the patience had amounted to what? Exactly what she didn't want. And this unfortunate woman's husband. Sandra had made a promise to him and failed to deliver.

She was aware that the rest of the people who were in there

were now leaving, and that the two ERT officers moved in. She heard their chatter, the sound of their footsteps on the thin carpet of the room.

Sandra couldn't take her eyes off Mindy. It never should have ended this way. But as she replayed Mindy's final moments, she understood how the situation might have looked through a sniper's lens. When Mindy raised her gun to hand it to Sandra, it could have been interpreted as her aiming at Sandra.

Son of a bitch... Her heart ached for Mindy Ashmore, despite all the hurt and damage she had caused today. She'd been a regular person tested beyond her limits. And while Sandra always aimed for zero casualties, she'd failed today.

"She was in the process of surrendering." Sandra was muttering, but she couldn't help herself. *It didn't have to end this way.*

"Come on, time for you to go," ERT Officer Willis said to Sandra.

One of the board members returned, likely a doctor, to tend to Beal and escorted her out.

Sandra gave one more look at Mindy's body before leaving. He was right, and there was nothing more to do in this room. Crime Scene would come in and process the scene, collect the cash, and return it to the FBI. None of this was her problem or concern. She'd done her job. Or at least she tried to do it.

The loss of life hit hard. Down the hall, she snatched the tissue box from Pamela's desk and wiped her face.

The metallic flavor of blood coated her tongue. Death. She was wearing Mindy Ashmore's life force. Her poor husband was going to be destroyed. And after all this, he'd still have debt from the hospital. There was no way they'd ever write it off now. If word got out they had, it would only encourage more events like today.

"Where did you put everyone?" Sandra knew that until all the gunmen were cleared from the building, the hospital was still in lockdown.

"Beal's office. It's the largest on the floor." He pointed to the right. The blinds in the room were now open.

Sandra saw Janie DeSilva and went inside to her. "Janie?"

"Yes?"

"I'm Sandra with the FBI. We spoke on the phone."

Janie nodded, but appeared somewhat distracted by Sandra's appearance, which must have been hideous. She'd still have Mindy's blood all over her.

Sandra continued. "I wanted to thank you for all your help and to also tell you I met your sister this morning at the cordon line."

"Oh, thank goodness." Janie put a hand to her forehead. "I was afraid she was inside the hospital too."

"She was running late."

Janie smiled. "She's always running late. Today, that was a good thing."

"It was. When you get out of here, call her right away, okay? Tell her I told you."

Janie bobbed her head. "I will."

Sandra searched the room, seeking out Dr. Cowan. They might still be able to get Phoebe Chapman that heart. She'd seen Valerie Cowan's photo before the breach. She spotted her at the same time as the doctor was making her way to Sandra.

"You're with the FBI."

"I am. Sandra Vos." The doctor didn't blink twice at Sandra's appearance.

"I'm Dr. Cowan. I'm scheduled to perform a heart transplant on a little girl at eleven o'clock."

"Phoebe Chapman."

"That's right. We're running close to the cutoff point, but if she's safe, I'd like to call the donor hospital and get her prepped for surgery."

"Give me a minute." Sandra went over to Officer Willis in the doorway for a status update on the fourth floor, just as a man's voice came over his radio.

"Officer Willis?"

"Go ahead, this is Willis."

"We have a situation down here on the fourth with Tom Sparling. That negotiation woman still with you?"

Sandra grabbed Willis's radio. "This is Special Agent Vos," she said, speaking up for herself.

"Yeah, well, Tom Sparling's saying he's not leaving the Chapman room, and he'll only talk to you. Get down here. Willis, you are to accompany her. Kemp can stay with everyone until the situation is all cleared."

Sandra was looking at Dr. Cowan as the news came in.

Willis snatched his radio back from Sandra. "You might have heard there's a crime scene up here. And a body. Kemp can't cover it all."

There was a groan. "Very well. Vos, get down here."

"The elevators available yet?" Willis asked.

"Not yet."

Willis handed her the keycard for the stairwell, and Sandra returned to Dr. Cowan. "I'm going to do all I can to save that little girl, so you can take it from there."

The doctor nodded, and Sandra headed for the stairwell. She jogged down the four flights, savoring the spike in her heart rate. The journey to the fourth at a clip was giving her more of a cardio workout than hauling the backpack up eight levels had.

She stopped at the door for the fourth level and took a few deep breaths. She must look frightening. Wiping her face with a dry tissue was better than nothing, but the blood remained caked to her skin as a macabre mask. Looking down, she had some of Mindy's blood on her shirt. But, oh well, they'd be getting her the way they got her. There wasn't any time to waste if that little girl's life was going to be saved.

She hurried past the nurses' station, happy to see that Jordon Maddox was no longer there. He must be on the way to the operating room for surgery. The same should apply for Nurse Mahoney.

The three ERT officers were outside Phoebe's room, positioned off to the side, likely in case Sparling fired through the glass. Sandra approached and stayed to one end.

"I'm here, Tom. It's Special Agent Vos." A formal introduction to make sure Tom recognized her authority and the seriousness of the situation. "Tom, you said you wanted to talk to me. Well, I'm here."

"Make the men with the guns go away," Tom said back.

"You know I can't do that, and you know why. There's a little girl in there, Tom."

"I won't hurt her."

"But you already are. She is scheduled for a heart transplant soon. Without that heart, she will die." Sandra didn't even know if that could still happen tonight, or if the poor child would need to return to the waiting list.

There were a few beats of silence. "Her blood will be on this hospital."

"No!" a woman cried out, and Sandra assumed it was Gail.

"Maybe the hospital will start to listen and be taught a lesson. They'd finally know what they do to people."

Sandra didn't care for how Tom spoke of Phoebe as a pawn he was willing to sacrifice to strengthen his statement. "She's innocent, Tom. She wants the chance to grow up, make friends, get married, find *her* soulmate."

"Don't bring my dead wife into this."

"Didn't you? That's why you're here, isn't it? Sure, having the money to pay off her medical bills was a side venture. But today was motivated by the love you have for your late wife. You did this for her. Or am I wrong?"

There was silence.

"Please, Tom. That little girl is only four years old. Her name is Phoebe, and she didn't take your wife from you. Neither did her mother or Nurse Torres."

"She deserved better." Grief strangled his voice.

Sandra assumed he was back to talking about his late wife's misfortune. "I'm sure she did. Tell me about her."

"She was a loving woman. She balanced me out, grounded me." A rough edge to his voice told her he was crying. "She saw the good in people."

"I'm very sorry for your loss, Tom." She wasn't just saying that to move things along. Her heart went out to anyone who had to say goodbye to loved ones.

"And... *And* I shot two people. There's no hope for me."

"Both men are alive, Tom. They're going to be just fine." A stretch of the truth as that wasn't a guarantee. Last Sandra knew they were stable, but that could have changed.

"That's good."

Sandra glanced over at the ERT officer next to her, who nodded. This was a good turn of events. Tom Sparling's conscience was making a comeback.

"The others have surrendered peacefully, Tom. They're all safe. You can put all this behind you too. Did you want to come out and join them?"

Seconds passed without a word.

"Tom?"

"No, I'm not going anywhere."

"What would it take for you to come out peacefully?"

There was silence, and it didn't feel good. Tom Sparling had nothing to lose. "Would you be willing to let Phoebe go so she can have her surgery?"

"And what do I get?"

Sandra racked her brain for what he might want, what might motivate him. He had done all this for family, for the love of his deceased wife. That told her he had family values. But this was also about making the hospital pay. He owed them one hundred and seventy-five K. There was two hundred and fifty K sitting upstairs that they could repurpose. But last Tom knew his medical debt was written off. "You should know something before we continue talking. Things didn't work out for your friend Alaya Princess." She went with Mindy's handle in case he didn't know her given name.

"Uh, what do you mean?"

"She's dead."

"You're lying."

"I wouldn't do that."

"Sure you would."

"I'm not, but if you want to take the chance I am, that's up to you. Did you know that if you die or go to prison, Tom, your wife's medical debt will pass to her daughter, Trudy Hall?" It was a bluff that Sandra hoped he'd believe given the heightened emotion of the moment.

"It would?"

"You basically just said Founders Hospital is unscrupulous. If so, they will get their money one way or the other. Trudy is your wife's flesh and blood. The hospital has powerful lawyers."

"What do you want from me?"

"I told you. Let Phoebe Chapman go. Once you do that, I'll get the cash to Trudy."

"You can say whatever you want. But no, I won't let the girl go, but I will release her mother. *If* you get the money to Trudy, and I want to see it."

"We have a deal." Sandra turned to the closest ERT officer. "Have someone bring in Trudy Hall ASAP."

The ERT officer nodded and got on the job.

Sandra ran for the stairwell and headed back up to the eighth floor.

Sandra was heaving for breath by the time she made it back to the top floor. She beelined straight for Megan Beal's office to talk to Dr. Cowan.

"Vos?" ERT Officer Kemp said as she bypassed him.

Dr. Cowan stood from where she was sitting. "Is Phoebe okay?"

"She's hanging in there."

"Then can I get her prepped for surgery? We're running against the wire, but if I call the hospital right now, they might cooperate and send the heart."

With the weight of Cowan's words, the possible repercussions sank in. If she couldn't pull off Phoebe's release in time, the organ would go bad and no one would benefit from it. She'd be responsible for another death.

"Agent Vos? Do I call them?"

They were already butting against that two-hour window, but surely, she could get Tom to surrender soon. At least she hoped so. But what if she was wrong and robbed someone else of the heart? She looked at her watch. The hospital had said they needed to know by nine o'clock. There was still time.

"Maybe hold off for just a bit longer. But remain on standby. Can you do that? Just for a few more minutes?"

Cowan's face fell. "Sure. But after nine, her heart could go to someone else. What's going on?"

"She's still being held hostage on the fourth floor." Sandra realized she wasn't telling the doctor anything she hadn't heard moments ago over Willis's radio.

Cowan rubbed her arms and hugged herself as if fending off a chill.

"The situation should be resolved momentarily." *If I have anything to say about it!*

Sandra hustled past Kemp and down the hall to the boardroom for the cash. Willis was standing at the door, and she blew by him.

"Vos? What are you doing?"

She was already stuffing the cash into the backpack. "A deal was made on the fourth. I need this money for that."

"This is a crime scene."

"In case you haven't realized it, this entire hospital is one, and right now, this cash is a girl's best shot at surviving. Do you want her life on your conscience?" The second the question left her lips, she wished to reel it in. "I apologize for that. Of course you don't. No one would. But this is the FBI's cash, and I'm the FBI, so I'm taking it."

"All right, have at it."

Sandra took the money back down to the fourth. "What's the ETA on Trudy Hall?" she asked the same ERT officer she'd asked to get her there.

"She should be here any minute."

While he was talking, a ERT officer strode toward them from the stairwell door with a woman in her early forties at his side.

"How did she get here so fast?"

"Detective Birch brought her to the scene to have on standby, in case we'd need her."

Sandra smiled. *That's my man!* She bridged the distance to the woman. "Trudy Hall? I'm Agent Vos. Did this officer explain the situation to you?"

"He did."

"Good. Now, you're not in any danger with this exchange. He just needs to see me hand you the money and for you to confirm it's one hundred and seventy-five thousand."

Trudy nodded.

Sandra gave a thumbs-up to ERT, then spoke in a raised voice. "Tom, we have Trudy Hall here, and the money for her."

The blind in the door went up, but it was Gail Chapman's face at the glass. She said something that was muffled by the closed door.

"Do you have the money, Trudy?" Tom asked.

Sandra handed the backpack to Trudy.

"I do."

"How much is there?"

Gail remained at the window as Trudy made a show of pulling out the bundles of cash. After a few minutes, she said, "One hundred and seventy-five K."

The blind in the door was dropped again, and soon the door was opening.

The ERT officers raised their guns, prepared to use them if things went sideways.

A woman's narrow wrists came through the opening. "Don't shoot," the woman called out.

"It's Gail Chapman," Sandra told them, but it had no effect on the ERT officers. They only lowered their guns when the door shut again.

Sandra went over to Gail. "I'm Sandra Vos."

Gail was trembling. "Phoebe's going to die if she doesn't get that heart."

"I know, and we're going to do all we can to ensure that she does. How is she currently?"

"She's hanging in there." In that moment, it was like Gail saw Sandra for the first time. Her eyes widened slightly. "What happened to you?"

Sandra had forgotten about the blood on her. It also explained the taken-aback look that Trudy had given her. "I must look a fright, but I'm fine. Now we must do what we can to get your baby girl out of there. If you'll excuse me." She motioned for an ERT officer to shelter Gail in a room down the hall. ERT would have cleared the adjacent ones. Sandra kept Trudy with her, thinking she could still be useful.

"Tom, we need to talk about the next steps," Sandra said. "That little girl needs a new heart." When there was no response, Sandra turned to Trudy. "Would you be willing to talk to him? We can see if he'll listen to you."

"Tom, Mom wouldn't be happy with what you're doing here," Trudy called out, moving ahead without responding to Sandra.

That wouldn't be the direction Sandra would have recommended, but Trudy would know him much better.

There was no reply from inside.

"Keep talking," Sandra encouraged quietly. "You're doing great."

"I know losing her was hard on you. It's been hard on me. I didn't even know her for most of my life. All that time I'll never get back."

"There's no going back," Tom said, his voice gravelly like earlier.

"But it's going to be okay, if you trust me," Trudy told him. "Mom wanted us to be a family, even if it was a different one. Do you believe she's watching us from heaven? I do."

There was more silence, and Sandra sensed an energy shift.

Trudy continued. "She loved you more than anything, Dad."

Sandra realized how generous the woman was being with *Dad* when Tom was technically the man who married her birth mother. He also wasn't someone she knew until five years ago.

"I love you," Trudy said, just as she started to sob.

Sandra wrapped her arm around her, and signaled for an officer to take her away. She'd been put through enough.

"Tom, did you hear all that?" Sandra asked him.

"Yeah."

"There's a future for both of you. People who love you don't cut you out of their lives. Prison won't stop her love. She'll be there for you, every step of the way." Sandra paused, but Tom didn't respond. "She's taken care of with the cash. Will you let that little girl go now?" Sandra's chest tightened as seconds ticked off.

"Yes, I'll surrender," Tom eventually said. "Tell me what to do. I don't really have a death wish."

Sandra let out a deep breath. "That's great to hear. Okay, well, I'm right here, outside the door." She didn't move from where she was. "You just need to open the door, and kick the gun across the floor into the hallway and then come out with your arms in the air. Can you do that, Tom?"

"Yeah, I'm... I'm doing it right now. Don't shoot me."

"No one will shoot you."

The door slowly opened. The gun came out first, followed by Tom Sparling. He looked at her while ERT officers moved in and apprehended him. Another went in for Maria Torres.

Shortly after, the nurse came out and walked right up to Sandra. "How is Jordon?"

"In surgery."

Maria threw her arms around her. "Thank you!"

Sandra hugged her back, taking a moment's comfort in the

embrace, the human contact. Maria hadn't seemed put off by the blood. Though, as a nurse, she'd be used to seeing it.

"I never should have gone back to get that man's phone. If I hadn't..."

Sandra put a reassuring hand on Maria's shoulder. "We can't know the future."

"Though maybe we can?" Maria lifted her hand and showed Sandra her ring finger. She grinned broadly. "He proposed, and I accepted. We've already started our family." Maria touched her belly.

"You're expecting too? Congratulations," Sandra told her, grateful she hadn't known before and had the added pressure.

"Thank you. Can I go check on Jordon?"

"I don't see why not."

Just then the regular lights came on with an announcement that the lockdown was lifted. It wasn't long before the hallways became busy.

Gail hurried down the hallway to her daughter's room.

That's my cue...

This time, Sandra took the elevator to the eighth floor. Hopefully, Dr. Cowan could pull off a miracle.

FIFTY-FOUR
9:15 PM

Sandra swung past the command vehicle to fill everyone in and to let them know she was off. They were all wrapping things up to head out themselves. Neal promised to update her on Jordon Maddox and Nurse Mahoney. She handed the keys for the Bureau car to Brice, telling him she was going to order a car service. There was somewhere she'd wanted to be since that morning and couldn't get there fast enough.

Sandra had updated Elwood, and he said, "Let's hope Maddox and that nurse pull through. I'll call the director and let him call Ilene Maddox."

Amen to that!

She ordered a ride on her phone and set out to the meeting spot, but her phone rang, stopping her in her tracks. "Special Agent Vos," she answered.

"Dr. Cowan. I wanted to let you know the good news. Phoebe Chapman is getting her heart. She's being prepped for surgery as we speak."

Sandra put a hand over her heart, sending out gratitude to the universe. "That's wonderful news. Thank you for letting me know."

"Thank you for getting that little girl safely through the day."

"Nurse Torres had a lot to do with that too."

"That's good to know. Take care." With that, the doctor was gone.

Sandra's heart was pounding. Tears beaded in her eyes, and she took a few moments to breathe. Today had taken a crap turn with Ashmore's execution, but this news just inserted some light. She started to walk toward the street.

"Hold up," Brice called out, stopping her. "Just one thing before you go. While you were in there, you'll be happy to know that I used the full backing of the Bureau to enforce the Fat Cats site be taken down. It's already offline."

"Impressive, and great job."

"We'll try to ignore the likelihood of it popping up tomorrow with a different name."

"Let's take the win for tonight." There were at least a few.

"Sorry that things went down the way they did in there with Mindy Ashmore."

"Me too, but it sounds like Phoebe Chapman has a bright future." She told him about the call she just received.

"Hallelujah. I tell you this job is one helluva ride."

"That it is. Night, Brice."

"Night. I hope everything works out with your mother."

"Me too." She turned to leave and came into Kreiger's path. *I might never get out of here.* But Kreiger just shook her hand and dipped his head.

Forty-five minutes later, due to a detour to the field office for her car, she arrived at Howard University Hospital. She had also taken time to clean up and change into fresh clothes from her to-go bag. Now, though she couldn't get to Margo fast enough. She headed to the floor where Dana told her to go and scooted down corridors toward her mother's room. She heard voices before she reached the doorway, and as she rounded it, the sight before her melted her heart.

Dana, Eric, and Olivia were sitting at Margo's bedside playing cards. Margo was laughing. She must be winning.

"Eric?"

He turned and stood. "You're here." He hugged her and pulled back, angled his head. "You all right?"

"I will be." While all trace from Mindy Ashmore's death was physically gone from Sandra's appearance, it was etched in her mind.

"Glad to hear it."

"Mom." Olivia hugged her.

"My little Sandra, you made it." Margo was beaming from the bed, and it was hard to reconcile the picture in front of her with a woman who had fainted that morning. Well, except for the bandaged wrist.

"Nowhere else I'd rather be." She gave her mother a squeeze and a kiss on the forehead.

"I'm winning." Margo snickered. "I think they might be letting me, but I'll take it!"

Dana shook her head. "You are winning fair and square."

"Whatever you say. Deal my Sandra in. My little ladybug." She winked at Sandra, and her heart puddled. That was the pet name she'd started calling Sandra not long after Margo and her husband had adopted her and Sam. It was one she hadn't heard in a long time.

"I'd love to play." What she'd like even more was answers, but this was a good moment, so she'd enjoy it as long as she could.

The four of them played Go Fish for a few rounds when Sandra's phone rang. She pulled it out, and while there was no caller ID, she had a feeling the call was important.

"Excuse me, I have to take this."

"That's my ladybug. She does important work." Margo hummed a tune.

Sandra touched her mother's shoulder as she stepped away and went out into the hall. "Special Agent Vos."

"Lieutenant Coleman here."

Her heart sank. "So...?"

"Jordon Maddox's and Colby Mahoney's surgeries went well. Both are expected to make a full recovery."

"That's great news." She told him about Phoebe's heart.

"Thank God. I didn't just call about Maddox and Mahoney. You did a great job today, Sandra. If you're like me you're probably giving yourself a rough time about Ashmore, but she's not your weight to carry. She made her decisions. You gave her every chance. Please remember that."

"Thank you for the kind words." That's about as deep as she could let them sink in. Words, surface level. She'd need to process what transpired today in her own time. "And I appreciate the updates."

"Don't mention it. Night."

"Night." She ended the call and put her phone away.

Eric came up and put his arm around her, resting his hand on the small of her back. She turned to him. "It's so nice that you're here. It means a lot to me."

He leaned in and kissed her.

"Did you pick up Liv?" She assumed he probably had when she saw Olivia here.

"I did. We've been here for about an hour."

"By the way, great thinking to have Trudy Hall on standby. She helped save the day." She gave him the overview, leaving out Mindy Ashmore's demise.

"Glad to hear everything worked out."

She pressed on a smile, which he saw through. His facial expression tightened.

"What didn't you tell me?"

"The shot caller died. It was tragic, unnecessary."

"Oh, Sandra. I'm sorry to hear that."

"The worst part? I was right there when it happened." *Her brain matter was on my face, in my hair, in my mouth...*

"You can't control everything. Sometimes bad things happen."

"Somber, but you're right."

"From my side of things, Stevie Cross will go away for his role in today's incident."

"As he should. Did he really think he'd get away with it?"

"You know what they say? Some people are stupid. But I don't really think he cared if he got caught. Cross seemed to think he owed his nephew. He was estranged from the boy's mother for several years. But he saw how Sullivan's death destroyed her at the funeral. So when Shane came to him for help, there was no way he was letting his nephew, or his sister, down again."

"What a person will do for family..." Her thoughts turned completely to Margo. "We need to find Mom's doctor."

"That's him there." He nudged his head toward a fifty-something man in a white lab coat striding toward them.

"Sandra Vos?" the doctor said.

"I am."

"I'm Doctor Friedman. If you have any other family members in the room you'd like out here, please, go ahead and get them. Considering Margo's mental state, I feel updating her would only confuse her more."

"I agree."

"I'll get Olivia and Dana." Eric swept into the room, and quickly returned with them.

Olivia came over and stood close to Sandra. Eric stood on her other side. Dana was next to Olivia.

"That's everyone?" the doctor asked, and Sandra nodded. "Your mother's condition is serious but not critical. She has a bleeding gastric ulcer, which we believe was exacerbated by her medication. Margo was taking a low-dose aspirin every day, a common recommendation for a woman her age. She was also on an NSAID for her arthritis. Both things are typically fine on their own, but they increase the risk of a peptic ulcer. The bleeding caused the anemia and resulted in her passing out. Her wrist only broke due to how it twisted when she fell. Her bone density is what one would expect of a healthy woman her age."

Sandra took a few seconds to find her voice. "What does that mean? A peptic ulcer? Is it treatable?"

Eric took Sandra's hand, and Olivia tucked into her side. Sandra wrapped her arm around her daughter.

"It is. We'd stop with the medication immediately and get her started with blood transfusions to build up the iron. Then we can do surgery to fix the ulcer."

"And the associated risks with that?" Sandra was afraid to take a deep breath in case she somehow jinxed the diagnosis.

"Once we get her iron levels built up, the surgery is considered low risk. Do I have your permission to start her on a blood transfusion, Ms. Vos? I understand you are Mrs. Davenport's medical proxy?"

"Yes, please, go ahead and do that."

"Will do so immediately." The doctor smiled at them and set off down the hall.

Sandra stood there, her head spinning. All that worry today for no real reason.

"Grandma's going to be all right, Mom." Olivia sniffled.

"That she is, sweetheart."

Olivia left with Dana and went back into Margo's room.

Sandra pinched her St. Michael pendant. "She's going to be all right." She parroted Olivia's words, trying to get them to really sink in.

"More than all right." Eric wrapped his arms around her, and she sank against his chest.

This had been one hell of a day, with all its twists and turns, but she got through it. She'd do so again tomorrow, too, if she could at all help it. And even better, she'd face the future with her family and Eric by her side.

A LETTER FROM CAROLYN

Dear reader,

I want to say a huge thank you for choosing to read *Every Last One*. If this book had you flipping the pages, you have every right to be excited because more Sandra Vos is on the way! If you would like to hear about new releases in the Sandra Vos series, just sign up at the following link. Your email address will never be shared, and you can unsubscribe at any time.

www.bookouture.com/carolyn-arnold

I hope you absolutely loved this installment in the Special Agent Sandra Vos series! The idea for this series hit during the Christmas holidays one year, and it had me so inspired. It was something a little different to offer fans of crime fiction while not completely abandoning the adored genre. Not the typical detective mystery, but more a thriller with an infusion of police procedural.

As most writers do, I took some creative liberties, and not everything will be exactly as it is in the real Washington Field Office or Washington, DC, for that matter. I take the reality of a setting and put my fictional twist on things.

I'd like to thank everyone who helped me with this book. George, my husband and best friend, is always my first mention. He helps me keep balanced and sane.

But I'd also like to make special mention of William Arnold, to whom this book is dedicated. Bill was my father-in-law and a sincerely special man. He always saw into your soul when he spoke to you, and he had such an incredible sense of humor. I dedicated this book to him because we lost him to a peptic ulcer (what Margo was diagnosed with) years ago. Unfortunately, in Bill's case, it happened suddenly. We never even knew he had one until it was too late. Bill had Alzheimer's like Margo too.

I'd also like to thank my editor, Laura Deacon, who sparks me to think of ways to further deepen the plot and tighten the pacing.

There are many others, too, and I appreciate everyone. And you, my beautiful reader, thank you for your support.

Speaking of, if you devour books, you'll be happy to know I offer several bestselling crime fiction series for you to savor, as well as series in other genres. I have two kick-ass female detective series—Detective Madison Knight and Detective Amanda Steele.

Then there is my Brandon Fisher FBI Series if you like dark serial killer novels. It's also an extension of Amanda Steele's world. Brandon lives in Woodbridge and is dating Amanda's friend. Now we have Sandra right in Washington, only forty-five minutes away... You'd almost think I gave some thought to linking them all...

And before I sign off, please, don't underestimate the power and influence of word of mouth. Talk to your family and friends about my books, your local bookstores and librarians, your neighbours, the people at the checkout counter, your dentist, your... well, you get the point. Thank you!

And last but certainly not least, I would love to hear from you if you're so inclined to drop me a note! You can reach me via email at Carolyn@CarolynArnold.net. You can also follow and interact with me on Facebook and Twitter (X) at the links below. To investigate my full list of books, visit my website by following the link below.

Until the next time, I'm wishing you a thrill a word and twists you never saw coming!

Carolyn Arnold

www.carolynarnold.net

facebook.com/AuthorCarolynArnold

x.com/Carolyn_Arnold

goodreads.com/carolyn_arnold

PUBLISHING TEAM

Turning a manuscript into a book requires the efforts of many people. The publishing team at Bookouture would like to acknowledge everyone who contributed to this publication.

Audio
Alba Proko
Melissa Tran
Sinead O'Connor

Commercial
Lauren Morrissette
Hannah Richmond
Imogen Allport

Cover design
Head Design Ltd

Data and analysis
Mark Alder
Mohamed Bussuri

Editorial
Laura Deacon
Melissa Tran

Copyeditor
Jon Appleton

Proofreader
Becca Allen

Marketing
Alex Crow
Melanie Price
Occy Carr
Cíara Rosney
Martyna Młynarska

Operations and distribution
Marina Valles
Stephanie Straub
Joe Morris

Production
Hannah Snetsinger
Mandy Kullar
Nadia Michael
Charlotte Hegley

Publicity
Kim Nash
Noelle Holten
Jess Readett
Sarah Hardy

Rights and contracts
Peta Nightingale
Richard King
Saidah Graham

Dear Reader,

We'd love your attention for one more page to tell you about the crisis in children's reading, and what we can all do.

Studies have shown that reading for fun is the **single biggest predictor of a child's future life chances** – more than family circumstance, parents' educational background or income. It improves academic results, mental health, wealth, communication skills, ambition and happiness.

The number of children reading for fun is in rapid decline. Young people have a lot of competition for their time, and a worryingly high number do not have a single book at home.

Hachette works extensively with schools, libraries and literacy charities, but here are some ways we can all raise more readers:

- Reading to children for just 10 minutes a day makes a difference
- Don't give up if children aren't regular readers – there will be books for them!

- Visit bookshops and libraries to get recommendations
- Encourage them to listen to audiobooks
- Support school libraries
- Give books as gifts

There's a lot more information about how to encourage children to read on our websites: **www.RaisingReaders.co.uk** and **www.JoinRaisingReaders.com**.

Thank you for reading.

www.ingramcontent.com/pod-product-compliance
Lightning Source LLC
Chambersburg PA
CBHW061520210726
48287CB00006B/1761